WHERE ANGELS FEAR

THE NEW
ADVENTURES

WHERE ANGELS
FEAR

Rebecca Levene
and
Simon Winstone

First published in Great Britain in 1998 by
Virgin Publishing Ltd
Thames Wharf Studios
Rainville Road
London W6 9HT

Bernice Summerfield was originally created by Paul Cornell

Cover illustration by Jon Sullivan

ISBN 0 426 20530 8

Typeset by Galleon Typesetting, Ipswich
Printed and bound in Great Britain by
Mackays of Chatham PLC

REBECCA'S DEDICATION

This book is dedicated – as promised – to Sue Driscoll (or
Mrs Dickinson as I called her when she brightened up my
school life, a rather frightening number of years ago).
And not just for her great kindness in letting me leave
A-Level biology.

SIMON'S DEDICATION

For Charlotte & Lorna.

Acknowledgements

We'd like to thank:

Ben Aaronovitch, David Banks, Daniel Blythe, Stephen Bowkett, Simon Bucher-Jones, Chris Bulis, Andrew Cartmel, Mark Clapham, Paul Cornell, Russell T Davis, Martin Day, Terrance Dicks, Andy Lane, Mark Gatiss, Craig Hinton, Andrew Hunt, Matt Jones, Paul Leonard, Barry Letts, Steve Lyons, David McIntee, Simon Messingham, Lawrence Miles, Jim Mortimore, Daniel O'Mahony, Kate Orman, Lance Parkin, John Peel, Neil Penswick, Marc Platt, Justin Richards, Gareth Roberts, Nigel Robinson, Gary Russell, Dave Stone, and Nick Walters

And all of Team Fiction:
Bodle, Whore-Slave, Kathleen, Food-Dwarf, the Positronic Man and Fish Boy

For making working on these books such a pleasure for us both.

There was no one there to select a preference for the INet news interface. Deprived of instructions, it defaulted to one of its standby personas, a rather podgy, jolly-faced woman whom 73.2% of those surveyed had considered to be both reassuring and trustworthy. She was always chosen when the news was very bad.

It wasn't the shots of bodies which were judged to be the most disturbing. News viewers quickly became inured to death – and corpses in sufficient quantities registered as little more than special effects.

It was the pictures of the university which were the problem. Its red, mud-brick buildings – one finally discovered – burnt with a curious green flame. Some had already crumbled into a darker red powder. Without its infestation of students, the sector's premier learning establishment looked like little more than a primitive preindustrial settlement in the wake of some barbarian raid. There was something terribly *wrong* about seeing such a venerable landmark in this state, like the feeling a child gets when it first catches its mother crying.

After the university, the vistas of destruction on the rest of the planet came as something of an anticlimax.

PROLOGUE

BEFORE ALL THAT

From a distance, the Worldsphere looked like nothing: just an emptiness where the star charts said there had once been a solar system. The solar system was still there, of course, but you had to move closer to realize that, close enough to see the great dark globe which a people more technologically advanced than any known to humanity had built around their sun. The globe that had once been seven planets, and rather more moons.

Now it was a self-contained habitat sheltering, at any one time, approximately four-fifths of the members of the society which had created it, a society which encompassed several different organic species as well as many orders of mechanical intelligence. There was no one else quite like them, and there had never been a collective noun for what they were – they called themselves the People.

The rest of the People were scattered throughout their local galaxy, many travelling on the sentient ships which were, themselves, also People. At that moment, a surprising number of those ships were hurtling towards the Worldsphere at speeds which insulted the laws of physics.

Most were returning from somewhere that, according to the People's strictest treaty, they weren't supposed to have visited in the first place. They didn't expect to get into trouble when they got back, though – they had, after all, been sent by God. Now God had summoned them home, and

3

many of them were wondering why; the hyperspace bands were filled with worried chatter and uninformed speculation. God – the ultra-powerful computer which handled much of the Worldsphere's running, and an all-round nice guy – had been unusually cagey about his motivations.

Everyone had the strong impression that they were not being told the whole story.

Billions of light years away, in the galaxy that the agents of the People had just deserted, a ship was twenty minutes from planetfall. Dellah had long since ceased to be a picturesque brown-green globe suspended in the middle distance. For the last hour, it had gradually filled the viewscreen until it was impossible to think of it as anything but the ground – towards which they were plummeting at an alarming rate.

Captain Adam Wantman watched the approaching planet sourly through the main leisure-lounge viewscreen. Behind him, he could sense several of his passengers looking at him askance. He could almost hear them thinking, If he's here, who's piloting the ship?

Dellah Spaceport Control, you morons, he thought back. His mood was always bad at this stage of the journey, when his job was over and he had to pass control of his ship to some officious prick who didn't care if she picked up the odd scrape when she landed because hey, the old girl looks pretty beat up already.

And now he'd been told that they'd been chosen for a random customs check. Which meant sitting on an isolation pad for eight hours while every square inch of the *Joanna* was taken apart and examined for contraband. And, if just one of his passengers was carrying something they shouldn't be, he would be the one to get the blame.

He turned his back on the viewscreen to glare at the ship's human cargo; most of them quickly dropped their gazes. A woman in the far corner glared back and Adam grinned at her; she'd been all over him a week ago when the journey from Tyler's Folly began, but her enthusiasm had waned with every day that brought her closer to Dellah and her husband and two children.

Someone else was meeting his gaze, too. Or, more accurately, staring through it. The guy wasn't much to look at – standard-issue low-level bureaucrat, with a soupçon of world-weariness, Adam thought – but he was a policeman on the Folly and that meant Adam was willing to treat him with more than the usual respect. Policemen tended to know people who could make trouble for people like Adam. He was a strange one though: really quiet, as if there was nothing going on inside him. Or maybe so much going on that it took all his energy just to keep it from getting out. He simply sat there, next to two salesmen, who didn't seem to say anything either. They looked to have lost weight in the past week too. Gaunt and silent: a delightful combination. He made a mental note to check on the catering after the inspection. Oh for the simple freight-carrying days when a small planet hopper like the *Joanna* could earn her keep without having to take on passengers, and Adam wouldn't have to defer to anyone.

There was a sharp jolt as the ship touched down, and the smell of Dellahan mud permeated the lounge. Adam expected to hear the gentle pattering against the hull which indicated that, true to form, it was raining outside. Unusually, the sound was absent.

'Customs check, people,' he said suddenly, and watched several of them start guiltily. His heart sank. 'If you'll all make your way back to your cabins, customs will come by to process you one at a time. Sorry for the delay,' he added as an afterthought.

He left a babble of disgruntled voices behind him and headed for the main hatch. The customs official waiting for him there didn't look like he could be older than twenty: a scrawny redhead with sharp cheekbones and no sense of style. Probably some student doing a part-time job to supplement his scholarship: just the sort of professionalism Adam had come to expect from the customs service.

'Anything to declare?' the redhead asked, without interest.

Adam instantly thought of a hundred and one responses,

each of which would have guaranteed him a week in detention while the *Joanna* was strip-searched down to its constituent atoms. 'Nope. But you're going to look anyway, aren't you?'

The student's eyes flicked up to his, and an expression that might have been amusement flittered across his features as, just for one moment, he acknowledged Adam as a fellow human being. It didn't last. The student's eyes flicked back downward, as if his flash of compassion had simply been switched off at source, and he continued with his rote recital in a bored voice: 'I'll be interviewing the passengers, one by one, in their rooms. In the event that one of them is found in possession of contraband, your ship and cargo will be forfeit until such time . . .'

Adam tuned him out and concentrated on worrying about whether the passengers who'd been stupid enough to smuggle something on board had also been bright enough to hide it properly.

Despite his – admittedly self-assessed – status as one of the People's most important agents in the region, Clarence hadn't been in Earth's galaxy when the evacuation began. As soon as he heard about it, he travelled to the Worldsphere's spaceport to meet the refugees, and wasn't surprised to discover that many of the People's other agents had done the same.

He could see them below him now, crawling like termites towards the gash in the sphere that let the outside in. Clarence beat his swan's-feather wings in graceful arcs as he flew. Although he didn't need them to keep afloat, and there was no one watching, he had been told that doing this made his chest muscles ripple in a pleasing fashion, and he took a moment to imagine how he must look with his angel wings, and his dark windswept hair, and his chiselled good looks, flying above the vast concave landscape of the Worldsphere.

Rather absurd, he decided. He felt a blush starting in his chiselled cheeks and creeping all the way across his chest. There was nothing sillier than a religious icon in the wrong place. He wondered, not for the first time, why God had chosen to place him in this particular form; it was a joke that only one person he knew could appreciate, and she spent most of her time in another galaxy.

Not that Clarence could complain. Although he was organic now (the thought still made him shudder), he had been very different once. Crammed into this humanoid shell were the remnants of an intelligence that had once been able to run a starship – that had actually been a starship. Then the accident had happened, and all God had been able to salvage of that once-huge intellect was so pitifully small that it could fit inside the body of an angel. Clarence had realized long ago that he could no longer really understand what he'd once been. It was like losing your hearing, and losing all your memories of sound at the same time.

Sighing, he folded his wings neatly against his back and allowed himself to fall.

Five hours later, Adam was finally beginning to believe that he might be in the clear. He had often thought that forcing a ship's captain to accompany a customs official on his rounds was a peculiar sort of torture. As they entered each room, his heart rate sped up and he found himself examining it as closely as the revenue man, wondering if this would be the one that cost him his entire journey's profit in fines. Maybe they brought him along so they could judge his innocence by how worried he looked. Or maybe they just enjoyed watching him squirm.

But now there were just three more passengers to check, and he was starting to feel positively blasé about the whole thing. Especially since one of them, the next one, was the Tyler's Folly policeman he'd caught staring at him earlier.

Policemen just didn't go in for smuggling. Or, if they did, they made damned sure they didn't get caught.

The student gave a cursory knock on the nondescript grey door, then pushed his way into the room without waiting for a reply. Adam grimaced and followed him in.

The policeman was sitting on the bed, his composure so

absolute that Adam wondered for a moment if he was either dead or meditating. He didn't acknowledge their presence in any way, and Adam saw the student make a little moue of displeasure, turning down the ends of his thin-lipped mouth.

The room was empty, save for one small case at the policeman's feet. The bed was entirely unrumpled, just slightly indented where the man's weight pressed it down. The place had a curiously unoccupied smell. Adam suddenly found himself imagining the policeman sitting there, immobile, throughout the entire journey. Never moving, never using the bed or the sonic shower, never eating and never pissing. Just sitting, waiting for them to land. Adam snapped his head sideways in irritation, trying to dislodge the absurd fantasy, but once summoned it refused to be unthought.

The student seemed entirely unaffected. 'Open the case,' he instructed in a voice that held just a hint of smugness. It was a voice which very clearly said: you've ignored me, and now I'm going to make you suffer in the only small, petty way I can.

The policeman didn't move.

The red-haired student's frown deepened, two perfect parallel lines on his milky-blue forehead. 'If you don't open it, I'll do it myself.'

There was a moment more of silence, then the policeman's eyes snapped up to meet them, like the sudden reanimation of a weeks-old corpse.

Half an hour later, a solitary figure emerged from the asymmetrical shade of the *Joanna* and trudged off through the perpetual Dellahan rain.

Once they'd disembarked from their various ships, the People's agents had congregated in a large park just outside the spaceport. The park, a wide green space dotted with bushes from a hundred different worlds tortured into shapes which nature had never intended, had been built by the Obscene Topiary Interest Group. It was too well executed to be actually amusing, although the fountain of milk that they'd incorporated into one of the nearby organic sculptures did raise a wry smile.

Clarence had spoken to many of the evacuees. Some of them seemed culture-shocked. They'd spent so long away from the Worldsphere that they returned to it almost as strangers.

He caught one of them, a hawk-faced woman, regarding him with an expression that might have been disapproval. He wondered if she was seeing him as one of the humans among whom she'd been living might have done. Did she think he was *blasphemous*?

Gradually, Clarence drifted to the outskirts of the group, waiting for God to speak to him. He could see God's distinctive yellow remote drone now, flittering from Person to Person, reassuring, explaining, joking. God's ikon, the two circles and two dashes of its projected cartoon face, was fixed in an expression of unshakable calm.

Throughout the rest of the Worldsphere, millions of identical drones were scattered, many of them also engaged in conversations with any of the People who wanted advice, information, or just a good gossip. God never allowed more than one drone to be visible at once, though, as if it was important to him to maintain the myth of his unity. Or perhaps to maintain the comforting illusion for each of the Worldsphere's inhabitants that, at any one time, they might have God's undivided attention.

'Hello, Clarence, I thought you might come.' God's voice was masculine, light and pleasant. The remote drone's ikon was smiling broadly at him, and Clarence was annoyed to realize that he felt flattered.

'I wanted to see for myself what was going on.' The spherical drone bobbed noncommittally, like a very heavy soap bubble on a very powerful breeze. 'So what exactly *is* going on?' Clarence continued after a moment.

'Just a precaution,' God said. 'We always knew how dangerous it was to put agents in that galaxy. It was one of the two strictest injunctions in the treaty. Our rivals don't want a war either, but they can't go on forever pretending that they don't know our agents are there. A break will do everyone good.'

'How long a break?'

'How long is a piece of string?'

Clarence paused to run the conversation through one of his remaining syntactic routines, and couldn't help noticing that God had carefully avoided using any conjunctions, thus producing a series of possibly unrelated statements rather than anything resembling an explanation. The other People were right. God, who'd never been caught out in a lie, was being extremely economical with the truth.

'So,' Clarence said, with studied casualness, 'is it worth my while waiting for Bernice to show up?'

'She isn't one of us, you know,' God said.

Clarence felt a number of heated responses poised to come out of him. The urge to let them out was so strong that it was almost physical. He had a quick-fire flash of images across the inside of his retina: Bernice looking at his naked, improbable form for the first time, and her lips quirking up in her trademark half-smile, the smile that told the world that it was welcome to share the joke too, but that she didn't really mind enjoying it on her own. Bernice drugged and weeping because she believed she'd destroyed the future and killed her friends. Bernice taking comfort in his arms and allowing him to find out, for the first and only time, what it felt like to be an organic kissing another organic.

For a moment, the intensity of the sensations almost let him remember what it was like to be able to think a thousand different thoughts a second.

He realized that his wings had reared up in an unconscious gesture of protest, and he settled them back down, shaking the pinions into order. He looked out over the inside of the sphere, at the landscape of fields and towns and seas and islands and mountains curving imperceptibly off until the eye could no longer follow it, but the mind knew that it finally curved right round to the beginning, leaving one standing on the horizon. There was a smell of freshly cut grass and absolute healthiness that Clarence had never encountered anywhere outside the Worldsphere.

'No, but she is a friend. And we owe her,' he said eventually.

God circled him as he spoke, forcing him to twirl round to follow the bright yellow drone. Like the dot on the subtitles telling you which words to sing, but the song was the unique landscape of their home, and Clarence didn't know the tune. 'The last time I saw her, I told her that I didn't risk my life to save her because she was going to die anyway,' he confessed.

The drone's pencil-thin eyebrows twitched in a facial shrug. 'It's true. I'm surprised she didn't understand.'

'Oh, she did,' Clarence said with a self-deprecating smile. 'That's why I have to offer her the opportunity to come here, and avoid whatever trouble it is that you're not telling us is coming.'

God began to drift away from him gently. 'You're perfectly free to ask her. But you know she won't come.'

Clarence frowned at the departing drone. 'Why, did you run another simulation of her? Do you always know better than the rest of us?'

'No, I just know Bernice.'

The figure had walked for miles to find the right place, the entrance which was needed. It ended where it had begun, inside a world.

He'd been alone for a very long time, not just as he marched over this planet's surface, searching for a way in, stumbling past muddy farms and unconcerned farmers to the cliffs that lay beyond the cultivated land. He'd been alone for as long as he'd been free.

But not any more. He could sense his compatriots ahead of him, deep in the earth, waiting. They wouldn't have much longer to wait.

Here, 'mid the bleak waves of our strife and care,
Float the green 'Fortunate Isles'
Where all thy hero-spirits dwell, and share
Our martyrdoms and toils.
The present moves attended
With all of brave and excellent and fair
That made the old time splendid.

J. R. Lowell

1

QUESTIONS RAISED

'And so that's where the band took their name from.'

'Oh. Not really a strong influence on their work, as far as I can tell. Though I did like that one about Earth: most helpful to one new to your galaxy.'

Bernice Summerfield wasn't entirely sure whether he was taking the piss. She was really starting to worry about Clarence. He had always been naive in a peculiarly knowing way, but she'd never known him talk so much without seeming to say anything. She clicked off the holo-screen on which she'd been showing him one of the highlights of twentieth-century Earth culture, and turned to regard him more fully.

'I'm glad you settled on Clarence, though,' he wittered on. 'Pygar doesn't really sound very me. And I don't think I would have reacted too well to the allusion to blindness. I mean, I know I miss the point a bit, and I –'

'Stop it, Clarence!' Bernice's words almost startled her more than the angel. The look of shock on his face and the flaring of wings unsettled her even more. She didn't, she realized, really feel comfortable shouting at an anthropomorphic construct embodying purity and love. It just wasn't the sort of thing you do. Maybe it was the raven-dark hair, not the imagined blond, that made him fair game: the hint of smouldering Valentino.

'Sorry.'

His forlorn tone snapped her back to herself. It didn't do to start linking religious images with romantic heroes; that way confusion, and possibly damnation, lay. 'No, it's my fault. I know you well enough to realize you'll say what you mean eventually. It's probably the lack of sleep.'

The image of Clarence looming over her in the middle of the night, waking her from a most promising dream, flooded her rather fuddled mind. Wolsey also clearly resented the intrusion on his nocturnal pursuits; there was real venom in the cat's half-closed eyes, as if he were considering whether or not the enormous feathered beast currently lounging on her sofa merited a heroic solo hunt.

'I liked the film, that's all. It was your idea to watch it.' The angel was clearly still upset, and cocooned himself in his perfect snow-white wings: a child in its den, eyes downcast. 'It was nice to see another angel; to try to understand what God meant when he gave me this body. To hear the punch line.'

'This is all to do with God, isn't it?' Bernice tried to keep her frustration out of her voice. Why do these things always have to crop up at five in the morning? she screamed inside. But she hoped that Clarence would see only the apology in her eyes.

'Yes.' Well, he was no longer rambling on. Remarkably succinct.

'In what way?' Still gently probing.

'In every way.' Patience.

'In which way that concerns me?' One last chance.

'Oh, for . . .'

Later. Or rather still early morning, and Bernice felt she was at last getting somewhere.

'So, you want me to leave Dellah and go with you to the Worldsphere for an unspecified period of time, and for no readily apparent reason.' The coffee had done her good, and the soothing jazz had diffused an earlier near-slapping incident.

'Yes, but it's not my fault I don't have the answers. I assure you I'm not attempting to be mysterious deliberately. You know I wouldn't do that to you.'

'I know. So, God's pulling out of the Milky Way, finally living within the terms of the treaty. But why now? Now of all times. It doesn't make any sense. I think somebody we know has taken to heart all that guff about working in mysterious ways.'

'I think you're starting to lose me again, Benny.'

Bernice pondered the whole situation, the absence of explanation and the labyrinthine workings of God's almost-infinite mind, and immediately decided on more coffee. 'God created you in the image of a religious ikon from a society in a distant galaxy that you had no knowledge of or interest in yourself. True?'

'Yes.'

'Couldn't he have chosen something from your own culture? A joke closer to home?'

Clarence seemed confused. 'There are no such figures. There never have been.'

Now it was Benny's turn to be lost. 'Maybe not now, but in the past. Even the almighty People must have had a primitive, superstitious period. A time when all the answers weren't found in science or near-limitless intellect. A time when you believed in gods, demons, imps, fairies, anything. It's only natural.'

The angel got up from the sofa, padded over to the window, and gazed out at the beginnings of dawn beyond. His wings fluttered and stretched. 'We've never believed in anything, Benny. That's the way we've always been. From our most primitive beginnings the People have known there was no God, no divinity. It's the very foundation of our society.'

'But then why bother with God; why create him? You appear to feel the need for at least the pseudo-divine. Creating your own all-singing, all-dancing deity. It's the same thing even if you use technology. It's the same need. Why start needing it when you were already so advanced?' Bernice felt sorry for the beautiful creature before her, could see he desperately wanted to explain all.

'Because.' He paused and turned away from the window, suddenly fascinated by the cat, the shelves, his feet, everything else but her. 'God once told me it was because we realized that everyone needs a god, or something to fill that role. If you make your own, at least you can make sure it's a nice one.'

After that Clarence withdrew even further into himself, further into his still-complex workings. He asked her the question again, as Benny knew he would. The look on his breathtakingly handsome face when she said no was childlike in its transparency. He *knew* she would turn him down, or rather God had probably told him she would. And he *really* seemed to want her to go.

'I'll miss you, Benny.' A note of finality. She was sure he had tears in his eyes.

'Don't be so silly. Pop in when everything settles down. You know how these things tend to work themselves out.'

'Not this time, Benny. If God won't tell me how long the evacuation's going to last, that must mean he knows it will last forever. I won't be coming back.'

And then he left.

It took fourteen hours for someone to realize there was a problem with the *Joanna*. The office was never highly staffed, but for some reason the unusually good weather around the spaceport had had a detrimental effect on the officers' health. It was, eventually, the Pakhar student earning a little extra on clean-up detail who made the discovery.

Covering her sensitive, twitching nose with a small plastic breather she pulled open the rather battered hatch. She should have realized something was wrong then, of course. The hatch was always left open. Open to mark a clean ship. Open to mark a ship waiting to be cleaned. And even with the mask on she still knew there was something very wrong. The stench was insufferable, stinging her eyes and coating her throat.

She saw the first of what she later found out were bodies, human bodies, just around the first turn in the main passage-way.

* * *

It took another four hours for a passing, and apparently under-the-weather, customs official to notice the smell and find the unconscious Pakhar.

Initially, he thought she had been attacked, injured in some way. Then he saw the reason for the dark stains on her body-fur, and it was all he could do to hold on to his last meal.

Braxiatel never really looked comfortable in the Witch and Whirlwind, and he certainly looked odd with a pint in his hand. He held his neat, sandy-haired head at an aloof angle, as if he'd seen it all before and hadn't been impressed the first time. But at least he's loosening up, thought Benny, just as her companion slammed his drink on the table, screwed up his thin features, and hissed, 'What does he want?'

Bernice spun round and scanned the darkened room: students drinking; students playing games; students laughing; students reading from an old book and holding hands; man impersonating a film noir private eye. 'Who, exactly?'

'Oh, come now, Bernice, you know. Him. The Mystery Man.' He emphasized the last phrase with unusually bitter mockery. Bernice, unlike most of his students, knew that Professor Irving Braxiatel was far less human than he let people believe. And far older than the thirty-odd years he appeared. So she was rather surprised to find him behaving like a teenage boy in a strop with his parents.

Her gaze returned to the Philip Marlowe in the corner. Every inch the retro-buff: shabby fedora, beige mackintosh with a raised collar, and filterless cigarette glued to his lower lip. His right hand gripped a tumbler half-full of what she assumed to be whisky – whisky suited the look, the attitude. His eyes, dramatically shaded by the hat, were piercing. With a start, she realized he was staring straight at her, and she looked hurriedly away.

'I see what you mean. Intense. Intensely weird. Becoming quite a fixture. I've spoken to him before, or rather he's spoken to me.'

After a moment she risked another glance over and saw a rather young and somewhat drunk student approach and point to the cigarette still wedged between the older man's lips. The student pointed to a group close by and gesticulated further in the direction of the plume of smoke. Piercing eyes turned on the student. The cigarette never left the man's mouth; no words appeared to be spoken.

Looking distinctly shaken, the youngster withdrew, back to his friends and the safety of resentment at a distance.

'I think he's actually smoking real tobacco, you know.' For some reason, Bernice also felt the need to whisper. 'And he's had the good sense not to give up drinking for Lent.' She glanced ruefully at the mango smoothie in her hand.

'He would.' Braxiatel's eyes never left the smoke-shrouded figure across the bar.

'Am I missing something here, Irving? Is there something you'd like to tell me?'

'He's doing it again!' Braxiatel's reply was somewhat unexpected, and punctuated by the resounding slap of his hand hitting the table.

Bernice turned to see the object of Braxiatel's attention raising his glass, and smiling an oddly bright smile, though the cigarette remained firmly in place, and his eyes never lost their intensity. She thought he definitely seemed familiar.

Something about the smile, never moving beyond the lips, made his gaze seem more threatening, and sent a shiver running down her spine. He wasn't looking at Braxiatel, he was looking at *her*. 'I think someone just walked over my grave.'

'What a remarkably fatalist phrase. I really would expect something a bit more upbeat from you, Professor.'

The high, cultured tones and sing-song voice dragged her gaze away from the mystery man and round to the relaxed neatness of a familiar good-looking thirtysomething. His simple suit was cut to perfection, tailored yet effortlessly unstructured, its high collar implying either a penchant for the military or a bent to the religious. The lack of any decoration bar a simple silver medallion ruled out the military. 'Well, if it isn't the Very Reverend James Harker. Not really your stamping-ground, Jim. Is the department of Comparative Religion on fire?'

'Another dazzling display of wit, my dear Professor. I feel almost out of my league joining you, but I have my reasons.' Harker's smile was the second one in as many minutes that seemed to hold no warmth. As he settled down, he sighed and brought one hand across his face, hunching behind it and sliding round into the shade cast by Bernice.

'Would these reasons be enigmatic and extraordinarily difficult to explain? Would you be reticent about any such explanation?' Bernice was becoming convinced that the last couple of days were specifically engineered to tip her over the edge. Peril she could cope with, but she really hated being out of the loop.

'No, not really. I just came to have a look at them.' His hand flicked almost imperceptibly in the direction of the group of students gathered around the old book. They were still all holding hands and seemed spellbound by the short, ochre-skinned humanoid reading to them. Bernice was surprised they could hear anything over the din of the bar, which, even though it was midweek, was as noisy as ever.

'If it's not too obvious a question, why do you appear to be spying on someone giving a reading in the bar? I mean, I know it's not exactly a one-way ticket to hipsville, but we are supposed to be pro-reading. And listening is also something I like to encourage in others.' Bernice was regretting the flippant tone of her words even as they spilt from her mouth, so she decided to silence herself quickly with her mango taste sensation.

Fortunately, her new and rather erratic bar companion was too intent on his study to notice her attitude and he answered with good grace.

'She's reading from the *Book of Maa'lon*.'

'That would appear to be as good a reason as any to spy on a harmless group of people in our care. Has forbidden knowledge been unleashed?' The brightly coloured concoction swiftly returned to her lips.

'For one who advocates listening in others, you practise it rather poorly yourself, Bernice. I've been here on several occasions when you have been discussing matters of faith with James. Maa'lon is a recurring theme.' Bernice had forgotten all about Braxiatel. A swift glance revealed him still to be attempting to stare down his aggressively unhealthy nemesis. Mind occupied with other things and still had time to make her look stupid.

Maa'lon? Of course, James – medallion – religious man – religion. Even when her brain resented the absence of some of the strongest and most poorly named ale in the business, she could still make a simple intuitive leap.

'But surely you should be happy that some of the student body have taken an interest in your faith,' she said brightly. 'Are attendances up, then? I never really thought of you as an evangelist, but I suppose it's all part of the job.'

'I can assure you, Benny, that I have nothing to do with this little gathering, or with the other seven that are also taking place elsewhere on campus tonight. With absolutely no assistance from me, the Church of Maa'lon is undergoing an unprecedented rebirth. I've been asked to give nine "blessings into the fold" already today, and I'm sure there are bound to be more.' The reverend had a haunted look around the eyes, and he hunched down further.

'It's still essentially a good thing though – I mean for you, isn't it? Look, they're hugging. That's nice; hugging's very healthy, I'm told. Not drastically my scene, but then nor are religion, smiling beatifically, and men who wear sandals. No offence, Jim.' Fortunately, the reverend seemed to be oblivious to her babbling, so she decided to try another drink and forget about commenting on her friends' footwear. It only ever got her into trouble.

Crossing the room, Bernice deliberately angled towards the young followers of Maa'lon. As she approached, she realized that the short humanoid with the distinctive yellow-brown skin was no longer reading. The lesson for the day was over, and the group now seemed to be moving on to group prayer and chanting.

'He is here.

He is among us.

He will save us.'

After a short pause they repeated the refrain, and then all locked arms and began to sing.

'Praise! The Redeemer is here.

Rejoice! The saviour of souls walks again . . .'

Bernice hunched over the bar, attempting to put her head as near to the main speakers as she could; however, she could still hear the cheerful but nonetheless discordant tones. Deciding extreme measures were necessary she ordered a dangerously large Virgin Mary.

As she wondered whether anyone would have either the heart or the guts to ask the impromptu choir to stop, someone did just that. She smiled when she recognized the young student who had earlier singularly failed to make an impression on the mysterious man in beige. This time the young man took no prisoners. He was firm and to the point. And he was also clearly much happier dealing with a group of students who sang and smiled and cared about other people's feelings, than with an unresponsive possible psychotic with an apparent death wish. In no time they moved on, all holding hands and gently humming.

'Heads up!'

Emile was nearly knocked to the ground as the girl flew past him, a blur of green topped with a trail of bright orange hair. He went down on one knee to pick up the contents of the bag which now lay strewn across the grass. As he began to gather his belongings, he felt ghostly eyes looking at him. The spectres of his past, laughing at odd little Emile and his amazing knack for awkwardness.

'Bloody glide-planks!' he shouted.

It was a conspiracy. He minded his own business, got on with his own life, and then crazed women on floaters came out of nowhere to knock him down and make him look silly. And she'd spilt his drink.

He sighed and shrugged it off. Never mind; on the whole, he was beginning to get the hang of this fitting-in business. The mud-red barrel-like buildings of the university looked much less daunting in the sun. They no longer loomed over him; the warmth and the stringy grass made him feel more alive, more involved. At least when he wasn't on his knees wiping raspberry slush off his palmtop.

He wondered whether he should get a plank, go for a new image. New Emile could fly around campus and dazzle all before him with loop the loops and hair-raising flips. He could grow his hair long, too. Though the spray-on one-piece would probably be unwise: his slight paunch and ill-defined muscles probably wouldn't help the overall look.

He was just adding up how much it would all cost, when he heard the crack and then the scream, the scream that didn't stop. He realized he was running and heard others shouting for the paramedics; then he rounded the corner and never thought of buying a plank again.

The room was almost totally dark, the only light coming from the small haze vaporizer on the coffee table. Two shadowy figures giggled from their respective positions on the two sofas. Then their laughter became more hysterical.

'No really, Fec, I just didn't know what I was supposed to be doing with girls at the time. It was all a mystery. Everyone makes mistakes. Though I'm not saying it wasn't awkward. But only for the next few years until I could get off-planet.' The tall speaker wiped the tears from his eyes and burst out laughing, throwing back his long ebony hair. Earrings and chains jingled, and he reached over to turn down the vaporizer.

'This stuff's doing my head in, man. I think I should only be saying this sort of shit to a counsellor. I mean, no offence, but I don't think you're really responding too well.'

'Healing power of laughter, Kal,' his short companion responded, in between giggles. The dark hairless head nestled between orange-clad knees, and his small, three-digited hands massaged the exposed broad discs of his feet. 'I just can't believe you thought it should go there. I mean –'

Whatever he meant was lost as an alarm blared and the room was suddenly flooded with light. The tall, pale human attempted to thrust his long arms into the sleeves of his orange jump suit and failed, falling off the sofa and knocking over the vaporizer.

'Shit! Shit! Shit! Where is it, Fec, man?'

His plum-coloured companion tried to focus on the readout attached to his sleeve. Eventually, he got the hang of fast-moving characters. 'St Sophia's, main quad. Plank versus people-mover. People-mover won. Two minutes away; start Clearance.'

In unison the two slapped small metallic pads on to their upper arms, groaned, and hurried out of the room.

Emile felt as if time was still moving slowly when the orange-suited paramedics arrived. He could only see the blood, the beautiful face and the blood. The girl who had been such a blur before, the essence of speed, was now so still, and utterly pale.

The paramedics ushered him out of the way and knelt over her. Emile could see just how serious it was by their clipped tones as they spoke to each other and by the speed of their unpacking. Soon equipment and foil containers littered the grass around the victim.

The taller of the two men took the girl's hand and leant over her.

'Miss. Miss, can you hear me? My name's Kalten, this is Fec. You've had an accident. Don't worry, you'll be fine. But you've lost a lot of blood; we have to give you some now.' As he spoke he began to unwrap one of the foil containers and Emile saw the red liquid inside begin to expand.

The Cham'di, Fec, peeled back the green spray-on, exposing more alabaster skin. He attached the blood-pac to a short sub-dermal and began to swab. As he was just about to pierce the skin the girl's eyes flashed open.

'No!' Her voice was quiet, broken, but full of strength. 'Don't put that thing in me, it's forbidden.' She reached up with a grunt and revealed a gold and amber charm which had been woven into her hair. 'I am Itari, and you can't force me. I know the law. I won't be tainted.'

Even that one small movement was enough to open the

wound further and the dark stain on the grass expanded. The girl sighed and closed her eyes. The shoulders of the paramedics slumped in resignation. Then they sat with her and quietly watched her die.

James Harker watched Bernice return from the bar. She held her little glass like a trophy, and was smiling at the retreating Followers. He always admired the way she wore her heart on her sleeve. Not for her the religious life. Not for her the soul-searching and denial. It was there for all to see.

'James here has an interesting dilemma, Bernice.' Braxiatel's words brought the reverend out of his reverie, and he looked back at the man who now knew it all. Knew the truth about him.

'Don't tell me. Though you discussed the matter in depth while I was at the bar, you now feel it necessary only to hint at the problem in my presence, thereby precipitating a tragic and disfiguring glass-related incident that is totally beyond my control.' James Harker suddenly realized how little he knew Bernice.

'Not this time, Benny,' Braxiatel answered with a thin smile. 'It appears that the recent upsurge in interest, and particularly belief, in Maa'lon is due to reports of his physical presence on Dellah, and eye-witness accounts relating to his performing miracles. Essentially, Maa'lon, as those rather tuneless students made clear, "is here".'

'On Dellah? Why here?'

The reverend now knew, as he'd often suspected, that Bernice hadn't been listening to a word he'd said to her over the last few months; but without a hint of annoyance he leant across the table to say it all once more.

'Because, Bernice, Maa'lon and the faith that takes his name are native to Dellah, to the small town of Tal'een a few hundred kilometres from here. It's from there that the faith spread out to the stars and to me. Five thousand years ago, Maa'lon walked among the people; he knew and spoke to their hearts; he provided the Code, which is the main part of the *Book of Maa'lon*, and then he travelled on to prepare the way for those that would follow. The Followers believe that he will return to show us the Way. And that would appear to be just what's happening now in Tal'een.

'The young reader that was leading the group here was a Hut'eri; she's native to Tal'een, and she says that she has actually seen Maa'lon.'

Bernice appeared to be puzzled by his explanation, and immediately voiced her concerns: 'Now you know I won't just accept the idea of a god abroad on Dellah but, even if it turns out to be true, I don't really understand why this would be a problem for you. Surely you'd be one of the big winners? It's the sceptics like Irving and me who would be in trouble.'

Braxiatel was clearly enjoying himself when he butted in. 'Ah, now we get to the root of the problem. It appears our young reverend has never believed what he preaches.'

Emile was just wandering. He wasn't exactly sure where he was, he just knew he needed to be out in the open. Away from that place. Away from everyone. He certainly didn't need to be bundled over for the second time that day. But it happened none the less.

The three figures looming over him looked hell-born in the twilight. Dark figures with tentacles writhing from their faces. They each bore large, menacing weapons covered in bright readouts. He wondered whether the shock had gotten too much for him, or whether his mind was being overly literal when trying to deal with demons.

'You are a St Oscar's student?' asked the largest of the three demons.

'Er, yes,' stammered Emile, hoping against hope that, given such a fifty-fifty opportunity to say what was probably the right thing, he had not already messed up.

'Good.' Emile's sigh was embarrassingly loud. 'Fact: we are looking for Professor Bernice Summerfield. Question: do you know her?'

Emile felt an overwhelming desire to say yes again and point them in the right direction, but he knew he couldn't do that to Benny. He took a deep breath and closed his eyes so as not to be distracted by the weapons.

'Might do. Depends what you want with her. Who are you?' He screwed his eyes even tighter shut.

'We are Grel. We seek facts. New facts on the planet Dellah. Professor Bernice Summerfield is an excellent source of facts: a fact catalyst, some have said. She understands how to find good facts, and good facts come to her. The Grel admire seekers after fact and we require her help in our search,' answered the central creature with a flamboyant display of tentacle waving.

'Oh, well that's all right then.'

James Harker was certainly going up in Bernice's estimations, and she wished she had paid more attention during their previous debates. It would seem her 'always controlled' drinking had allowed her to miss the finer points of a most complex and remarkably rational man. She made a mental note not to switch off when people started talking about their religious beliefs. Well, not for the first half-hour at least.

'. . . all that seemed a bit silly, really. Superstition born of its age. But the Code, that's really something. A great way to live your life. Full of love and compassion; moral but never harsh; a guide rather than a manual for intolerance. That's what drew me. For a confused teenager desperate for answers and understanding, it's a profoundly moving tract. I've never been without it since an aunt gave me a copy on my sixteenth birthday. You should read it. That's why I became a Follower and why I decided to spread the Code. We would all be living in a very different galaxy if more people had that one little book.'

The reverend seemed relieved to be able to explain himself, to work the problem through before them.

'But if Maa'lon is walking the streets of wherever and doing all manner of nice and godly things, why not just go and see him? That should conquer the faith problem.' Bernice had the distinct impression that she didn't sound quite serious enough given the circumstances. 'I mean, you like his ideas, and now you could get the proof that would make faith irrelevant.'

Harker toyed with his medallion as he spoke: 'I appreciate what you are trying to do, Bernice, but faith is a prerequisite of being a Follower. Only those who believe will be shown the Way. Only those who are true to Him will follow. And as one of the more prophetic texts makes clear: "By sight alone shall He know the truth of you, and ye shall be judged." Now, obviously the "ye" and the "shall"s are human embellishments, but I think they set the tone rather well, don't you? Anyway, all that matters is that I have lived a lie and will be judged on that lie. There's really nothing more to say.'

Bernice could think of lots of things to say, but she was fortunately distracted by the fight that broke out by the entrance.

The fight hadn't lasted long at all. In fact, it hardly really qualified as a fight. The starball team – four strapping lads, a particularly violent-looking Goll, and a diminutive, chitinous insectoid with truly evil eyes – had clearly drunk enough to take offence at being pushed out of the way by three bizarre humanoids with squid-like tentacles erupting from their mouths. The sportsman-and-booze correlation ran true to form, and the blows rained down. After about ten seconds of grunting and one disturbing scream it was all over and the bar manager called for the paramedics. By the time they arrived the three Grel had already joined Bernice's party and were attempting to wave their tentacles in an innocent manner while wiping the blood off the butts of their dataxes.

James Harker didn't feel entirely comfortable around the Grel. Although when Bernice had explained who they were she had also assured him they were essentially non-hostile, he couldn't get the image of them clubbing the drunken sports team out of his mind. He certainly wasn't going to take them to Tal'een, and he definitely wasn't going to let them anywhere near Maa'lon. Not a chance.

Fortunately Bernice didn't seem too keen on them either.

'I don't understand why you're even interested in the subject. You worship facts, not gods. You don't believe in anything but knowledge. You have faith in nothing. Meeting a god, if there is one there anyway, would be pointless. You'd only annoy him.' Bernice's voice got louder and higher as she went on. 'And you'd annoy me.'

'Facts about gods good facts. Proof make faith fact, so we seek good messianic facts,' responded the central Grel, the only one to speak so far. 'Grel already know many good Maa'lon facts, now need to complete data stack. Grel will prove useful; have many good facts at your disposal.'

The reverend found he was having real trouble understanding the alien's rudimentary speech patterns, and hoped the others were having similar problems.

'Why would we need you? We have a Very Reverend Follower of the Way here; he knows it all. Go on, ask him anything about Maa'lon. We don't need your facts where we're going,' Bernice said, pointing at the reverend and taking a large swig of whisky.

The Grel master turned to the smaller of his companions, on his left, and waved his tentacles in an oddly enigmatic manner. Peering into a little display on the side of its still blood-spattered weapon, the Grel said, ' "When Maa'lon first came among the Hut'eri he knew not his own name. None recognized him, and none would bathe his feet in the milk of the a'tsch. For seven days he wandered homeless and nameless, until a child named him and then all knew his name." Fact required: what type of animal told the Sacred Child the hidden name?'

The reverend's heart sank. He felt Bernice's eyes on him. Braxiatel looked at him expectantly. The three Grel did distracting things with their tentacles.

'Well . . .' Play for time, he thought; inspiration may strike. Then a sudden idea. 'Well, it was the sacred gh'see, of course.'

'Bad fact! Incorrect response. The Sacred Child knew name of Maa'lon all along; it was the Sacred Child who told all the animals of the great forest of Tal'een: "and the multitude of beasts beat out the name Maa'lon in the ancient tongue with their hooves and claws and paws. And then all knew his name, and they washed his feet in the milk of the a'tsch." '

'Bugger,' muttered Bernice as she headed back to the bar.

'That was just too weird, man. And, believe me, I've seen weird.' Kalten leant forward to rummage through the detritus littering the room. He smiled as he found the remains of a snack bar. He was soon munching noisily.

'Too weird,' was all Fec felt it was necessary to say. Swaying round, feet high in the air, lying flat on his back, the Cham'di turned his large bloodshot eyes to his companion. 'Extremely weird.'

Kalten was disappointed when he finished his snack so quickly. There didn't seem to be anything else to eat. He tried to empty his mind of food thoughts; he needed to distract himself. The wrong thought occurred.

'I mean, what makes someone do that kind of shit? Believe that crap. Just lie there and die; we'll just twist in the wind.' Kalten could feel the anger rising within him and wondered where best to direct it.

'When it comes down to it, Kal, the sickness was in her head. No blood-pac can help that. She was screwed.'

Kalten knew he was just saying it, talking shit to blur the issue. Just trying to help. He wanted it to work, but he knew it wouldn't.

Slowly, with all his joints cracking loudly, he stretched across to the vaporizer and set it to maximum. The machine's hum shifted up in tone, and it was soon impossible for them to see each other.

Bernice went back to Braxiatel's study after the bar closed. She knew he wanted to tell her something; she just had to let him do it in his own time. She turned down a whisky and sat down, defiantly sipping a small orange crush while he unlocked the tantalus. After a few moments of silent endeavour he came and sat next to her, placing his cognac on

31

the exquisite eighteenth-century coffee table. The moment of truth.

'They want me to come home, Benny.' Not exactly what she'd been expecting. 'My people want me to leave Dellah.'

'Do you know why?'

'No. Which is obviously something that worries me. I don't like it when they get all mysterious. I've spent too long doing it to other people to appreciate it when it's done to me.' Braxiatel seemed to be searching for something deep within his golden drink.

'Are you going to go?' An obvious question, but one which needed to be raised.

'No. Rest assured, Benny, I'm not leaving my home. I've invested too much time and effort in Dellah to leave it all behind. And anyway, I haven't lived there for centuries, and I didn't even like it much then,' answered Braxiatel, giving his cognac a swirl. He smiled and chuckled to himself.

Bernice felt cold all over. Braxiatel was trying to cheer her up, trying to make her feel better, to stop her being scared. Which meant that Braxiatel himself was scared.

'What else did they say, Irving?' She was sure he would notice the steel in her voice.

'Very little. Well, very little of use. They called me back, just as they've called all my people back. When I said no, they took my machine. I couldn't get there now even if I wanted to; they're sealing themselves off. They didn't say why, but that's the long and the short of it. I'm on my own. Or rather, we're on our own. Actually, I'm finding the whole thing quite invigorating.'

Bernice felt her heart sink.

2

A DAY IN THE LIFE

Clarence sat on a high rock and gazed out across the desert landscape spooling out endlessly below. He liked to come to this piece of the Worldsphere when he was brooding; it was one of the wilderness areas that had been left to grow naturally while the rest of the giant habitat was given over to the People as their plaything.

He could allow himself to believe that he was alone here.

But none of the People was ever truly alone. Above him, the planet Whynot floated, its absurd cartoon face composed of continents and islands smiling down at him. All the People's jokes were so large, they weren't really funny any more. Was he one of those jokes? And, if he was, who was getting him?

He knew the answer. He was God's joke. And, when the punch line came, it would be God, he was sure, who would deliver it.

'Hello, Clarence.'

He turned around, expecting to be met by God's eternally bland, smiling face. It wasn't him, though. Just some other drone sent to keep an eye on a depressed angel.

'Hello,' he said, warily.

The drone wobbled from side to side in an enquiring manner when he didn't say any more. It was long and thin, almost missile shaped, and the hologram of its facial ikon stuck out from the sides of its body like the shocked expression on the face of a human cartoon character. Clarence didn't think he knew it.

'I came here to be alone,' he said eventually, rather pleased at how rude he sounded.

The drone didn't seem put off, though. It drifted gently sideways in a sudden gust of dry-smelling desert wind, then settled on the rock beside Clarence and leant its small body backward so that its unreal face was staring up into his.

'I'm with ARIG, by the way,' it said.

Clarence deliberately turned away and gazed out across the yellow-brown plateau beneath them. 'Really?' he said with optimum disinterest.

'My, aren't we sulky today?' The drone sounded amused rather than offended. 'I wasn't sent by God, if that's what you were thinking.'

That got Clarence's attention. 'But you know who I am,' he said neutrally. The drone didn't respond, and they sat in silence for a further three minutes and forty-eight seconds. Clarence sighed. It was clear that no amount of standoffishness would make the drone go away. 'All right then,' he said, resignedly. 'Who are you?'

'I thought you'd never ask!' The drone's facial ikon beamed happily at him. 'I'm just a remote: a stealth drone from the *B-Aaron*.'

Clarence was impressed despite himself. The *B-Aaron* was one of the most aggressive of the People's Very Aggressive Ships. Its kill count during the recent War had been second to none. And, unlike many other veterans of the War, it had experienced absolutely no visible guilt about it afterwards. Consequently, it had been welcomed gladly back into the bosom of the People, and invited to dinner parties that the more troubled veterans, with their discomfiting talk of death and responsibility, were not. Yet another blunt irony of the only conflict his pacifist race had managed in living memory.

Clarence had a horrible feeling that he might have known the *B-Aaron* before the accident, but he no longer had any memory of it. 'Have we met before?' he asked cautiously.

'Oh no,' the drone said cheerfully. 'I knew of you, of course, and I heard about the . . . well, you know. But we didn't share any of the same interests.'

'ARIG,' Clarence said, remembering. 'That's the Apocalyptic Religions Interest Group, isn't it? Well, I suppose I can guess why I might be of interest to you now.'

'Yes, but you'd probably guess wrong,' the drone said, then added, 'Do you know that my stealth capacity is so good that I can shield this conversation from anyone, even God?'

Clarence's head jerked up involuntarily to glance at Whynot, home of most of the intelligence of God.

'Of course, he'll realize that we're having a shielded conversation, but I quite like the idea of the old bugger trying to work out what it's all about.'

'So what is it about?' Clarence asked.

'Operation Ragnarok.'

Emile was experiencing the lassitude unique to the last ten minutes of an early-morning plate tectonics lecture. Beside him, Elspeth was snoozing lightly, thereby aligning herself with the majority of the students in the hall.

Professor Uraz seemed indifferent to the effect he was having on his listeners. His dull monotone resonated flatly through the high-ceilinged mud-brick room.

After several more minutes he flicked a switch on his hand unit, and the miniature hologram Earth on Emile's pad was replaced by an almost identical one on which, if he squinted really hard, he could just about make out that the continent of Antarctica had shifted a couple of millimetres downward. And this, Emile thought with resigned horror, was just the beginning: over the course of the term they were due to examine the tectonic shifts on every planet of major archaeological interest in Earthspace. This was not the thrilling student life he had imagined when he ran away from his home to join the university.

He realized that he had almost drifted off to sleep when he was jolted sharply upright by the end-of-lecture chime. As he woke, he experienced a brief subliminal flash, an image of a twisted body and the copper smell of blood.

That could have been me, he thought. There was a time when I might have made the decision she did.

Beside him, Elspeth stretched her arms upward and yawned languorously. The movement pulled the material of her T-shirt tight over her small, firm breasts, and Emile made his usual token effort to find that arousing. And, as usual, he found himself far more intrigued by a fair-haired boy in the next row who had clearly come to the lecture straight from the running track. The loose cotton of his track suit was glued to his body by sweat, and Emile could smell the musky evidence of his exertion from ten feet away.

Suddenly, the boy turned round and caught Emile's stare. He smiled broadly, the white of his teeth flashing in the glare of the overhead spotlights. The boy's gaze flicked briefly down to his own pad, then back up at Emile. His smile became even more dazzling for a moment before he turned and exited the hall at a fast jog.

No one should be that attractive, Emile thought, an out-of-body vision of his own rounded, unfinished-looking frame flashing through his mind. He sighed and dropped his eyes to his personal pad, ready to switch it off.

Then he felt a clenching in his chest which emerged as an embarrassingly loud gasp when he saw that the boy had sent over his room number and the call-up code for his pad.

'You don't want to get involved with him,' Elspeth said from over his shoulder. Emile jumped. For a moment, his world had narrowed down to him and the boy and all the wonderful things they might do together.

'Why not?' he asked, instantly defensive.

'He is, you could say, in with the wrong crowd.' Elspeth's forehead was creased in a frown beneath her black bob, and Emile saw that she was being uncharacteristically serious.

Emile let his dreams of the perfect romance fade away into the never-never land where they belonged. Maybe his dad was right: he would never meet the right man because wanting a man at all was wrong. Maybe he should work harder on finding Elspeth attractive.

She slipped her arm around his shoulders now, and he wondered if *she* found *him* attractive. Probably not. He was just safe.

'Never mind, Emile,' she said softly, her Tyler's accent momentarily stronger, all soft Rs and long vowels. 'You can do a lot better.'

Emile blinked owlishly as they emerged from the relative gloom of the lecture theatre into an unusually sunny Dellahan morning. 'Better than that?' he said disbelievingly. 'In some of my more implausible fantasies, maybe.'

Elspeth laughed – a raucous squawk which always took people by surprise emerging from such a slight, delicate frame – and Emile felt the warm glow of friendship. Less intense than love, but with less potential for pain, too. And a lot more than he had ever known before he came to Dellah.

Around them, their fellow students were loitering and mingling in twos and threes, none of them too keen to proceed to the next hour of tedium.

To one side, a larger group had joined hands and seemed to be engaged in some kind of open-air prayer meeting. Several of the other students were pointing at them and laughing, covertly or openly. Emile tried but couldn't really find it funny. There was still a part of him that yearned for that, for rules about what to believe and how to behave and who to be with. Even a religion that told you that everything you wanted and were was sinful and wrong could be more comforting than no religion whatsoever. Nature abhors a vacuum so much that she will rush to fill it with anything at all.

Elspeth, he realized, was also staring at the student congregation with an expression that was very far from amused.

'Do you mean he's one of them?' Emile asked, as understanding began to dawn.

'Not quite. Similar medium, different message. Dark, secretive, occult mumbo-jumbo, I heard.'

Emile stared down at the numbers and letters on his keyboard, wondering if there was some cabalistic meaning hidden there. 'There's a lot of it about these days, isn't there?' he said softly. There'd been a noticeable upsurge in recruitment to old religions in recent months. Even the Sultan, that old traditionalist, had noticed it, and responded by offering a grant top-up to anyone engaged in regular acts of worship. As if, Emile thought, a few shillings could be enough to make someone change their fundamental beliefs.

Elspeth snapped him out of his reverie. 'There always has been,' she said. 'Doesn't mean we have to play follow my leader.' Elspeth's mercurial temperament had switched to boundless cheer again. 'Come on, I don't think I can face the chronological techniques lecture after that. Let's go and worship at the shrine of strong lager.'

Irving Braxiatel had avoided thinking about, or indeed tackling, any of the major problems on his mind by spending the morning tackling every trivial task that he'd spent the last few weeks avoiding.

Now he really was down to the dregs: writing advertising blurb for the numerous productions the theatrology department put on over the course of a term. As head of department, it was his duty to do this. As a rational being, he found it utterly absurd.

Hence the program he'd written to handle the task. He was rather proud of it. By cross-referencing with the sociology department database, he'd found a list of the most strongly push-button words correlated by species, gender, genre, and other less important variables. He'd linked this up with a straightforward syntax routine and a creative writing crib-program which the English department had confiscated from one of its brighter, but less motivated, students.

Now all he had to do was enter each synopsis and a perfect piece of blurb would emerge, guaranteed to contain all the key phrases that would leave the punters gasping for more. Or at least keep the other fellows off his back for a little longer.

Currently, the first years were putting on a season of erotic mime. Braxiatel had always considered the art form to be a crime against sentience, and had briefly toyed with the idea of spending all the advertising budget on state-of-the-art therapy for Professor Mordechai, whose idea it had been. The only thing less erotic than watching a being perform simulated acts of sex with a garden vegetable, he had decided, was watching a being performing simulated acts of sex with a simulated garden vegetable.

Fortunately, the program prevented his own distaste from spilling over into the copy. He was quite pleased with the result it had produced. He was particularly fond of the phrase 'darkly bizarre eroticism' which the program had chosen to use in its description of no fewer than four of the mimes. It was so evocative yet utterly meaningless: the essence of good advertising copy.

He pressed DELIVER and watched as the text was whisked away from his screen and into the university central core. He was rather startled when, a few moments later, it bounced straight back with the message 'Delivery failure; Reason: Rejected by Dean's morality buffers' attached, along with a seal that appeared to read 'by order of the Sultan's New Moral Army'.

He was still staring at it in puzzlement when Renée Thalia burst into his office in a swirl of expensive perfume and inadequate clothing.

He flicked his eyes over her, taking in her outfit in one appalled rush, then allowed them to travel the same territory more slowly, hoping to make his disapproval plain.

Not that Renée paid the slightest bit of notice. She smiled widely and flicked her head to the side, bouncing her curly fair hair on her shoulders as she perched on the edge of Irving's desk. Her pose was clearly designed to show off the maximum expanse of milky-white thigh. An objective observer, Braxiatel mused, might have described the body so blatantly on display as a little on the plump side of average. In the real world, he'd only ever heard it called 'lush', by almost every fellow of the university at one time or another since she'd arrived four months ago.

'I just thought I'd drop by to check the final arrangements for the concert tonight,' she said. Her voice, where one might have expected something husky and sensuous, was actually rather crisp and no-nonsense. Would that the rest of her were the same, Braxiatel thought wearily.

'What exactly did you want to check?'

'Oh, you know, the music we'll be playing, the protocol, my outfit . . .'

'You're intending to wear that?' Braxiatel could not keep a squeaky note of incredulity out of his voice.

Renée pouted, suddenly looking startlingly like Marilyn Monroe. 'You don't like it?' Lurking far back in her blue eyes was a sparkle of mischief that danced merrily as she spoke.

'Not at all,' Braxiatel said dryly. 'I was just wondering whether you might like to put on a skirt, or whether you thought that belt would be adequate.' He realized that he was running his hands through his usually immaculate hair, mussing the sandy strands. He stopped himself instantly, folding his long fingers neatly on the desk in front of him.

She pretended to spend some time considering his question. 'No,' she said eventually, 'on balance I think this probably suits me better.'

Braxiatel nodded. 'I'm glad you're taking this more seriously than you usually take your performance commitments. The Sultan of the Tashwari is one of our major sponsors – the whole university is only here on his sufferance – and it's important that we impress him.' He allowed his eyes to reconnoitre a little more of her body before scurrying back to the safe territory of his hands. 'Which I'm very sure your – erm, what precisely does one call that item of clothing?'

She looked down at her own ample chest. 'A basque.'

'Hmm, yes. Which I'm very sure your basque will do.'

Renée rose from the desk and clasped her hands delightedly. 'That's wonderful. I was a bit concerned, you know, that a being as conservative as the Sultan might consider the whole outfit a little . . . immodest.'

Braxiatel sighed. 'On the contrary, I'm sure he will love every square centimetre of it.'

She smiled slyly and sashayed towards the exit. 'All five

of them,' he murmured, just loudly enough to be sure she heard him as she closed the heavy oak door behind her.

Her scent lingered a little longer than she had, lending an unwontedly floral air to an office whose main olfactory themes were usually wood and leather. Braxiatel found himself wondering whether a bunch of flowers might brighten the place up occasionally.

He shook his head irritably and returned to his study of the blurbs which the Dean's office had so unexpectedly rejected. 'By order of the Sultan's New Moral Army.'

What New Moral Army? He knew that the Sultan had experienced something of a resurgence in his own faith recently – rumour had it that he'd been the recipient of a visitation from his god – but it was unlike him to impose any of his beliefs on others. For the first time, it occurred to Braxiatel to wonder exactly what the Sultan's god had said to him during his visit.

What would Renée say, he thought, if she knew some of Braxiatel's work had been rejected on the grounds of being immoral? Renée . . . She was performing a cello concerto in front of the Sultan tonight. Perhaps he should pay a visit to her tomorrow to debrief her, find out what the old eccentric was up to.

For some reason, the thought made him strangely cheerful.

Later that day, Emile emerged from a lecture that should have been given by Bernice Summerfield, and might have been more interesting if it had been, to find the woman herself waiting for him outside.

She was standing beside an alien, one of the Grel he had met earlier. It was the servitor with the dark splash of colour over its eye, and its leather-like head was turned towards her in an attitude of intense concentration, or interest, or possibly adoration. Professor Summerfield has found another admirer, he thought. He smiled at her and nodded at the huge creature as he approached, feeling a brief twinge of excitement mingled with apprehension.

'Hi, Professor, is anything up?'

41

Bernice grinned and slung a companionable arm over his shoulder. The rough fabric of her jacket chafed against his neck and he noticed for the first time that she was dressed for travel. Both the excitement and the apprehension leapt up a notch.

'Is there somewhere you want me to go? The next lecture's on faecal analysis, so almost anywhere would be an acceptable alternative.'

She frowned as she led him towards her rooms. A stray lock of dark brown hair blew into her eye, lending her an incongruously coquettish air.

'Actually, Emile, I'm the one who's going. I was rather hoping you might do something for me.'

'Well, I did have a vacation to the Eye of Orion planned, but I suppose I can cancel it if you really want me to,' he joked feebly.

Bernice laughed generously, clapping him on the back in a suspiciously 'hail fellow well met' kind of way as she led him into her shambolic quarters. The Grel, Emile was amused to see, followed them in, ducking his tentacled head to fit under the door and then looking around with an expression that, even on his unfamiliar features, registered as amazement at the astonishing mess.

Bernice swept an armful of papers off the sofa to make room for Emile and herself to sit. The alien remained standing, perusing her bookshelves with obvious fascination. Bernice glared at it, then shrugged and returned her attention to Emile.

'I hate to ask this, but I have to go away, and there's something I'd like you to look into for me,' she said, bending down to fumble through the detritus on the floor.

'What is it?'

'Aha!' She sat back up and waved a remote control around in triumph. 'At least I live in an orderly mess. Well, Emile, I suspect that what I want you to investigate isn't unconnected to the thing that I'm going away to study. But take a look. I hope you have a strong stomach.'

* * *

42

Emile, it turned out, didn't. Halfway through the recording, he'd been forced to use Bernice's surprisingly spotless bathroom to say goodbye to the beers and bar snacks he'd shared with Elspeth earlier.

'You want me to investigate the murder of an entire spaceship's crew.' Emile stopped, momentarily at a loss for words to express the absurdity of this idea. 'Aren't there people more qualified to do this than me? Like, on a rough estimate, several billion of them.'

He turned from his fixation on the final frozen scene on her screen to look Bernice in the eyes. He was startled to catch an expression that might have been guilt in them.

'Fact: you have good cult knowledge. Fact: all evidence suggests these murders are cult killings. Fact: Professor Summerfield has faith in you. Conclusion: you are appropriate investigator.' Unexpectedly, it was the alien which had spoken, the cilia around its mouth waving gently in time to its speech.

After a second, the import of its words registered with Emile. *It knows that I was in a cult. She told him about that. How could she?*

When he looked at Bernice again, she had dropped her head so that her dark fringe shielded her face from his view. *She knows she had no right to tell him,* he thought angrily.

But when she looked up again, her face showed only a kind of steely resolve. 'I have a bad feeling about all of this. All these new religious groups: they can't be unconnected. Uncovering the cult responsible may involve infiltrating it, and at least I know you're wise to them. Once bitten, twice shy, as I'm told they say.'

'Nice analogy, Professor. I would have said it was more like sending a recovering alcoholic to infiltrate a brewery.'

To his surprise, she laughed. Then she reached forward and gently cupped his cheek in her palm. 'Oh, Emile, don't keep underestimating yourself. You're much tougher than you realize. The police will be investigating this too, of course, but I have a very strong feeling that any answers they find won't be the important ones. A friend of my ex-husband's –' a note of disapproval entered her voice '– has arranged for all the police files to be sent over to your personal terminal. Just do me a favour and see what you make of them.'

She let go of his face and leant back. 'Why the sudden interest in religion? And why now?'

Something caught her eye on the low plastic coffee table in front of them and she reached forward to pick it up. It was a single perfect white feather. Gently, she stroked her index finger along its length, a thoughtful expression on her face. 'And Clarence . . .' she muttered. 'Why now?'

The room was dark once more; the two shadowy figures reclined casually and took deep breaths, always inhaling through the nose. They began to giggle.

'This stuff's starting to totally do my head in, you know,' snorted Fec.

'Too true. Life in the Haze; rose-tinted. Beats the shit out of the outside.' Kalten became suddenly fascinated by his hands, which he was sure shouldn't have so many fingers. He began to giggle.

'You're a maniac.' Fec attempted to get up and then thought better of the idea. He looked round at Kalten sheepishly to see if he had noticed. His tall friend smiled knowingly back at him.

They both burst out laughing; tears streamed down their faces and they rolled about the floor clutching their stomachs.

It took Kalten a while to realize he had heard the door smash open, and the fast tread of booted feet. He struggled to understand what was going on. The feet nearest to him looked distinctly military. Military feet in the university: he had to lay off the Haze.

The vaporizer smashed with a sharp red flame.

Kalten looked up at the obscured figure looming over him. The voice was deep, utterly no-nonsense.

'Morality code violation. This is the only chance you're gonna get. Get a life, boys; get a god.'

And then they disappeared.

Renée was going to be late for her recital, she knew. It would annoy the hell out of Irving Braxiatel, which was a definite bonus, but it might also prejudice her rather cushy position at the university. 'Orchestral Attaché to the University of Dellah Theatrology Department' was a great title. It certainly beat 'That woman in the corner who'll play the cello for her bed and board' which had been her most impressive previous moniker to date.

She was going to be late, she thought, as she hurried along the square-paved concourse leading from her rooms to the concert hall, her cello case bumping uncomfortably against her back and the rain, which had been unable to stay away for long, turning her carefully styled hair into a sodden mess in the Dellahan twilight.

I'm going to be late. It was no good, no amount of self-induced panic could make her start running in *this* outfit. If she opened her legs wider than about a centimetre the skirt would be bound to split. And then Braxiatel's amusing prudishness might actually be justified. Besides which, she knew from experience that she looked a lot sexier moving at a fast walk than a slow, out-of-breath jog, and she was rather enjoying the glances of admiration her frantically swaying hips were garnering from many of the students she passed.

When she arrived at the hall she was, of course, fifteen minutes late. Every face in it (most of them the Sultan's native Dellahan retinue) turned to watch her as she staggered up the aisle towards the stage. By this time, her cello had ceased to be merely an encumbrance and had graduated to being the heaviest object in known space.

Halfway up the aisle she paused to get her breath back, enjoying the feeling as rain dripped from her hair and into the deep cleavage of her basque. She felt several eyes tracking the progress of each water droplet. Two of them, belonging to a thin, peculiarly dressed human, seemed to be watching them with particular envy. As she finished her journey to the stage, she flashed him her 'if you ask for my number later, I'll probably give it to you' smile.

So it didn't occur to her to wonder why he stared at her so intently during the performance.

* * *

It was two in the morning, and Emile still had plenty more to do. That was OK, though. After everything he'd already seen, he didn't plan on sleeping at all that night. He had no intention of giving the images lurking behind his eyelids a chance to pounce.

His room was transformed, wallpapered with pictures from the doomed ship: torn flesh and blood and the messages written in blood which had been found scrawled on the floors, and on the walls.

The police were already working on identifying the victims; with the state they were in, it would only be possible on a genetic rather than a physiological level. They'd run DNA tests on the sludge they'd swept off the floors, and found fifteen distinct lifeforms. The ship manifest listed thirteen passengers and the captain, and then there would have been the customs officer.

Ergo everyone on the ship was dead. Ergo the killer had been someone else, someone from Dellah, from one of the many growing cults.

Emile couldn't fault the logic, but couldn't shake the feeling that they were all falling for some sleight-of-hand too obvious to see, like someone who'd been tapped on the shoulder and had twisted round the wrong way to catch the culprit. No point worrying about it, though; nothing definite could be known until all the genetic prints had been cross-matched to produce positive IDs. Only three people – the captain, the customs official, and a female Dellahan passenger – had been positively identified so far. It would take weeks or even months to do the rest, tracing back the various passengers to their home planets and checking the central registries there for their DNA data.

Better to leave that side of the investigation to the police, he'd concluded, and concentrate on the messages themselves.

He'd spent an hour just staring at the pictures before writing down the messages, the ones the police had translated and the many that they couldn't. It was all nonsense about fear and God and war and other typically apocalyptic religious rantings. If it was unusual for anything, it was for its ecumenicalism: so far, at least seven distinct languages and nine different registered religions had been identified among the rambling, bloody text.

Emile stepped back from the wall, where he'd been studying one of the plainest scrawls: Allah Akbar, God is great, written on the floor beside what might have been the remains of an entire body. For a moment, Emile felt the stink of old blood in his nostrils, the phantom smell of death.

By all the laws of fiction, Emile ought to be well on the way to becoming a serial killer himself by now. Or, according to the logic of censorship, he ought to have become desensitized to it all, indifferent to the horror around him. In fact, he found it increasingly disturbing and repulsive as time wore on, as if the implications of such a barbaric act were too huge to take in all at once.

He had realized one thing, though. The writing wasn't all by the same hand. That supported the police hypothesis of a group of cult killers, naturally, but Emile didn't think that was it.

The writing on the walls all looked the same. It was the stuff on the floor that varied. A very strong intuition told Emile that the victims had written those gory messages themselves. Prayers to their various gods written in their own life-blood.

It was all very gothic. And he wasn't really sure what it meant, except that perhaps it was wrong to disregard the importance of the ship's passengers altogether, to dismiss them as simple victims.

Emile stretched his neck upwards and rotated his head, trying to ease the tension in his shoulders. It was no good; he needed a break. Elspeth was always still up at this time of night. He would cadge a cup of coffee from her, and they would chat about something trivial, and he wouldn't have to think about all this death for a while.

Before he left, Emile sent off his deductions so far, limited as they were, to wait for Bernice on her personal terminal. He had to make sure she was totally up to date, in case anything happened to him before he could complete the investigation.

He considered this last train of thought, and realized that he was probably being rather melodramatic.

Then he thought about it some more, and it occurred to him that he was almost certainly just being sensible.

After that he decided not to think about it at all. The last thing he needed was to make himself any more frightened than he already was.

'It's the end of the world, isn't it?'

The little drone moved up to Clarence, bumping against his leg in its excitement. 'No, no, that's a common misconception. Nothing ends, but everything changes, and a lot of people die.'

'Ragnarok. *Operation* Ragnarok. And this is something I should know about?'

'Know about?' The drone looked amused. 'You've just taken part in it. It's God's name for the evacuation of Earth's galaxy.'

'According to whom?'

'Oh . . . I have my sources.'

Clarence raised an eyebrow.

The drone ducked its face sheepishly. 'All right then, I did my usual spherewide media-scan for any references to ARIG-related matters, and Operation Ragnarok came up.' It moved closer to Clarence, so close that the hologram ikon of its face passed through Clarence's real flesh-and-blood one. 'Even though there hasn't actually been any reference to it in any of the media; I checked. Interesting, isn't it?'

'So God just planted it there for someone to find.' Clarence hunched his wings preparatory to doing some serious thinking. 'Why? Who did he think would find it?'

'Me, presumably,' the drone said. 'God must have realized that ARIG would stumble across it sooner or later. Did he expect me to come and tell you, though?'

'And why would he want me to know? What does it mean?'

'And what is he expecting us to do?'

Clarence and the drone looked at one another. 'We're not going to out-think him, are we?' Clarence said. 'Not even you, and you're several million times smarter than I am now.'

The drone shuffled away from him, probably embarrassed at the mention of his accident. 'Second-guessing a deity just isn't possible; ARIG know that better than anyone.'

'So what *do* we do?'

'Nothing,' the drone said firmly.

'But then what's the point –'

'No, listen. Anything we do might be what God wants us to do. And I'm damned if I'm going to dance to his tune. All we can do is investigate, try to find out more about what's going on. With better information, it might be clearer how we should act. Or, if nothing else, we could go public with it, shame God into owning up.'

The sky was beginning to darken as false night swept across the eternally stationary sun of the Worldsphere. The drone's mat-black body faded into the background, leaving only the luminous semaphore of its facial ikon visible.

' "All *we* can do . . . how *we* should act." What does this have to do with me?' Clarence realized how petulant that sounded. 'I mean, why did you come to me?'

'You're one of the only veterans who was part of Operation Ragnarok, and the only ship. Although not entirely –' the drone hesitated, and Clarence was sure that if it had been an organic lifeform it would have been blushing '– not completely the ship you used to be. But our kind weren't often allowed into our rival's galaxy. Too obvious for them to ignore.'

One of the only veterans . . . Until now, Clarence had never been able to remember if he had taken part in the War. He'd never asked, too ashamed to admit to his lack of memory. And too afraid of what he might have forgotten.

With the onset of night, the temperature dropped dramatically, and Clarence wrapped his wings around himself for warmth. The desert suddenly felt very lonely indeed. 'Does it really matter anyway? Isn't it just an interesting puzzle for ARIG to work out?'

The drone paused for a long time before answering. Clarence suspected that he was about to be given the first totally honest answer of the day. 'Ragnarok was the last battle,' it said eventually. 'The great battle yet to come. The whole power of the Norse gods was built on deceit and treachery, and they knew that one day they would have to pay for what they'd done. The Greek gods were safe in Olympus, and Jehovah was safe in his heaven, but the Norse gods knew that they were never safe in Asgard, that one day their doom would come marching over the rainbow bridge to get them.

'It all began when Loki broke his chains. He'd been their friend once, a god of fire and mischief and Odin's blood brother, but he killed Odin's son Baldur out of jealousy and spite, so they imprisoned him underground and left him to rot. When he broke free, he became one of the leaders of the forces of evil, leading the march on Asgard.

'All the great Norse gods squared off against their enemies, and they all fell, one by one, taking their foes with them. The sun was swallowed by a huge wolf, all life was driven from the face of the land, and the earth itself was consumed by fire. It was reborn again, of course, but none of the old gods survived, and mankind was reduced to a remnant of a remnant.'

The drone turned to look out across the landscape, into a darkness that only its sensors could penetrate.

'That's some pretty serious shit,' it said. 'If God knows there's something like that coming, then I want to know about it too. Ragnarok was so big that no one could stand on the sidelines. Everyone had to choose sides.'

Clarence turned to stare at the drone. 'You weren't friends with !Ci!ci-tel and WiRgo!xu, were you?' he asked.

'I knew them,' it replied blandly. 'Look, every veteran learnt something different from the War. Do you want to know what I learnt?' It didn't wait for Clarence's response. 'I learnt that I like fighting, and that I'm very good at it. Other People discovered that, too, and hated themselves for it. I didn't; I'm not ashamed of what I am. If there is a war coming, I want to be involved. I want to be able to choose sides.'

'We can't though, can we?' Clarence said bitterly. 'We've all hidden ourselves away in Asgard, and drawn the bridge up behind us so no one else can get in.'

The drone smiled slightly. 'In Norse legend, the rainbow bridge gets destroyed at the start of the battle, burnt by the sons of the fire giants. I love metaphors, don't you?'

3

THE MANY-COLOURED VALLEY

The Grel were not always mighty masters of fact, guardians
and seekers after the life-blood of the universe: knowledge.

> *When the first Grel subdued the beasts of the plains and
> mountains, they gave thanks for their mastery of the
> paradise that was Grellor. For truly there was never a
> more beautiful world than this land of marshes and dark
> moist places, and truly there was never a more blessed
> race than the mighty Grel. For strong they were and
> handsome of feature; not for them the blighted feature-
> less faces of the other savage and simple beasts. Their
> tentacles rippled with pride as this brave people recog-
> nized their mastery of all before them. The land was
> theirs, as were the thick abundant oceans.*
>
> *As inquisitive as they were handsome, the Grel
> sought the reason for their good fortune, looking to the
> land, the seas, and the skies. But no answer was
> forthcoming and the mighty Grel despaired. Then one
> came among them who knew the answer to the riddle of
> the Grel's blessing. He spoke to them of the mystery of
> their mighty race:*
>
> *'Behold, children of Grellor, for you are thrice
> blessed. You have mastery of this jewel of a land; you
> are handsome beyond measure; and your minds can
> solve even really tricky problems. In short, you are the*

answer to the riddle we have set ourselves: you are the proof of the divine. I have wandered the southern marshes and there I had a vision; the pungent odours of that dismal swamp brought revelation and enlightenment. I heard the voice of Him who made us. For we are chosen, children of Grellor; we are blessed.'

Those gathered round understood the sensible nature of this revelation and demanded to know more of their creator.

'It is well that you should want to know more, for He is wroth with you,' cried Shenke, for that was his name, and he brandished his tentacles in a most angry manner. 'You have forgotten Him, and must now appease Him.'

Cowed by Shenke's words and the wild motions of his tentacles, the Grel asked how they might appease this wrath. His answer was simple.

'You must build a mighty triangle, made of fine stone and gold, which will reach toward the heavens and bring me closer to Our Lord, that I might talk further with Him, and placate Him.'

And so the Grel toiled. And toiled. They used all their skills and strength to build the mighty triangle. Many died bravely in its construction, and Shenke blessed them for they had pleased the Lord so much in their labour that He had called them to Him.

After eight years, the building was completed. Shenke blessed the construction and passed within its fire-bright majesty. There he stayed for a whole year, sustained only by his faith and the many offerings the Lord demanded. The Grel without became worried, for they knew not whether the creator was still wroth with them. Finally, Shenke emerged, pale and cowed, as if seeing the sun for the first time.

'Children of Grellor, I have spoken many times with the creator this past year. I have sought to placate Him for you. But His anger is mighty. He demands another offering.'

The surrounding Grel bowed in shame and fear, their tentacles drooped in defeat.

'Fear not, my children. For all you must do is build a mighty tower, in the style of this fine triangle. The tower will reach even further toward the heavens, and my entreaties will hold more sway with Our Lord.'

The Grel groaned mightily but moved to their tools as before, mindful of the need for toil and precision. But one among them spoke out:

'Suggestion: if He really is so angry, why don't we all just speak to Him and explain that we didn't mean anything by our ignorance. Can't you just ask Him to come before us?'

Even as he spoke thus, this bold Grel cast his eyes to the ground, fearing he had misunderstood the mysteries Shenke had unfolded before them. Shenke drew his tentacles together in the traditional gesture of contempt. At last, eyes tightly shut, he gave his answer:

'You are not yet worthy to put your case before Him. He demands, in His wisdom, that you must prove your faith before He reveals Himself in all His majesty. Only I have proved my faith, and so I am the vessel of His will. The tower will be a measure of your contrition and faith. Perhaps on its completion He may relent, but not before. So go now, and build the tower for His glory!'

Then the bold Grel, Melkan (for that was his name), spoke up once more:

'So, you're saying we need to keep building these really large things until, and there is no guarantee of this, the creator relents and decides we are worthy of conversation.'

Shenke knew all eyes were upon him. His tentacles toyed with the end of the staff he had recently taken to carrying everywhere, and he answered with a mighty dignity, 'Yes.'

'And, if we don't build the tower, what will happen?' queried Melkan the Bold.

'Then He will be wroth with you, and He'll probably smite you as well.' Shenke raised his staff in a very confrontational manner.

'Well, two of my brothers died building that triangle, and I don't really fancy starting the whole thing over. I think I'd just prefer to get the smiting over with now, if that's OK.'

The other Grel gasped and threw themselves to the ground, fearing the wrath of the creator. Shenke cast his gaze skyward, called forth the strength of his Lord, and pointed his great staff at Melkan.

'As you wish, cursed child of Grellor,' spat Shenke as the young Grel cowered before him.

When nothing happened, the crowd became uneasy and began to mutter with increasing volume. They looked from Shenke to Melkan and to the heavens, whence nothing came. They honked in frustration and confusion. But Shenke's voice still held all its power as he bellowed, 'This will only take a minute. Please bear with me.'

Shenke was still brandishing his mighty staff, on the steps of the great triangle, when the sun set. The other Grel had left that place long before, to follow Melkan the Bold, the first Master of Facts, and never to speak of the triangle again.

From *The First Book of Grel*
Chapters 1–4, 'The Awakening'

'It's very you, isn't it ?' said Benny as she threw her bag into the landcruiser, catching the Grel Master full in the face with it, and flashing him a dazzling smile.

James Harker didn't feel very reverend; he felt uneasy. Sitting in the back of the Grel landcruiser, flanked by the towering figures of the two servitors, wasn't doing him any good at all. For some reason they kept brandishing the cruel implements they referred to as dataxes, and then hooting with laughter at his obvious discomfort. One hand strayed to the chain around his neck; the other held his tiny, battered copy of the Code. Neither brought him any peace.

Bernice's driving added to his unease. Why she had demanded to do something for which she was clearly unqualified, he couldn't fathom. Her laughter as the great vehicle sped along the autoroute away from the university was in marked contrast to the anger of other drivers they met on the way.

When they had been initially flagged down for dangerously inept driving, the Grel Master alongside her was forced to claim diplomatic immunity, and to extend it to the eccentric archaeologist. Indeed, she seemed to take pleasure in embarrassing, and sometimes scaring, the taciturn creature. As if she were desperate to show who was in control.

As they left the islands of the university and the city behind, Bernice appeared to settle down. At one stage they were even overtaken. He had already told her she had a lot of driving to do, and that it wouldn't all be fun. Tal'een was over a day distant. The lands of the Hut'eri were mountainous, the soil poor quality, and it had never been viable to extend the great autoroute into the heart of their domain. The Hut'eri would not have wanted it, anyway. They were a very spiritual people, the people of Maa'lon; none was more devout.

Harker thought back to the first injunction of the Code: 'Those who find the Way will feel the path beneath them'. He had always thought the Hut'eri over-literal for their insistence on bare feet, even during the harsh mountain winters. He had interpreted the words as a reflection of the personal revelation that was the Way, that it was unique to each individual, but now he wondered whether Maa'lon would approve of his mode of transport. It would not do to offend Him before he had even had the chance to explain his absence of faith. Not a good start at all.

Bernice was beginning to worry about the reverend, and to regret deciding to drive herself. Pissing off the Grel was a minor victory when placed alongside the muscle spasms caused by trying to drive a vehicle designed for a being a metre taller and three times stronger than her. She would ache all over as soon as she stopped. Though that hadn't happened yet, and James clearly needed a pick-me-up. Inspiration struck.

'How about a game of I-spy?' She tried to sound as upbeat as possible but only succeeded in being embarrassingly high-pitched.

'Query: I-spy?' The Grel Master looked up from the dataxe in which he had been zealously interested throughout the high-speed departure from the university.

'It's a very simple game, ideal for travelling. All you have to do is look around, choose an object or animal or some such, tell us the first letter of the word that best describes it, and then wait for one of us to guess it correctly.' She was suddenly worried that the explanation made no sense, and that she had missed something vital out. 'Oh, and you have to start the game by saying, "I spy with my little eye something beginning with . . ."'

'Query: with what?'

This was going to be painful. 'With the first letter of the word that best describes it.' She tried to sound assured, but the potholed track they were travelling along didn't help. After pitching around wildly for a couple of hundred metres she brought the landcruiser to a halt. 'We'll take a break here, and James and I will demonstrate the game. OK, everyone, James?'

'Oh, fine, Bernice.' He clearly hadn't been listening to a word she had said.

'Right, James, I spy with my little eye something beginning with "R".'

James looked confused for a moment and then seemed to grasp the meaning of her words. He cast about uncertainly, searching the rocky terrain. Rocky terrain. They were surrounded by rocks. Dull grey rocks of all shapes and sizes. Occasionally covered with moss. And lichen. Nothing else. As soon as she had opened her mouth to start the game she had noticed the one fatal weakness in her plan. It was misty at this high altitude, and they had stopped in a rugged valley that looked more like a moonscape than a Dellahan rural idyll.

'Er, rock?' asked the reverend after a detailed search of his surroundings.

'Yes. Rock. That one actually.' She felt the need to point it out.

'An excellent game, Professor,' the Grel Master chimed in. 'Training for the eye is vital in the search for knowledge. I will play your game. Question: I spy with my little eye something beginning with "G".' The Grel Master then made a particularly flamboyant gesture with his tentacles.

Bernice, James, and the two servitors all began to look about the valley. Bernice could only think of 'ground' or 'Grel' and didn't have the courage to suggest them. James still seemed in a daze. The servitors picked up some nearby stones and thrust them into the tentacles around their mouths before casting them away.

At last servitor one, the marginally smaller of the two with a flash of maroon over his left eye, jumped up and exclaimed excitedly, 'It's a gh'see! A gh'see!'

'Where?' asked Bernice.

The servitor pointed into the mist. The master clapped his huge hands together and accidentally activated a screen on his dataxe. 'Excellent eyes, servitor. It was indeed the gh'see you now see so clearly before you.' The Grel gathered together and looked expectantly at Bernice and Harker.

They both continued to look into the mist.

Fifteen minutes later a small, white, short-haired animal not unlike a goat came into view. 'I assume that's a gh'see.' Harker nodded to Bernice. 'Right. How about a different game?'

Deciding to let the Grel drive turned out to be a good idea. The terrain became increasingly difficult as they headed higher into the mountains. The great vehicle lurched crazily as it sought purchase on the uneven ground, and Bernice knew she would have been way out of her depth behind the wheel.

'The Hut range is the largest on Dellah, with Maa'lon's Spear the highest point on the planet at 3,524 metres above sea level.' Servitor one, sandwiched between Bernice and Harker in the back of the cruiser, had become almost chatty. He was constantly reading out highlights of the Grel files on Dellah as they scrolled across the largest screen on his dataxe. 'This area is known locally as "the roof of the world", a moniker shared by primary geological formations on 8,734 other planets known to the Grel. And we have been described as unimaginative.'

Bernice almost missed his last sentence. She had long ago stopped actively listening to the litany of facts and the Grel idea of anecdote. But unless she was very much mistaken the massive creature next to her had just made a joke. Or an attempt at a joke. The Grel Master and the servitor driving made repeated snorting sounds and flared their tentacles, so Bernice assumed they found it funny. A Grel sense of humour; these were indeed strange times.

'I think it's time we got some rest,' she said after a moment. 'It's getting dark and I don't really fancy falling off the side of a mountain. Let's make camp.' Benny was tired. Her arms and legs ached. She needed sleep. But, most importantly, she needed to talk to James. The white-faced reverend had not spoken for over three hours, and she thought there might be something seriously wrong.

'I can't tell you what to believe; I can only tell you what *I* believe, and even that constantly changes. I can't tell you what to think or feel; I can only tell you what I've come to know, through the filter of my own experiences and preconceptions, and let you filter them through yours and come to your own conclusions. Put your trust in no one, least of all me.'

Renée chewed her lip as she read the first paragraph of *The First Book of the Grey* for the five thousand, four hundred and sixty-third time.

It still pissed her off. The Liar Paradox: too damned clever for its own good. For the four hundred and thirty-second time, she considered converting. Judaism seemed like a good candidate: a religion that not only told you what to believe, but what to do as well.

She submitted a quick query to her COG Uplink, and discovered that two thousand and four members of the Church of the Grey had converted to Judaism over the course of its history, the last in 2498. So that was out: nothing worse than following last season's fashions. Idly, she tried to think of the most obscure religion she could, and was quite pleased when she came up with Mithraism – only to have her hopes dashed when she discovered that three former COG members had beaten her to it: in 2102, 2333, and 2378 respectively.

There really was nothing new under the sun. The only way she could remain unique was by remaining a member of the Church of the Grey, the only practising member left in the universe, as far as she had been able to ascertain.

For the five thousand, four hundred and sixty-third time, she decided to keep the first paragraph of *The First Book of the Grey* as the first paragraph of her own *Book of the Grey*.

She leant back in the chair, unwinding her body in a luxurious stretch. Her fingertips brushed against the wall behind her, and she left them there, enjoying the feel of the velvety fabric she had pinned up to cover the functional beige of a standard-issue visiting academic's room.

Her relaxation was interrupted by a brusque knock on the door, a sharp rat-tat-tat. Renée smiled as she realized that it could only be Irving Braxiatel. No one else's knock could contrive to sound so desiccated and self-contained. And no one else bothered to knock. Everyone knew she kept open house.

'Come in,' she called, deliberately remaining in the same pose, just to see its effect on Braxiatel. She wondered what she would do if she ever did actually get him to proposition her. Run a mile, probably.

There was a slight hesitation, as if the person on the other side of the door was having to psyche himself up to enter, then Braxiatel strode through, holding his body even more rigidly than usual.

It struck Renée how out of place he always looked, no matter where he was, with his old-fashioned manners and his expressionless eyes that seemed to see so much more than everyone around. He appeared particularly inappropriate in her room: a stiff pale blue shadow in a riot of colour and fabric suspended from the walls and ceiling like a cheap Aladdin's cave.

He somehow contrived to look less real, or at least less there, than the room around him.

She saw his nose wrinkle slightly as it took in the lingering scent of incense from a recent late-night session with one of the students. 'Charming,' he said tersely, then, 'Renée, I have a favour to ask you.'

'Oh? What sort of favour?' She endeavoured to make it sound as salacious as possible, but her heart wasn't really in it. Braxiatel was clearly genuinely worried; she didn't like to imagine what could worry someone as generally unflappable as him.

He smiled thinly. 'Actually, it is indeed that sort of favour.'

Renée felt her eyebrows rising involuntarily. 'Don't tell me: the outfit last night was finally too much for you.'

Uninvited, he moved to perch on the edge of her desk, its metallic corner making a neat dent in the cotton of his trousers. 'It's not for me,' he said.

If her eyebrows rose any further, they would be crawling off the top of her head. 'So, er . . .' She was annoyed to realize that he'd managed to fluster *her* for once. Why did she find the idea of his trying to set her up with someone else so very irritating?

Crossing her arms over her chest, she made a firm effort to collect herself. 'Lecturing not paying the bills any more, Irving?'

'I beg your pardon?' Ah, now she'd managed to faze him. Good.

'It's just, I never quite pictured you as a procurer.'

He dropped his eyes, and she realized with a shock that her jest was not as far off the mark as she had assumed. 'You have got to be kidding me!' she exclaimed.

Before he could reply, his gaze alighted on her leather-bound copy of *The First Book of the Grey*, and he frowned, pulling on his lower lip distractedly. 'I didn't know you were religious, Renée.' He made 'religious' sound like an insult.

'I've told you about the Church of the Grey, Irving. In fact, I mentioned it in my interview.'

'I must not have been paying attention.'

Renée ran a hand through her hair, patting the blonde curls into place. 'Funny how that seems to happen whenever anyone starts talking about religion.'

Braxiatel grimaced. 'Yes, I'm beginning to wonder how many important things I've missed because of that.' He paused, then suddenly resumed with, 'He was at your concert, Renée. He couldn't take his eyes off you the whole time.'

Jealous? Renée wondered, astonished. But no, it didn't seem that way at all. At least now she thought she knew who he was talking about. This was going to be fun. 'Well, thanks for watching the audience and not me –' a shadow of a smile curved Braxiatel's lips '– but why exactly are you trying to set me up with this man? Old friend of yours?'

'No, but I know his race, and I can assure you that intellectual stimulation is absolutely the last reason he's here.'

Renée grinned. ' "Intellectual" stimulation wasn't exactly on my mind, either.' She saw that Braxiatel was frowning at her, and decided to let him off the hook. 'So you want me to seduce –' he winced '– this person. Feel like telling me why?'

Irving shuffled himself forward on her desk, invading her personal space. The slightly musty odour of his clothing was suddenly joined in her nostrils by the unfamiliar spicy-salty smell of his body. She had never been this close to him before, she realized; she wasn't sure if she liked it.

'I don't know,' he said, his voice lowered in a conspiratorial whisper, as though he thought they might be overheard. 'I just know that his being here can't possibly be good news.' He smiled self-mockingly. 'Trouble is his business. And he's deliberately tormenting me. I see him in the bar, or in a concert hall – I know he wants me to see him – but I can't even find out where he lives or what he is calling himself.'

'And you want me to ask this man out?' Renée said, feigning incredulity. 'You make him sound like some kind of axe-murdering loon. Are you trying to tell me you think he's my type?'

Braxiatel looked pained. 'I'm probably asking the impossible, but he did seem interested in you. I just thought, if he does suggest meeting up, or if you did see him again, you might consider letting me know what you find out.'

Renée couldn't help smiling as she finally prepared to play her trump card. 'Oh, we've already arranged to meet up,' she said, enjoying his shocked expression immeasurably. 'He's called John, by the way; I asked him. I'll tell him you sent your regards, shall I, Irving?'

'Cold light of day.'

Fec turned to his companion on the bench and nodded. His large bald head was still wet from the recent rain.

'Not sure I like it.' Kalten's voice had a wearied tone. His back was hunched. 'Used to think this place was really cool. Fun, you know? Look at it; we can't have been that whacked off our minds.'

'The times they are a-changin', Kal my friend. Uni's going down the toilet and it looks like we're going with it. What I wouldn't give for the Haze.'

'You heard what the stormtrooper said, man. Time to lay off it, at least till everyone decides to chill out. Besides, I'm still having trouble shaking off the image of those jack-booted loonies. Not what you want when you're in a delicate condition.'

Fec could see the slightly haunted look in his eyes and placed one broad-fingered hand on his shoulders.

'You're right, Kal. We'll play it straight until all this blows over. No pissing about.' He smiled what he thought was an encouraging smile.

After a few moments of silence, he removed his hand and moved it to the left knee pocket of his coveralls. He awkwardly removed the little book he had put there, and began to read about Ahriman the Great.

The roof of the world. The words echoed round in James Harker's head as he looked down on the mist clouds spread out before him. Maa'lon's land. The home of His people. The site of His resurrection. His judgement would come soon. Judgement on a fraud, a man who had lied nearly all his life. A man who had clothed himself in faith, but been empty inside.

'Penny for them?' Bernice's quiet voice dragged him from his contemplation of the clouds.

'Sorry?' He seemed to be missing the point a lot recently.

'Penny for your thoughts, James. What's wrong? You've hardly said a word all day.' Benny's brow furrowed attractively. Her worry was plain to see, and lifted the reverend's spirits.

'Same as before, really. Just that being up here, being where it all started, makes it that bit more immediate, more real. It's so beautiful. And that beauty is reflected in the Code. That's something I never understood before. I always avoided these mountains, the Hut'eri, Tal'een. I thought they were rather embarrassing. The home of superstition, I suppose. Something I tried to block from my mind. Fear of the irrational, you see. That's me. The rational reverend. Oxymoronic man.'

'Well, we find out tomorrow whether Maa'lon walks these mountains again. Personally my money's on either a hoax, a stunt from the tourist board, or the discovery of a particularly large and potent psychotropic fungus. Gods don't just turn up like this, believe me. And I've seen some really odd stuff.' Bernice stepped closer to the edge of the plateau, looked down, and hurriedly stepped back a few paces. 'You are not going to be judged and cast into perdition.'

'Can I have that in writing?' James forced the smile on to his face. 'Some form of guarantee would be awfully sweet.'

Bernice purposefully advanced on him, fixing him with her uncompromising gaze. She flicked a stray lock of hair away from her eyes. 'I think someone needs a hug.'

Extract from the diary of Bernice Summerfield

Harker's living on his nerves. He's got that haunted look to the eyes that spells trouble. I even tried hugging him to break the spell, and that's definitely not me. I think I'm out of my depth here. This is not my field of expertise. I like my gods to be firmly in the past. Footnotes in history. Marble fodder. This is all a bit immediate.

The Grel, surprise surprise, are not helping either. Constant questions about Sacred Children, animals, and names seem to be whipping him into even more of a frenzy. Though I've got to hand it to him. He's holding on to the core. He won't even consider the idea that the myths have a basis in fact. He's firmly in the allegorical camp and he's fighting his corner well. The Grel are their usual prosaic selves, expecting the scene to be as it was written. They want it all to be fact.

They really do make lousy travelling companions. And their camp-fire singing is appalling.

Extract ends

It wasn't Renée's idea of a dream date. When John had suggested that she should come and visit him later, the candlelight she had imagined had been more connected to romance than to esoteric and possibly banned magical rituals.

His room was amazing, but not in a good way: a great, high-ceilinged stone gothic cathedral, filled with the paraphernalia of a thousand different religions, none of them nice ones. The light from the many bloated black candles did not penetrate the dark corners and crevices of the room, and she stopped herself speculating on what else she wasn't seeing. She also carefully avoided thinking about the recent news items on the bizarre slaughter of the spaceship crew.

Maybe, just maybe, Irving was right about him.

'So, John,' she said, steepling her fingers and leaning forward in unconscious imitation of Braxiatel at his most severe, 'tell me about yourself.'

From a distance, he had appeared dashing and potentially handsome. Up close, he was a thin, scruffy, *yellow* man. She suspected that, even illuminated by natural rather than candlelight, he would have been of that hue, as if the cigarette he was smoking had somehow infused and dyed not just his clothes but his flesh and bones, too. He had the most lived-in-looking body she'd ever seen – even though, chronologically speaking, he only appeared to be in his mid-thirties.

He smiled, giving her the chance to determine that, yes, his teeth were also stained a faint yellow. He was humanoid but not human, she was quite sure of that. For the first time it occurred to her to question her previous unthinking assumption of Braxiatel's humanity. If you cut him up to see what he was made of, what would you find inside?

The unusually morbid thought disturbed her, and she shivered in her thin silk wrap.

'Oh, I'm terribly dull,' he said suddenly. She jumped, startled to remember that she had asked him a question. 'Just a traveller passing through.' One of the candles beside him guttered and died, leaving half his face in deep shadow. 'I like to go to interesting places.'

Renée shifted in the antique chair, unsuccessfully trying to find a comfortable position against its carved ivory back. 'And you think Dellah is interesting?' She attempted to inject a light note of mockery into her voice, but the slight quaver betrayed her.

'May you live in interesting times. That's an old Earth curse, you know.' He was leaning towards her now, and something in his posture or manner reminded her of Braxiatel. But, while Brax was an old, dry stick insect, there was something spiderlike about this man, weaving a web that its prey would only see when it was far too late.

Unable to look at him, she let her gaze trail over the room. She didn't know why he'd invited her there, but she was damn sure it had nothing to do with physical gratification. She couldn't escape the unpleasant feeling that she was being used as an unwitting middleman between this person and Braxiatel, being given messages that she wasn't meant to understand.

As her eyes roamed, she began to notice cases and boxes piled here and there in the room, matched by corresponding empty patches on shelves and floor. Was he packing or unpacking? she wondered, then saw the squares of cleanliness surrounded by dust where objects had been removed. 'But now you're going,' she said. 'So we can't be that interesting after all.'

'Running away to join the army,' he said, and she blinked at the non sequitur. He seemed to notice her confusion, reaching across to grasp her hand in a snake-fast gesture. 'I'm speaking of you rather than myself, of course.' He turned her hand over and ran dry, cold fingers over the lines of her palm. 'I see it in your future.'

At that instant, Renée knew precisely what she saw in her future, and it involved getting far away from this lunatic as quickly as was humanly possible.

Her companion looked into her eyes and laughed lightly, as if in response to her last thought. 'I'm sure you can show yourself out. And do send Irving my regards.'

The descent into the Tal'een valley was hampered by having to leave the landcruiser behind. Two Hut'eri, wearing simple purple tunics over their ochre frames and nothing else, informed them – bizarrely, Bernice thought – that the vehicle was an offence to Maa'lon.

Things got even stranger when James Harker stepped down. Initially, they bowed and touched their hearts. But the venom in their eyes when they saw his simple black boots seemed to chill the reverend. He hurriedly removed them, but they had clearly made up their minds about something and kept muttering to each other and shaking their heads. Bernice knew she was missing out on something.

'Benny, take off your shoes!' hissed the reverend.

'Why?'

'Didn't you read that copy of the Code I lent you?' Harker's tone held a mixture of panic and annoyance.

'Of course I didn't. You know it's not my kind of thing. I was being polite.' Bernice felt herself resenting the reverend's anger, but knew it was necessary for at least one of them to stay calm. 'Just tell me why I need to take my shoes off. And try not to be all snappy, OK?'

Fifteen minutes later, Bernice was regretting her tolerance of the beliefs of others. The rocky road was cutting her feet to shreds, and she kept having to force the Grel to slow down. Typically, beneath their armoured battle boots, the Grel had great, broad, rubbery feet that seemed to mould to any terrain, and also seemed impervious to even the sharpest of rocks.

Fortunately, James Harker was doing even worse than her. His lily-white, dainty feet seemed to have attracted particularly nasty shards. Bernice couldn't help wondering whether the trail of blood he left behind him was somehow symbolic; then she told herself to stop being portentous and to concentrate on where she was treading.

Head down in this manner, she initially didn't notice Tal'een or the crowds. But a loud hoot from servitor two and a gasp from Harker made her look up. She stopped in her tracks. Tal'een, at one end of the small valley before them, was beautiful. Small round buildings, fashioned from the purple granite-like stone all around them, topped with white, conical roofs, formed the circumference of a great circle. At its centre, another building, similarly purple and white but with an outer ring of columns, rose high above the town. Its white roof was covered in what looked like birds and possibly flying reptiles. Below, the circle was a heaving mass of Hut'eri, with other races apparent here and there, poking up above the short dark-skinned beings.

The mountains rose massively behind the town, and before it, filling the gentle slopes of the lush green valley, was a sea of tents. The valley was patchwork, multicoloured, and Bernice could see families cooking over fires and children playing between the canvas homes. 'It's Woodstock,' she said, rather inappropriately she immediately realized.

Harker seemed overwhelmed by it all, and Bernice had to drag him down the path towards the town and through the vast, colourful suburbs. The crowds recoiled from the Grel as they picked their way down the hill. The dataxes looked particularly dangerous in the morning sunlight. Soon, the path gave way to well-trodden grass and Bernice felt able to pick up the pace. Harker, clearly in pain, stumbled along behind her.

The tents were occupied by a cross-section of Dellahan society. All barefoot, simply dressed, and wearing the interlocking circle pendant. Most were Hut'eri, eyes bright with joy in their dark faces, but nearly all the races of Dellah seemed to be represented (though there weren't many Golls) and quite a few off-planet ones.

Bernice recognized a few students from the university and waved. The ecstatic smiles on their faces as they waved back made her wonder whether the place bore other similarities to Woodstock, but she ploughed on to the town in the wake of the Grel. Behind her, James Harker had taken to muttering under his breath. She was going to have to do something about him.

At last they reached the ring of stone houses, but were forced to stop by the weight of the crowds. Bernice could feel the crowd's excitement, their expectation. 'Is Maa'lon here?' she asked a stocky Hut'eri male who held his small child on his shoulders.

'Yes, He's in the House. He is due to speak soon, though I doubt we'll hear much this far back. But I want little Si'tan here to see Him.' He nodded up to the smiling child on his shoulders.

Bernice grinned at him and turned back to the Grel. 'Right, Maa'lon is due on soon. It would suit our purpose better if we were nearer the front of this lot. Do you think you can get us through?' The enthusiastic nods in reply made her nervous, but she grabbed Harker and followed in their wake once more.

Forcing her way to the front of a religious gathering was not something that Bernice had ever imagined doing in her life. It wasn't a particularly enjoyable experience. The Grel were not subtle in their methods and several Followers were forced to turn the other cheek. Fortunately, they made it to the front before anything really unpleasant happened, so Bernice only felt ashamed, though Harker looked mortified.

'I don't suppose you'd mind explaining why you felt the need to do that,' said the beautiful Hut'eri who emerged from the House before them.

Harker was just trying to keep himself together. Maa'lon was right in front of him. Had spoken to him, had invited him into His House.

After the initial horror of His arrival, Harker had settled down into a simple continuing panic. Even Bernice had seemed tongue-tied when explaining the Grel's actions. The Grel remained quiet, trying to look contrite probably, and the reverend had tried to hide behind them. But he had been noticed. Maa'lon had asked all of them into the House after the sermon, and He had looked long and hard at James Harker. He was judged.

They all sat around the fire in the centre of the high-ceilinged room. The wood smoked heavily, but also gave off a sweet, fruity odour that seemed to relax them all. Bernice was discussing the architectural style with servitor two, and the other Grel silently contemplated their dataxes, tentacles gently rippling.

'I hope you all like ka'h,' said Maa'lon, as He entered carrying a small wooden tray laden with earthenware cups and a tall steaming jug. He sat down on the floor before them and began to pour the lavender-scented green-hued drink. 'Bernice, this should warm you up.' He passed her a cup. 'Demka, that's yours.' The Grel Master's eyes widened in surprise as he reached for his drink. 'Grenke and Shemda, there you go.' The two servitors took their cups.

'And now for you, James, my very reverend servant.'

Harker felt the nausea building within him. It was time. His hand shook as he leant towards Maa'lon. As he grasped the small clay cup, he spilt some of the piping-hot liquid on to his robe. He gasped and looked fearfully back to Maa'lon.

The Hut'eri fixed him with His beautiful clear jade eyes. Harker tried to keep his bowels from loosening.

'You're a bag of nerves, James. Don't be so worried. You have nothing to fear from me. Your heart is open to me. And it is a good, pure heart. Have confidence in yourself.'

With that Maa'lon got up and walked out of the room, returning a few moments later with what appeared to be a bowl of warm water.

'Now, James, let's have a look at those feet of yours.'

Extract from the diary of Bernice Summerfield

Well, I must say, I'm surprised. This is not turning out quite how I expected. Maa'lon seems rather normal, and nice. Nice is indeed the word. I've never really gone in for nice myself, but it certainly beats the other choices you generally get with gods. If he is indeed a god.

As you would expect, he's a head taller than the average Hut'eri. Somehow height seems important in a religious ikon. His skin is that bit smoother too. Most of the Hut'eri I've seen so far have rough, almost scaly skin, suitable for the elements up here in the mountains. Maa'lon's yellow-brown skin is perfect and looks soft to the touch. And those eyes: two chunks of bright jade framed in pure white that look right into and through you. Weird.

Now, I admit the trick with the names was good, and it really freaked out the Grel, who are obsessively secretive about theirs with outsiders, but it's not exactly proof of divinity. Though I've never seen water work the wonders it did on James's lacerated feet. That was good. The reverend is now a picture of adoration and relief, which certainly beats his previous line in paranoia and depression.

So, one minor miracle and a good parlour trick. Jury's still out.

I really hope he can't read this.

Extract ends

They rose early in the House of Maa'lon. The Hut'eri that served there woke Bernice with some fresh ka'h at dawn. They had opened some of the solid panels that made up the inner barrel-shaped quarters, and the sun streamed in between the columns. The ka'h's sweet lavender fragrance seemed that much more cloying so early – obscenely early – and Benny knew she wouldn't be able to hold it down. Typical, she hadn't had a drink for weeks (the one Virgin Mary, she felt, didn't count, as that had been an emergency measure), but she still felt delicate in the mornings. Her body was set in its ways, refusing to accept its new temple status.

Rather than face the ka'h, Bernice decided on conversation with the young serving girl. The timid creature must have been scarcely more than a child and kept her head low as she bathed the professor's feet. Occasionally her bright eyes flicked up and then darted back down to her work, careful not to spill any of the milk in the small bowl in her lap.

'What's your name, dear?' asked Bernice.

The young Hut'eri looked up fearfully and then cast about the room. 'Tan'a, Professor,' she whispered, and then returned to her work.

This was not going to be easy. 'Where's Maa'lon, and the people I came here with?'

The girl set down the bowl, looked up again and smiled. 'He is blessing the fields and the animals. They are with Him.'

'Does that work then? Blessing, I mean.' Bernice hoped she didn't sound flippant.

'Oh yes, Professor, the crops have never been so good, nor the harvest so early. In the days since Maa'lon's arrival everything has ripened beyond measure. The land is lush and green. This valley was the most fertile of the Hut'eri lands, but the soil was still poor. Farming has always been a struggle, and that struggle formed part of the Way.' Once the girl got started, excitement filled her every word and movement.

But just when Bernice thought she could really start to talk about Maa'lon, and particularly his arrival, he returned. His smile never left his face. Nor did the adoring gaze of James Harker, who walked alongside him. The three Grel followed, talking among themselves and somehow conspiring to look shorter than she remembered.

'Bernice,' James enthused, 'you should have seen it. The fields respond to his touch and word. His glory is reflected in the fruits themselves. Look, this only appeared on the vine yesterday.'

He lifted the muslin covering on the pot he had just set down on the floor. Inside were several large fist-sized plum-like fruits, each a deep maroon streaked with orange. They looked delicious.

'Try one, Bernice.' Maa'lon's voice had a honeyed tone.

She thought about it, considered the lush fruit before her. She was hungry, and it certainly looked tempting. But there was something holding her back. Something about fruit hovered at the back of her mind and made her uneasy. Everyone was looking at her. There seemed no sensible reason to turn him down. She reached into the pot.

'Maa'lon! Maa'lon!'

All eyes turned to the desperate-looking out-of-breath Hut'eri who ran in through the columns and collapsed before his god.

'What is it, Ham'tha? What troubles you?'

'I am sorry to disturb you, Lord.' The Hut'eri's words came in quick gasps. 'It's the N'a'm'thuli. They attacked our village, and killed my wife while I was out in the fields. They took our children, Maa'lon. You must help us.'

4

IT'S FUN FINDING OUT
ABOUT CULTS

The Hut'eri of the Great North Ridge were the most
hardy of that people and the most unfortunate. For on
the Plain of Tumas, a short distance from the Hut'eri
homeland, the Morkai practised their own dark ways,
worshipping a being of darkness that demanded constant sacrifices. Only the screams of innocents would
appease their dark lord: a wrathful god with no name.

The Morkai soon tired of slaying their own kind to
slake the thirst of their god, but an enterprising priest
suggested their Lord would be satisfied with the lives of
their enemies, though in greater numbers. And so the
great hunt began.

When the Hut'eri were discovered struggling to raise
cattle and crops in the forbidding mountains, the
Morkai rejoiced. Here was a small, weak race, a race
whose very way of life abjured violence. They soon
became the cattle themselves. For months the Hut'eri
were slain in the rude temples of the plain, the cloying
odour of their burning flesh a sweet perfume to the
nameless god. Hundreds died. Thousands of the northern Hut'eri fled higher into the forbidding range.

They sent word to Tal'een seeking guidance and
help. The response was simple: 'Follow the Way and

Maa'lon will protect you. The Way is all you will need.'

Though they took some comfort in these words, the northern Hut'eri knew they were now alone, and that they would continue to die on the altars of the dark lord. In terror they fled further into their bleak domain. But the Morkai continued the hunt and many were still found, and slain. And now many more died in the harsh conditions of the upper peaks. In the secret meeting halls, hewn from the rock, the Hut'eri despaired. They knew they could not endure this new hardship as they had done all before.

Then one old and wise Hut'eri staggered into the greatest of these halls and demanded to speak. The huddled children and broken adults were struck dumb by this man's bizarre appearance. Every part of his body was covered in scars, his dark skin obscured by maroon scabs that clearly pained him as he moved. In places the wounds reopened and blood ran down his chest to stain the loincloth that was his only garment.

In his right hand he carried a bundle of stinking pages, each made of stretched animal skin and covered in a deep red scrawl. 'Behold,' the old man screeched. 'Behold the Book of Blood!'

The gathered crowd was confused by his words and muttered uncertainly, but the old man carried on. 'I have been shown a new way, a way that will ensure our survival. For too long have we been led down the wrong path, left prey to the strength of others. But we too have that strength within us, and we must let it save us. Has Maa'lon come to our aid? Has He dealt with those who would make sport of us? No, He has not! And why? Because He is a false idol, a child's dream that we have foolishly believed!'

The crowd now became uneasy as their god was questioned so openly. But in the hearts of many the same questions had already been asked, and the same answers drawn.

'This book will show us a new way. A way that will take us down to the lush lands of the plains that should be ours by right and which we will now take by might alone.' The power of the old man's presence and his remarkable appearance added strength to these revolutionary words. Those who had been praying to Maa'lon for respite now questioned their own actions. Maa'lon had not aided them. While hundreds of the devout died horrible deaths, their saviour had stood by, as had the rest of their people.

'Within this book are the teachings of the real God. Our true Lord. He that has been hidden from us, but now comes to us in our time of greatest need. This He has revealed to me.'

At the end of that savage winter, the Morkai once more prepared to head into the mountains to harvest the northern Hut'eri. But as they gathered in the foothills, smiling in the spring sun, they heard a great cry. In the woods all around them weapons were beaten and screams rang out. The trees were alive with dark shapes. Then, as one, those who had made the terrifying sounds emerged.

At first the Morkai didn't recognize those before them. They thought they beheld new twisted beasts that haunted the forests, though as they looked closer they recognized the vestiges of their old prey. These Hut'eri were very different from the timid creatures that had always fled from the Morkai warriors. Each was covered in scars and walked near-naked into the cold light of day. Each had twisted stripes painted across face, arms, and body. They wore horns upon their heads and carried cruel blades in their hands.

The Morkai were still taking in this sight when the Hut'eri attacked them, streaming out of the woods on all sides and screaming at the top of their voices. The Morkai never had time to shake the fear from their bones. They were slain where they stood. Hacked to *pieces. Burnt on huge pyres. All save their hearts, which were consumed by the warriors.*

The Morkai villages and towns never knew what hit them as the crazed Hut'eri advanced. Everyone was killed. An entire race that may have been an offshoot of their own. Only the children were spared from the Hut'eri slaughter. And when the entire plain was taken, and all the lush lands belonged to the Hut'eri, the children were gathered together.

The Hut'eri had begun to build a great temple, a place to worship their lord. A building that would become the heart of the new capital, N'a'm'th ('Vengeance' in the old Hut'eri tongue). The temple would be consecrated with the sacrifice of over a thousand Morkai young. Soon the stench of flesh once more drifted across the plain, in honour of the new god who had led the Hut'eri of the north to victory, a victory that would sunder them forever from those of their race who were still following the teachings of Maa'lon, and from their own promised land. A god who had no name.

*The N'a'm'thuli Schism and the
Dark Heart of the Hut'eri*
Jonaas Brenkler
Professor of Ancient History (Indigenous),
University of Dellah

Maa'lon looked down on the distraught man before him. His jade eyes seemed to moisten as he considered his personal tragedy. Bernice felt herself tense up while she wondered what his reaction would be. What the scope of his reactions could be.

'Sit down, my son, and drink.' Maa'lon's words were soothing and the ka'h eagerly taken. He gently stroked the Hut'eri's ear. 'Don't think of it for a while. Concentrate on the aroma of the ka'h. Let it infuse your spirit.'

Bernice could see what He was doing, see the frantic Hut'eri beginning to nod his head and close his eyes. More parlour tricks? Hypnotism seemed rather un-godlike. But she knew the man needed it, needed to escape from himself. Maa'lon cradled his head as he sank down into sleep. There was definitely a tear in his eye now. He sighed as he released his charge and turned to his companions.

Someone needed to say something, and Benny felt it was her role. 'So? What will you do? The faithful are threatened: is it time for righteous vengeance?' It was only when she had finished speaking that she realized how rude she sounded. It was not a time to be glib, but before she could take it back Maa'lon spoke:

'Vengeance is never righteous, Bernice. Killing is killing is killing. That is not my Way. When this poor soul wakes, his pain will be eased somewhat, but it will still be within him, part of him. That will form a part of his own journey along the path and will allow him to find the Way. It will mould him, and my love will reward him. There is nothing more that I can do.' His words grew quieter and quieter as he spoke, and his hands returned to the distressed Hut'eri's head.

Bernice felt foolish. Childish. Arrogant. She just wanted to get out. Into the open air where she wouldn't feel closed in by such godliness, a purity she had to admire but which contradicted everything she held dear. Maa'lon had to be a charlatan; it all had to be parlour tricks. Anything else was just too ridiculous to contemplate.

'Sorry,' she muttered as she ran out of the House.

'Really, don't you think this is all faintly ridiculous?' Irving scanned the room disparagingly. Gothic mansion out of Hammer Horror by Poe. No wonder Renée had been so disturbed. He should never have sent her into this man's den, he thought, feeling a brief protective urge towards her. Then he imagined her sitting opposite this person, crossing her legs so that she could show him a flash of thigh, and smiling that provocative smile of hers, and he let a small smile of his own twitch his lips. Perhaps Renée had been exactly the right person to send.

'Ridiculous in what way?' There was a strange rusty quality to the man's voice, as if it had been a very long time since he'd last spoken. Or, Braxiatel thought, since he had last spoken any human language.

'I feel like I've entered the lair of a pantomime villain,' Braxiatel said. 'I would have thought all of these trappings were beneath you.'

'John' regarded Braxiatel with mocking graveness from beneath his heavy brows. 'Soon, you'll understand exactly why I have chosen this particular decor. I just pray that, when you do, it's not too late,' he murmured, quoting the cliché with melodramatic relish.

'Stop this nonsense!' Braxiatel snapped, surprising himself with his level of irritation. 'I know who and what you are. You know what I am, too. And you must know I am the last of my people left out here; all the others have scuttled home, as they usually do at the first sign of trouble. And now you're here, arriving at the first sign of trouble, as your people usually do. I want to know what's going on!'

'I'm sure you do. Why you think I should be obliged to tell you is another matter.'

'Either tell me or don't tell me,' Braxiatel replied, attempting to calm himself. 'But end this absurd theatre. Besides, you should know that, in light of recent events, this "cryptic master of the occult" role is a very dangerous one to play. If you're not careful, you may find yourself on trial for multiple murder.' He paused his diatribe to draw a long, steadying breath. 'If that happens, I should like to assure you that I will be right behind you: laughing all the way to the gallows.'

'How kind,' John snapped, with what sounded for the first time like genuine annoyance. He too seemed to take a moment to calm himself. 'I wish I could explain,' he said softly, then chuckled slightly. 'The trouble is, if I did you might believe me. All I can tell you is that faith is the key – to a door you don't want to open. And you and I are in far more danger, and are far more dangerous, than them.' He swept his hand round in a gesture that seemed to encompass the entire campus and its lively, oblivious population. 'Your kind have always sent others in to do their dirty work; I would recommend that you don't break the habit of several lifetimes. That rather buxom young human you sent to me –' he leered appreciatively, and Braxiatel felt one of his hands clench into a fist '– I understand that she's a believer. Traditionally, it is the armies of light which overcome the armies of darkness.'

Before he could continue, they were interrupted by a young man dressed in a severe black suit. A pair of thin wire-framed glasses were perched on his nose, and he frowned over them at Braxiatel, before saying, 'Departure plans are prepared as you specified.'

Braxiatel's companion smiled thinly and waved the young man off, saying, 'Good news; we'll talk about the details later.' Then, when they were alone again, he added, 'My secretary. Marvellously efficient: I don't know how I'd manage without him.'

Braxiatel stood. 'You know, I don't think you're being cryptic because you have to. I think it gives you a cheap thrill. If you do ever decide to fill me in, I'm sure you know where to find me. That is if you haven't already deserted the sinking ship by then.'

He had almost reached the door, his footsteps echoing behind him hollowly in the vast, dark room, when the man spoke again. 'I have to confess, I do get a cheap thrill out of giving you a taste of your own medicine. Or hadn't the hypocrisy of you accusing me of being needlessly mysterious occurred to you? Just why do you hide out here, Braxiatel, giving such a good impression of being a dusty old professor that I've begun to wonder if you remember what you really are?'

Braxiatel turned to face him, his eyes raking over the esoteric paraphernalia around him. 'I never forget for one moment what I am: a collector. That's what I've chosen to do with my life; everything else is just an accident of birth.'

His companion hung his head wearily, as if finally tiring of the encounter. 'I agree: we all make our own destinies. And you made yours when you chose to leave your people and live among the dirty, messy bustle of the younger races. You've become one of them, Braxiatel. All this time you imagined you were standing on the sidelines, you've actually been playing the game. You dipped your toe in the current of the universe, and now you're in danger of getting swept away by the tide.'

'But it's ridiculous!' Fec's voice took on a much higher pitch as he threw the book across the room. 'Even I can see it's bollocks, and I'm hardly the brightest, am I?'

Kalten quickly lunged over to pick the book up and return it to his friend. He looked round nervously, waiting for the sound of booted feet. Nothing. He relaxed slightly.

'Don't think about it, learn it. Use that shot-away memory of yours, and keep quiet. Walls have ears.'

'Only in the Haze.' Fec chuckled to himself, but shut up when he saw the serious look on Kalten's face.

'I don't give a monkey's what it says; we agreed on Ahriman, and we're sticking with it. You were the one who fancied the girl handing out the books. Just read the thing and shut it.'

Kalten looked down at his own book, and tried to forget how he sounded.

'But the inconsistencies, Kal. It's absurd. It's almost as if they're talking about two different things.'

Kalten fixed the Cham'di with what he hoped was a withering look. 'You know that; I know that. Anyone slightly more evolved than a fish knows that. But with any luck this mumbo-jumbo will keep us out of the zone of weirdness. The place where the soldiers live. OK?'

'OK. OK. I'm learning the mumbo-jumbo, already.'

James Harker felt high. 'High on life' was a term he'd often heard but never really understood. Now he did. Everything was all right. He felt like singing. All that worry, fear of judgement, terror of Maa'lon, was now gone. He did indeed feel high.

The incident with Ham'tha had sealed it. He could feel the

love. All that compassion. All that anger caged by his own principles. That was the essence of Maa'lon; he too was bound by the Way. At His core lay the Way itself, always more powerful than simple emotion. James knew He had wanted to help Ham'tha. He knew that He desperately needed to destroy the twisted children that had left Him long ago. Ham'tha's own pain mixed with Maa'lon's feelings of betrayal and shame at the new path of the N'a'm'thuli.

But Maa'lon had not given in to this pain. He was the example. A perfect being capable of understanding the power and lure of emotion, but always considering the larger picture, the fate of all above the pains of a few.

All those years he had been right to follow the Way, without even knowing why. By sheer luck he was here, with the saviour of them all. He had been given the opportunity to help Him in His divine mission. He had been given one great chance. He would never let his Lord down again.

For a brief moment, the image of the packing crate wending its way through the quads of St Oscar's was pin sharp. Suddenly, there was a violent jerk in the picture, an upside-down image of grey skies, then nothing but the hiss of static.

Braxiatel swore. He had left ten micro scanners floating in the gloomy atmosphere of John's rooms. Five of them had already been out of commission by the time he'd returned to his quarters to tune into their transmissions on the holo-monitors. Over the last three hours he had watched all the rest blank out one by one, this last one an agonizing few seconds before he finally saw where the crate had been heading. The object of his surveillance must have known that the bugs were there right from the start. He had simply chosen to disable them at the most annoying moments possible.

Braxiatel shook his head. He probably ought to forget about this obsession, anyway, and concentrate on problems closer to home. He was becoming increasingly worried about the Sultan's behaviour. At last night's University Council meeting he had discovered that students who were not members of registered religions were being refused residency permits. It was absurd. The Sultan had always maintained a secular regime; it was one of the reasons St Oscar's had been happy to locate itself in his domain.

And now, suddenly, the university seemed to have found itself in the middle of a theocracy.

But was it so sudden? Braxiatel thought. The signs had all been there: petty rules, little financial incentives, rumours. It was he who had chosen to ignore them. So concerned with the details, he failed to see the bigger picture. He scowled. There was a time when that would never have happened. What had gone wrong? When had he lost the necessary distance to see things for what they truly were?

Braxiatel was almost relieved to be interrupted from his brooding by a timid tapping on the outside door. Maybe it was Renée, he thought. It had been over a day since he'd seen her, and he had been wondering if she was fully recovered from her disastrous date.

But it wasn't. The spindly, translucent-skinned being standing outside could have fitted inside Renée's more generous frame several times over. In fact, Braxiatel thought darkly, if it was a student here, it almost certainly had fitted inside Renée at one time or another; he sometimes wondered if he was the only member of the university who hadn't. 'Yes?' he snapped.

The alien looked slightly taken aback at his tone. Or at least, there was a wash of blue coloration into its delicate face, and the cilia on its head wriggled backwards, as if trying to escape. 'Irving Braxiatel?' it asked nervously.

'Hmm?'

'I'm here on behalf of the New Moral Army.'

The first thing Emile saw when he woke up, pressed right up against his nose, was a picture of a bloody mush of flesh and bone. He felt a hand clamp down on his shoulder, and let out a shrill scream that he was instantly ashamed of.

'Take it easy, Emile.' Two large brown eyes under a mop of straggly black hair stared down at him.

He struggled to speak, coughed dryly, then tried again. 'Hello, Elspeth.'

Blinking the crusty residue of sleep from his eyes, he finally noticed the expression on her face. Horrified would probably have been the best way to describe it. Or possibly alarmed *and* horrified.

He sat up, and looked around his room. It looked like the inside of some museum of carnage, decorated with mementos of all the worst crimes in history. 'Um . . . this probably isn't what you think,' he began tentatively.

Elspeth frowned. 'So Professor Summerfield hasn't asked you to nose about in the Dellahan Demon Slayings, then?'

'The Dellahan Demon Slayings?' Emile asked disgustedly.

'That's what Channel Nine's calling them. Are you going to answer my question or not?'

Emile lowered his eyes. 'Bernice did ask if I'd look into it for her,' he confirmed.

Elspeth cursed colourfully. 'What are you, Watson to her Holmes? And what's she up to while you're in way over your head –' her gaze swept round the room '– and risking your sanity doing this? She missed her lecture this morning. Has she swanned off on holiday somewhere?'

'Bernice is exploring other avenues of investigation,' Emile said stiffly. Elspeth snorted. 'Look,' he said more firmly, 'she thought this was important, and I believe her. It's actually a bit of an honour that she trusted me enough to do this.' He knew he didn't sound convincing, even to himself. 'What do you care, anyway?'

Elspeth harrumphed, and sat in the only chair which wasn't covered in the detritus of his research. 'I worry about you, Emile. You need looking after.'

'What are you, my mother? No, look, I'm sorry. It's just, well, I'm at a bit of a dead end, and there's only really one way I can think of proceeding. Actually, I think it's the reason Bernice picked me for the investigation in the first place.'

He moved to the blinds and drew them, letting a wash of pale morning light into the room. 'Everyone's sure the culprits are in one of these religious cults,' he continued. 'It's obvious where to go to look for them. And, as you pointed out, they do seem to be having a bit of a recruitment drive at the moment.'

Bernice was staring at the abundant yellow fruit on a low bush when she noticed the Grel.

'Question: what are you looking for, Professor?' The Grel carried his dataxe uneasily and worried at its blade.

'Imperfection, my dear Shemda.' The Grel visibly quailed before her. 'It is Shemda, isn't it?'

'Yes, Professor, I'm just not used to hearing it from the mouths of strangers. Question: why do you seek out imperfection?'

'It would make me feel better. I like things warts and all. There must be some warts somewhere or I'm going to have to make some rather novel life choices that I'm really not sure about.'

She paused, and studied the Grel carefully, but its face was a blank. 'Have you not thought of the ramifications of Maa'lon's divinity, if that proves to be the case?' she asked.

'We are here to observe that divinity, Professor. To gather all the facts.'

'Yes, but have you actually thought about what it means if he is the saviour, the one true god. It's his way or perdition. And for his Way you gotta have faith. Not really my strong suit.'

'Question: why would faith be an integral part of this new life? Maa'lon has already supplied enough proof to be considered divine.'

'That's it! Proof! I knew something really obvious was capering about right in front of me, and I just couldn't see it. There you go, Shemda, you're a genius. Where is faith if you're going to have proof?'

'Question: could we start again at the beginning of this interchange?'

Extract from the diary of Bernice Summerfield

I should have paid more attention at whatever time someone was banging on about proof and faith. This clearly isn't my forte. All I know is the whole idea of most religions comes down to the fact that God just isn't going to prove he or she's there. That would be too easy. No, you have to believe in them first and get the proof later. When you're dead. No faith, no proof. Simple. Compare to the actions of one Maa'lon. Discuss.

Extract ends

Benny was asleep in the House when they brought the child in. The chattering crowd and the wails of its mother woke her from a rather disturbing dream in which she and Maa'lon were walking the fields arm in arm, her heart warmed by his smile. She quickly got up and pulled her jacket on. It was cold up in the mountains and she was sleeping in her trousers and her T-shirt. The floor was cold under her bare feet.

The crowd was gathered around the fire in Maa'lon's room. Benny couldn't see what the focus of all the attention was, so she pushed her way through. Some of the Hut'eri seemed to resent her gentle pressure, but most recognized her as a guest of Maa'lon and moved aside. When she got through to the front her heart caught in her throat. Before her lay the body of a young Hut'eri, like a broken rag-doll. The girl was no more than a metre tall and clearly would grow no more. She would die that night.

Most of her limbs were broken. Her ribs poked through her rough skin. She must have taken a fall. The mountains were treacherous, and Hut'eri young seemed to be encouraged to fend for themselves.

'She must have lost her footing, Maa'lon. She's always been such a good climber that we've never worried.' The mother was hysterical, shaking as she spoke. Behind her a stern-faced man, obviously her husband, held her by the shoulders. Tight.

'She has fallen far, Bree'tha. She will not survive the night. It is a tribute to her strength that she survived the journey here. You should be proud. Your fine daughter will find her own way now.' Maa'lon seemed weary as he spoke and his smile never reached his eyes.

86

'No! No! She's too young. Must you take her now? She's our light, our treasure.' Bernice was taken aback by the vehemence of the father's words.

'Yes, Lord. You are here, and you decide when all find the Way. Can you not spare this little one and let her make you truly proud of her?' added James Harker.

Maa'lon looked round at the expectant faces of the crowd, and held Benny's gaze for a few moments. 'If I do this thing, it must be this once. For I must respect my own laws and the laws I gave to you. Will no one ask me again to perform such a task?'

'None will, Lord,' James assured him after glancing around the room for approval.

'Then so be it.'

Maa'lon closed his eyes and knelt over the girl. He placed his hands on her chest. The crowd seemed to be holding its breath. After a few moments Maa'lon's hands became translucent, lit by an internal fire. The fire spread through the girl's chest and body, flashing brighter for an instant where the skin was broken, and then disappearing. Maa'lon stepped back from the young Hut'eri and seemed almost about to fall. Tears welled in his eyes.

Everyone looked from him to the broken child on the floor. Then they realized she was no longer broken. Her skin was unblemished and smoother somehow. Her chest started to rise and fall with vigour, and her eyes flickered open.

'Be'tha!' cried her mother as she hugged the child to her.

The room looked like a bomb had hit it, albeit a bomb that had some peculiar affinity to the sexual act. The remnants of food and drink scattered throughout would have done a Bacchanalian orgy proud. Most of the bedding was on the floor. The rest of it was twisted uncomfortably around Renée's hips. Which was just as well, because the gawky, translucent alien walked into her bedroom without bothering to knock, and he didn't seem like the sort who would have appreciated a panoramic view of her naked body.

Renée didn't think she'd ever seen a being appear more

mortified. Still half asleep, she wondered for one confused moment if he might be from a species that could actually die of embarrassment. He had quickly averted his eyes from her half-uncovered body, but she could see that he was now struggling with the problem of finding somewhere to look that didn't contain evidence of the disreputable things she'd been doing with that body in the very recent past.

'Are you here to see me, or did you just want a look around?' she asked.

The being shuddered delicately, and fixed its large, watery eyes on her face. 'I'm from the New Moral Army,' it said, somehow managing to inject both fanatical fervour and nervous hesitancy into its tone. 'Professor Braxiatel told me I'd be able to find you here. He said you were just the sort of person we're looking for.'

James Harker felt elated but confused. He felt drained by the experience. He had seen a miracle, asked for one. But in doing so he had asked his Lord to alter His plan. He had dared to ask a boon of Maa'lon, He who had given him so much already. He had been unable to stand the child's condition and he had thought to make his Lord do his bidding.

But it was still a miracle. Life from death. There for all to see. That should settle it for Bernice. She clung to her scepticism as her own religion; she had such faith in the rational. Surely now she could make the leap, take the chance. For him it was now sealed. Maa'lon walked among them; on Dellah as He had once before. His time had come and He was showing them the Way. James Harker was going to be right by His side as they walked the path. Barefoot.

Benny watched the Grel talking animatedly among themselves. The Grel Master, Demka, was waving his dataxe and pointing to the sky. The second servitor, Grenke, hooted his agreement and fluttered his tentacles. Shemda, the maroon splash over his eye vivid in the morning sunshine, shook his head and pulled his tentacles tightly together.

A Grel argument? A rare enough occurrence to warrant her attention. She moved within earshot and discreetly examined the local flora.

'Supposition: the Grel search for knowledge has been a path chosen to allow the Grel people to recognize and test our God once we gained sufficient facts and skills. Our vast stores of knowledge cannot explain that which we have observed. I have had the datarunner check all xenobiological and technological databases: the occurrences we have witnessed cannot be explained. Conclusion based on the facts before us: Maa'lon is a god. He has proved himself before us.' The Grel Master had clearly already made his point at least once; he stared hard at Shemda and flailed his tentacles; he also fiddled with his dataxe menacingly.

The other servitor nodded his agreement and added, 'It is only logical that we should follow Maa'lon and seek further enlightenment. Query: why do you not see the strength of the Master's supposition?'

Shemda sighed, an action which rather startled Bernice, particularly when she realized he was looking straight at her. 'Because of what someone told me about the nature of faith. That it is the key to divinity.'

Bernice could feel the weight of his words and the expectation behind them. The three looming Grel were all staring at her now. She could sense Shemda silently begging her for support, or at least some answers. He realized there was more to life than fact and proof, but he didn't know what; he didn't even know where to start. Grimly, she decided she had enough on her plate without taking on strays. She turned quickly and headed away out of the village.

Emile had woken himself up with a strong mug of coffee in the college buttery. Then he had fortified his nerves with a shot of vodka in the Witch and Whirlwind, ignoring the comments about students who started drinking at eleven in the morning. Then he had taken another shot, because the first one didn't seem to be working. After that, he had decided that he needed some food to line his stomach and prevent the alcohol going straight to his head.

It was now twelve-thirty, and he was running out of excuses. Not to mention room in his stomach.

He had seen a prayer meeting going on outside as he'd entered the buttery. The participants had looked as if they were settling in for a long haul, so Emile could be pretty certain that they'd still be there if he left now. And they'd been actively evangelizing, so he could also be certain that they wouldn't turn him away. In fact, there was absolutely no reason why he shouldn't go right ahead and proceed with his plan to infiltrate the cults.

No reason at all. Emile sighed gustily, then lifted feet that felt as heavy as lead, and marched out to rejoin a society that he'd once believed he'd escaped forever.

The steep sides of the valley were heavily wooded, and it was there that she sought her solitude. The trees were all very old and gnarly and bore a fruit not unlike an olive. Except that it tasted foul. And the taste really hung around, glued to the sides of the mouth: a bitterness that seemed to build. She was soon desperate for water, anything to wash her mouth out.

After an interminable couple of minutes, she heard what she assumed to be a stream a little further into the trees. She ran as fast as her bare feet would carry her and nearly fell into the tiny rivulet as she slipped on the lichen-covered stones at its side. She righted herself and plunged her head into the flow. Now was not the time for delicately cupping hands and sipping; she needed the closest she could get to a torrent.

After a few minutes of the freezing flow, Benny had finally shifted the vile taste, and so she sat back on her haunches and drew a deep breath of the clear mountain air.

'Ate a j'lee then, miss?' said the small child sitting in the lower branches of the nearest tree.

'Sorry?' Bernice said, startled. She tried to pull herself together. Time for a little dignity.

'I just thought that, as you came running over here practically screaming and then tried to drink the whole stream, you might have eaten a j'lee. Very bad straight from the tree. It takes weeks of soaking them to make them edible. Even then they're pretty rank. One of the things I'm kind of hoping Maa'lon will change. No one should have to eat j'lee stew, especially one of the faithful.'

As the child spoke, quickly and with amazing confidence for one so young, Benny studied him. He was only slightly taller than the Hut'eri that had been brought back to life. She assumed he must be around ten years old. His eyes shone with mischief. His jade eyes. He looked like a miniature Maa'lon; his skin was equally smooth and its deep ochre colour was only partly concealed by his pure white robe.

'Who are you?' asked Benny, trying to regain some control.

'Kor'no.' The child flashed a brilliant smile and leapt down from his perch. 'AKA the Sacred Child.'

'What?' Bernice wondered whether she had 'mug' stamped across her forehead. Perhaps j'lee made you delusional.

'The Sacred Child, silly. You know, I'm the one who told the animals His name. They then beat it out and all Tal'een knew He had come. I'm really good with animals; they seem to like me for some reason. Probably the Sacred Child thing, I suppose. Do you want to come and meet some of them? They're practically tame now; there are always loads of them up in the grove. At least there have been ever since He came back to us. You coming?' He began to head off across the stream.

'Just a second, I'm not sure I've completely washed my mouth out.'

Fec knew he was out of time, but his large feet just weren't that suited to dancing. And you never heard anyone say: 'That Cham'di, he sure has natural rhythm!' The curse of his people.

He tried to move further back in the crowd, bringing his broad hands loudly together in what must have seemed like a one-man attempt to fill the gaps left by everyone else's clapping.

He bumped into someone, and turned to see Kalten's

madly smiling face. The tall human looked deranged: his long, dark hair leapt about his face, and his jaw looked set in a rictus grin.

Fec moved alongside him and grabbed the tambourine from his belt. Anyone could shake a tambourine. He raised it above his head and shook it wildly. Just as everyone else fell silent.

At least fifty people turned to stare at him. He tried to make himself appear small. And failed.

The prayer leader cleared his throat and the crowd returned their gaze to him. The tall blond human smiled down on them from his podium and pulled his bright woven cloak about himself.

'That's all for now. It is time to spread the word. Go out and teach of the Light of Ahriman; share your love.'

The prayer leader bowed and stepped down. Many of the Followers patted him on the shoulders before turning away and heading off to spread the word. Fec grabbed Kalten's arm and started to lead him away, anxious not to have to link up with some of the more zealous Followers.

Their way was blocked by two soldiers. Humans with broad smiles on their sallow faces. 'Hello, boys,' said the more elaborately dressed of the two.

'Er, hello,' answered Kalten awkwardly.

'Guess what?' The soldier's grin broadened. 'You're in the army now.'

The town was heaving when Bernice returned. It seemed as if all those camping outside the Hut'eri settlement had tried to force their way into the House of Maa'lon. Hundreds, thousands squashed together and shouted for their god. It took Bernice nearly an hour to fight her way through to the House. She only made it at all because Shemda eventually heard her arguing with some of the faithful and came to her aid with customary Grel efficiency.

Inside the House, she found a grizzly sight. Maa'lon was weeping, as was James Harker. Before them lay the twisted bodies of what looked like young Hut'eri. It was difficult to tell as each of the corpses was headless and burnt beyond recognition. On some of the bodies the ribcage had been ripped open and others had hands removed at the wrist and feet at the ankles. Someone had clearly had fun killing these children.

'Bernice,' Harker sobbed. 'They were left for us to find. A fruit-gathering party, twelve children, all under eight years old. Tortured and murdered. It's evil.' As he spoke, Bernice saw him look across at Maa'lon.

'Who did this?' she asked.

'Who but the N'a'm'thuli could do this, Bernice?' Maa'lon had real steel in his voice. 'They have darkness in their hearts, a darkness that will never go away, that will only grow stronger with the blood and screams of their victims.'

'Something must be done about it.' James's eyes flashed with anger as he looked back at the charred remains. 'If only we were not constrained by the Code.'

Maa'lon's gaze returned once more to the children; the tears stood out on his cheeks; his eyes blazed like jade coals. 'As we have seen so recently, circumstance can dictate change. Nothing must ever be set in stone. Peace is my goal and my gift to my children. But the N'a'm'thuli were once my children too. They could not endure the test I left for them and they strayed from the path. My inactivity made them the monsters they are today. I cannot abandon them again. We will give them the only peace they can now have: death. I must rid the world of the curse of the Morkai.'

Emile clasped the hands of the people on either side of him, and joined in a rousing chorus of 'Ahriman is the Green Shoot in the Flowerbed of my Life'. The Church of Ahriman the Great had been only too happy to recruit him, and the mixed group of students from numerous species had welcomed him into their number with an enthusiasm that had made him feel like a total heel. When they'd suggested that he join in an open-air sing-along to encourage new recruits, he hadn't had the heart to refuse. Which, he was beginning to realize, he certainly should have.

He stared steadfastly at his feet, desperately trying to avoid the joyous gazes of his fellow worshippers and the jeering looks of the passing students. He decided to concentrate on how much of a fool he felt. It was preferable to thinking about the happy glow of belonging, of once again being part of something bigger than himself, which he could feel lurking in the reptile centre of his mind, waiting to grab him.

He had formalized his plan of action, such as it was. He would spend a maximum of two days in each cult group, enough time, he hoped, to get an idea of the sorts of things they got up to. And whether those things might include the horrible murder of an entire ship's crew. After that, he would move on to the next one, and so on, until he had done them all. With the diversity of Dellah's spiritual renaissance, he reckoned it could take him his entire university career just to make a significant dent. Still, at least he could spend his evenings on his alternative investigations of the killings.

It was pretty weak, he knew, but he just couldn't see any other way to go about it. And as he'd sat and stared at the gory pictures of the crime, gradually letting sleep overcome him, he'd come to feel that Bernice was right. The bloody symbols had begun to speak to him in some wordless way, like a subliminal hum that, if only he concentrated hard enough, might resolve itself into speech. He'd become gripped by the certainty that, if he ever did manage to translate their message, it would be the most important thing he'd ever heard in his life. And the most frightening. Or perhaps he really was being turned into a killer himself, gradually sinking into a madness that felt increasingly like sanity.

He was snapped out of his gloomy reverie by a peal of particularly unkind laughter. Unable to stop himself, he glanced up, straight into the mocking gaze of a beautiful, fair-haired young man. Emile was horrified to realize that it was the student he'd admired in yesterday's plate tectonics lecture, the one who had given him his room number.

Emile attempted a sheepish smile. The student smiled brilliantly back, then drew away from his coterie of friends to lean casually against a mud-brick wall to one side of the prayer meeting, waving his friends off when it looked like they might wait for him.

He continued to stare at Emile throughout the rest of the prayer meeting. After that first, startled glance, Emile had once again dropped his eyes, but he remained painfully aware of his watcher, as if the lad's regard was exerting some physical pressure on him.

When the meeting broke up – its leader exhorting the worshippers to head straight for lectures, because Ahriman approved of the educated mind – Emile stayed rooted to the spot. He kept his eyes downcast until the fair-haired Adonis approached so close that his shoes impinged on Emile's averted gaze and he could no longer pretend that he wasn't aware of him.

'Hi there,' the lad said with a cheery disregard for Emile's discomfort. 'I'm glad I caught up with you; I was hoping you would give me a call.' He smiled again, shyly this time, like the nerdy teenager at a party asking the prettiest girl for a dance. Only everything was back to front.

Emile realized he was expected to say something. 'I, um, I've been a bit, well you can see . . . Um . . .'

'It's Adnan, by the way,' the young man said, taking Emile's hand with casual familiarity and leading him towards a wooden bench at one side of the meeting.

As he pulled on Emile, Adnan's crisp white shirtsleeve rode up his arm, and Emile saw with a shock of disgust that his flesh had been multiply and recently scored with what appeared to be knife wounds. It was undoubtedly deliberate, and almost certainly self-inflicted. And the symbols thus carved looked horribly familiar to Emile: he was sure he'd seen their twins written in the blood and flesh of less willing victims on the doomed spaceship.

He realized that he'd pulled away from Adnan in alarm when the young man turned round to look at him. The members of the Church of Ahriman had all dispersed, and he and Adnan were alone in the red-walled quad. He found himself looking around frantically for some means of escape.

Adnan noticed it too. He smiled, the same wide friendly smile, but this time Emile found himself looking for the steel beneath the velvet. He backed away another step.

Adnan held up his hands in a gesture of surrender, or possibly conciliation, exposing more of the symbols carved into his flesh as he did so. 'You've found me out,' he said breezily, as if Emile had merely discovered that he'd been stealing bread rolls from the buttery.

Emile tried to back away another step, and found himself pressed up against the mud-brick walls of the quad. He imagined he could feel every single rough contour of the bricks pressing into his back. He was very conscious of the smell of his own sweat. 'How did you discover me?' he stammered. 'Was it the computer search? I knew I should have invested in better ICE programs.'

'You know, I don't think we're on the same wavelength at all,' Adnan said in a puzzled tone. 'What exactly are you talking about?'

'No, after you,' Emile stuttered. He wondered what cruel game Adnan was playing; or was he just following the edict that killers are supposed to toy with their victims first? Emile's breathing was so laboured, he was beginning to wonder if he might pass out. At least that way he wouldn't be conscious for whatever Adnan had planned for him.

Adnan reached an arm out towards Emile in apparent concern, but stopped at Emile's nervous flinch. He sighed. 'All right. Well, you know I noticed you in the lecture, and I was thinking of inviting you along to a new group that I belong to. We're . . . interested in that which is hidden, and I thought that maybe you might be too. Then I saw you hanging out with that bunch of saddos, and it seemed a bit of a waste. I hate waste. To put it bluntly: don't join them, join us.'

The air whooshed out of Emile's lungs in a long, relieved burst. He smoothed his sweat-soaked hair back out of his eyes with a trembling hand. Adnan wasn't toying with him. He really wasn't going to die. The sudden realization was the most wonderful of his life. It was higher than any drug high.

Adnan was frowning at him, a single line creasing his perfect chocolate-brown brow. 'You thought I was going to hurt you,' he said incredulously. He actually sounded a bit wounded.

Emile managed a sheepish smile. 'It did cross my mind. What with everything that's been going on, and everything. Anyway, why do you want me? Erm, I mean want, as in want me to join, not the other sort of want, which I wouldn't –'

'The Church of Ahriman the Great,' Adnan said with light contempt. 'You can do better than that.'

Emile blushed. 'They're nice people,' he countered half-heartedly.

Adnan's smile was definitely predatory this time. 'Don't you know that nice guys finish last?' He rolled up his sleeves fully to reveal the scar-tissue symbols on his arms, and traced one pentangle with his finger. 'The old powers are reawakening,' he said with deadly seriousness. 'It's all much bigger than a dry old university now. Some of us have realized that, and some of us are not content just to worship gods. We can have their powers, too.' He snapped his fingers with a dry click, and for one second Emile thought he saw a ball of light hover above Adnan's hand. He blinked, and the image was gone.

Adnan shrugged. 'We're still learning,' he said apologetically. 'An economics major doesn't really prepare you for this sort of thing.'

A cloud passed over the sun, and Emile felt as if his world had narrowed to himself, Adnan, and the choice he had to make. But there wasn't really a choice at all. He knew that, wherever Adnan led, he would follow. Because there was every chance Adnan knew why those people on the ship had died; maybe he even knew the killers. Because Adnan was one of the most attractive men he'd ever met and, incredibly, he seemed to be interested in Emile.

And, somewhere hidden from his conscious mind, because the power he had glimpsed for just one moment was terribly, terribly tempting.

'I'm in,' Emile said.

Adnan clasped Emile's shoulders, and dropped a whisper-soft kiss on his lips. 'You won't be sorry you picked the winning side,' he said.

Extract from the diary of Bernice Summerfield

Things have all gone rather pear-shaped. In one afternoon, Tal'een has been turned from a hippy festival into a boot-camp. I'm still not sure which I prefer. Maa'lon has stirred the faithful; their cause is righteous; the place is alive with the kind of zeal I can only dream about. What makes me different? Why can't I see it their way? Why am I holding back?

The N'a'm'thuli deserve it. I saw those kids. Kids. All so young, dying in so much pain. Why? To settle a thousand-year-old score, or just because they are evil? Probably both. Well, now they're gonna get it. And, fellow traveller though I might be with the Maa'lon movement, I'm gonna have my say too. There is something so primal about harming kids. I may not be the galaxy's most maternal woman, but the feelings are there. As the N'a'm'thuli will find out.

Note: Never trust anyone or anything with more than two apostrophes in it. It's sinister.

Extract ends

5

WAR, WAR IS STUPID

It took two days to ready the faithful for battle. The beauties of the valley and Tal'een were subsumed in harsh shouts and the clash of steel. The Hut'eri all carried their own gl'ai: a simple, shining blade that hugged the forearm and curved viciously up beyond the elbow. Around the wrist-hold it fanned out into a lethal-looking bracelet of spikes. Though the weapon appeared to be primarily defensive (the arm's blade providing a comprehensive guard) these spikes sent a chill through Bernice. The Hut'eri were now beyond mere defence. They, and their God, were coming for the N'a'm'thuli.

As well as these traditional blades, many of which were lent to the Followers outside the town, the burgeoning army of Maa'lon bore more recent mechanisms of death. Bernice had no idea where all the weapons came from, but within hours of the call to arms many of the latest firearms were being distributed amid cheers and chanting.

What had once been a town of peace, awash with smiles and hope, was now a grim place that stank of ozone and where the nights were lit by the pulses of energy weapons. Even the students and other off-worlders that Benny had seen on her arrival took great glee in cleaning and charging a variety of guns that they had clearly brought themselves. Songs were sung and nightmarish targets were hit to much applause. Bernice made a mental note to have a word with the dean about gun control: she seemed to be the only person on the planet who was not tooled up.

On the third day Maa'lon came out of the House for the first time since he had told his children to prepare for war. He looked resolute; the jade in his eyes gleamed dangerously bright; his white robes shone once more in the morning light.

'Come,' he said, in a quiet voice that still carried across the armed horde before him. With only that one word, they went to war.

A day's journey across Dellah, the Sultan of the Tashwari was girding himself for a different kind of battle. Although, if it came to the more conventional sort of war – well, he was prepared for that too. Membership of the New Moral Army had quadrupled over the last day alone. This morning, for the first time, he had received a protest about the formation of the religious militia from one of the humans on the University Council.

It was too late, the Sultan knew. They should have protested when he first started the recruitment drive, using the 'carrot and stick' methods he had learnt from the humans themselves. They should have protested before the New Moral Army outnumbered the University Council by a hundred to one. Now, any protest would be silenced.

His God had been right, the Sultan thought, with the same blazing rush of joy which always accompanied the recollection. You must use your power to bring people to the faith you have found, his God had told him. But move softly: the unbelievers will stop you if they can. Be sure that they do not know there is something to be stopped until they are powerless to do anything against it.

Why give people a choice between good and evil, his God had asked, when there is always the chance that they may choose evil?

So the Sultan had ensured that, when the time came, the inhabitants of his university would not have the chance to tread the wrong path. The Sultan had made the choice for them, before they could know that there was a choice to be made.

'You were stunning.'

'Well, I suppose so.'

'No, I mean, you were spectacular.'

Clarence examined the holo-footage of the starship in flight, elegant and frighteningly powerful as it spun in an intricate mechanical dance. It looked like a Ship, but it no longer looked like him, the person living in his skull. He realized with a twinge of sadness that he felt more recognition for the humanoid face that gazed at him from mirrors than for this Ship which he had once been.

Sara!qava gazed at him through his big brown eyes, pushing aside a sweep of blue-grey hair to get a better look. 'You seem like a man who could use a hearty bowl of pasta,' he said.

They were inside Sara!qava's house in iSanti Jeni, a wonderfully homely place that never seemed full despite the hordes of children who inhabited it. The atmosphere was thick with the smell of baking and unconditional love. Clarence set aside the holo-recording of his old self and took the proffered dish, juggling it between his hands until it cooled to a manageable temperature.

As Sara!qava sat opposite him, still studying him with a mixture of concern and curiosity, Clarence shovelled up a mouthful of pasta, allowing the ends to dangle before sucking them in with an enjoyably inelegant slurp. His stomach rumbled appreciatively, and he realized how long it had been since he'd last eaten. A slave to my body, he thought gloomily.

Sara!qava gently drew the holo-projector towards himself, clasping the ovoid in his fine-boned hand. He continued to watch the brief film of the old Clarence in flight, delicately touching the tip of his tongue to his lips in thought. 'Is this the only footage you have?' he asked eventually, casually reaching across to prevent a lumbering toddler falling into a cauldron of soup.

101

Clarence let the bright twitter of seaside birdsong fill the room for a few seconds. He leant back so that the sunlight streaming through the window warmed his face and chest. When he opened his eyes, Sara!qava was staring at him.

'It's all God gave me,' Clarence replied. 'I never asked for more. I never wanted it, but now I'm beginning to wonder if God would have given me any more even if I had asked.'

'Thinking of joining the Pointlessly Paranoid Worrying About God Interest Group?' a jolly, disembodied female voice asked, and Clarence remembered that the House was sentient, too.

'Feel like going for a walk?' he asked Sara!qava.

The House harrumphed bad-temperedly. 'I know when I'm not wanted,' it said in a martyred tone. 'I'll just keep quiet if my input isn't appreciated.'

Sara!qava grinned at Clarence and rolled his eyes. 'You know you're just being nosy,' he told the House. 'We're going for a stroll along the beach. You can send a remote to listen in if you're that interested.

'There's no such thing as privacy on the Worldsphere,' he said to Clarence. Clarence wondered how many people really understood that.

Kalten was knackered. He wasn't built for running around all the time. Short bursts, OK, but three whole hours: it was sick. And the boots were killing him. Fec was lucky they hadn't planned on weird feet.

He adjusted the strap of his rifle but it still bit into his shoulder. It had continued to grow heavier, and Kalten wondered whether that was some deliberate part of the training.

Fec ran slowly alongside him; they were both nearly a hundred metres behind the squad now. After a few moments, the others disappeared down a rocky defile, and Kalten put his hand on the little Cham'di's shoulders.

'Rest time, I think. Looking a gift horse and all that,' he gasped as he came to a halt and doubled over.

'I think I'm going to lose my breakfast, which in one sense is not such a bad idea,' whispered Fec as he collapsed.

They remained in silence for a moment, their lungs still burning.

'Aren't you bad little soldiers?'

They both leapt to their feet and spun round to face whoever had spoken. The blonde female officer laughed at their inept attempts to salute and dropped down from the tree. No wonder they hadn't seen her.

'There's no place for slackness in the Army of God, you know. And I certainly see slackness before me now. I think a flogging may be in order.'

'Shit.' Kalten muttered the word louder than he intended.

'Profanity too? You boys'll be sleeping on your fronts for weeks.'

Heads bowed, they followed the officer back to camp.

It was only after she'd been marching and climbing for a few hours, with the sun high in the sky, that Bernice realized her feet had toughened up considerably in the few days since her rather awkward arrival. The bathing in herbs had certainly had the desired effect, leaving her feeling less of an outsider. At least her feet were in tune with the people of Maa'lon, even if her heart lagged strangely behind.

They had arrived in Tal'een from its southern approaches, and so she was surprised at how much harsher the northern route to the plains of the N'a'm'thuli proved to be. The steep north face of the valley rose for a thousand metres before allowing them access to a series of narrow defiles that housed vicious shrubs shrouded in interminable mists.

'We rarely come this way, Professor,' said Tan'a at her side. 'The N'a'm'thuli hunt throughout the northern range; without Maa'lon we would not have the courage to face them.'

The child seemed to have grown up swiftly in the few days since Bernice had met her. She now wore a simple crossed pattern of steel webbing over her plain tunic. Her gl'ai seemed a bit too big for her, but her eyes looked old enough to do the job.

'Tell me all you know about the N'a'm'thuli, Tan'a.'

Bernice's eyes were drawn to the snub-nosed gun strapped to the girl's thigh. 'I always like to know my enemy.'

Tan'a's eyes grew cold and she began to toy with the gun at her side. She did not even seem to notice when the barbs of one of the mountain plants cut into her left arm. 'There is little to tell: they are evil. They have a darkness in their hearts which led them from Maa'lon and into the hands of another. They take delight in the pains they inflict on the Hut'eri and Maa'lon. For this they will die; Maa'lon will no longer suffer them to exist.'

Bernice knew she was hearing the words of a father or a mother, but she could feel Tan'a's belief in them. 'What are they like, though? They're the same people as you, surely?'

'They are nothing like us. We are the people of Maa'lon. A people of peace seeking the Way. They have no souls, no hearts. They live for blood. They are nothing to the Hut'eri.'

Tan'a cut viciously at a bush with the gl'ai to clear a path, and walked on in silence.

'I remember so little,' Clarence said. 'And God always told me it was better to move on than look back.'

'But now you're beginning to have doubts about God,' Sara!qava said slowly, 'so you are beginning to doubt everything else as well.'

Clarence doodled in the sand with his toe. The water was silky and blue in front of them, lightly ruffled by the morning breeze blowing in from the shore. 'How do I know I'm even who God has told me I am?' he said. He realized that he'd drawn an inane smiley-face with his toe. He quickly scrubbed it out. 'No one else will talk to me about my past, either,' he said.

Sara!qava waded out until he was knee-deep in the tepid water. Frontlit by the rising sun, he looked rather heroic and handsome, his yellow freckles glowing like flecks of gold in his pale face. He gazed at Clarence sympathetically. 'Maybe they want to spare your feelings,' he said, 'not dredge up painful memories of the accident.'

'Or maybe they want to spare their own,' Clarence said

sourly. 'Nothing makes people more uncomfortable than talking to a cripple about his injury.'

Sara!qava reached out a hand, beckoning him forward into the water. Clarence joined him, enjoying the sensual swirl of the wavelets around his feet.

'I remember when my mother died,' Sara!qava said.

Clarence's head snapped up, startled at the change of subject.

A small smile twisted Sara!qava's lips. 'Don't want me to talk about it, do you?'

'No, I was just a bit taken aback. I mean, if you want to . . .' Clarence flustered.

Sara!qava's smile transformed into a full-blown chuckle. 'No, you don't. It's awkward. I remember right after it happened, people I'd known for years would cross the street to avoid me. I don't think it was me they were scared of. It was themselves: their own discomfort at not knowing what to say. They were terrified they would say the wrong thing. Terrified of embarrassing themselves.'

Sara!qava grimaced, as if tasting the bitter note that had entered his voice. 'I just mean . . . Oh, that I understand, I suppose.'

'Well, I'm glad you do,' Clarence said. 'But that's not what I wanted to talk about.'

'Oh,' Sara!qava said. 'Well, what then?'

'I'm sorry, I don't mean to be rude,' Clarence said. 'But embarrassment seems too easy an excuse. I'm beginning to wonder if that's just what God wants me to think. Maybe nobody talks about my past because nobody really knows it. Everybody seems to have known of me, but I haven't yet met anyone who actually knew me, first hand. What if God didn't really transfer the remnants of a Ship's mind into the body of an angel; what if he created me this way?'

Sara!qava glanced up at the ever-present smiling globe of Whynot. 'Oh dear. Angelic existential angst.'

Renée was doing push-ups. She'd never done push-ups before in her life, and had fully intended to spend the rest of her existence in blissful ignorance of what they felt like.

Thank you very much, Irving Braxiatel.

'Come on, you irreligious scum!' the drill sergeant barked. 'Put some welly in it!'

Renée reckoned it was worth the effort to lift her head and treat him to the full force of her glare. Unfortunately, he wasn't looking at her, and a salty trickle of sweat from her tangled hair stung her eyes. She hung her head defeatedly and carried on with the push-ups.

After ten rather feeble efforts, she felt a stinging slap on her raised posterior. She twisted her head round to find the gawky shape of Sergeant Salmon looming over her, swagger-stick poised for another blow. 'You,' he said, 'are the most pathetic, useless, ugly excuse I have ever seen for a recruit in all my years! Keep your bloody arse in and your shoulders square! Do you understand, you horrid little person?'

Renée rolled over into a sitting position. 'I should like to take issue with the word "ugly",' she said.

Sergeant Salmon spluttered in apoplectic rage.

'I should also,' she continued, 'like to point out that, while spanking is not outside my range of interests, I usually prefer to administer rather than receive the punishment.'

Sergeant Salmon's face was now a deep red colour that augured heart problems in later life. 'You . . .' he raged. 'You . . .'

'At ease, Sergeant.' It was the Sultan. The compassion in his wizened, orange-scaled face and the kindly glint in his two remaining eyes looking like they belonged in a different universe to the livid fury on Sergeant Salmon's face.

Renée, catching herself feeling rather grateful to the old codger, sternly reminded herself that this was actually all his fault. The small part of it that wasn't Braxiatel's fault, anyway.

The Sultan, oblivious to her seething thoughts, smiled benignly down at her and then back up at the sergeant. 'I think that's enough for today, don't you, Sergeant? We don't want to so exhaust our recruits that they have no energy left for their devotions. This is, after all, the New *Moral* Army.'

'Yes, sir,' Sergeant Salmon said stiffly. In his mind, 'army' was clearly the more significant term.

Hugely relieved, Renée clambered to her feet, pulling her unflattering khaki uniform into some semblance of order. 'Thank you, your eminence,' she said graciously.

'Not at all,' the Sultan replied. 'I was delighted to hear that you'd joined. I want the ranks of my army to swell with the growing numbers of the faithful. It is the moral duty of all believers to spread the good word.' He hesitated, and coughed embarrassedly. 'Although I had not, to be honest, been aware that you had any particularly strong religious convictions.'

Renée laughed breathlessly. 'I'm lucky enough to belong to a religion that is not incompatible with my lifestyle.'

But the Sultan didn't seem to be listening to her any longer. His ageing gaze swept over the muddy Dellahan playing-field, littered with the slumped forms of the New Moral Army's latest recruits. 'I have recently rediscovered my faith,' he said dreamily. 'It was wonderful. My god spoke to me in a voice like thunder.' He looked back at the red huddle of St Oscar's. 'I want other people to enjoy the same epiphany I have. And, as Sultan of the Tashwari, I have the power to ensure that they can.'

Renée did not like the sound of that at all.

They found more bodies hanging in the trees as they were looking for a place to camp. Harker could feel his blood beginning to boil, and knew the rage would need an outlet soon. This time they were women. Their eyes had been taken, then their skin peeled back from the fingertips. Each wore a necklace fashioned from her own internal organs.

James helped to cut them down. Maa'lon blessed the bodies, and then the trees themselves were cut down to make a pyre. Maa'lon made it clear that purification was needed. James was only too happy to help the poor Hut'eri on their way.

He spent much of the evening sharpening the blade of his gl'ai (a gift from Maa'lon, no less) and talking with his God. Though talking was a rather redundant term. Maa'lon knew his thoughts and heart, knew he would fight for Him till the bitter end. James now understood more of the Way. He knew that peace was an ideal, but that the N'a'm'thuli would never understand that; they were lost. He could see the pain in Maa'lon's eyes when He talked of His lost children; He could not forgive Himself the test that led them astray. Harker wondered whether he himself would pass such a test.

'Of course you would, James,' said Maa'lon as He washed the reverend's feet.

When Braxiatel knocked on Renée's door, there was no response. After a moment's hesitation, he knocked again, more firmly this time, but still nothing. Odd. He was pretty certain he'd seen her come in. And he knew she had spent the day, the last several days, training in the New Moral Army; he couldn't imagine she'd have gone out for a night on the town after that.

He felt a small twinge of worry; he'd involved her in his business, and it wasn't beyond the realms of possibility that she'd suffered for it. He wasn't sure he'd be able to forgive himself if that was the case.

Unbidden, all sorts of visions swam through his head. Renée unrecognizable, just a pool of blood and mangled flesh like the poor unfortunates aboard that ship. His adversary standing over her still-warm corpse, laughing at Braxiatel for taking it all so seriously. Renée with her wrists slit, because she'd finally worked out what was going on, and it was too much for a human mind to bear.

Braxiatel's hearts' rate sped up painfully. He reached inside his jacket for his master key, and thrust it urgently at the door.

He stopped it inches from the lock, as some alternative scenarios invaded his consciousness. Renée, unclothed, enjoying the company of one of the students. Renée enjoying the company of several of the students, and various pieces of equipment being involved. Renée enjoying her own company . . .

Braxiatel sighed. It was no good; he had to know. He set his keycard against the lock and pushed open the door.

He stopped just inside to study the unusual sight in front of him.

Surrounded by the garish, fabric-strewn clutter of her quarters, Renée was soundly asleep. She must have collapsed on to the bed as soon as she entered the room, still clothed in her dirty khaki uniform. One arm was sprawled up above her head, the other curled underneath her chin in an endearingly childlike pose. Her face was softer in repose; stripped of the self-knowledge which animated it when she was awake, it looked strangely bland, not really like her at all. Braxiatel smiled: the day's training must have exhausted her.

He moved until he was standing over her, then reached forward and smoothed a strand of curly blonde hair from her brow.

She stirred slightly, and her eyes flickered slowly open. She looked directly at Braxiatel, and for a moment the expression on her face was unreadable. Braxiatel felt his hearts speed up again, and could not for the life of him understand why. Then memory seemed to return to her.

'You utter bastard!' she said. She pushed herself into a sitting position and threw her pillow at him.

Braxiatel was too surprised to ward it off, and it struck him squarely on the nose before tumbling to his feet.

'You sent them to me,' she said. 'And they told me that, unless I joined up, they'd stop my salary. I've just had three days of hell because of you, and you haven't even had the courtesy to come and apologize.' She glared fiercely up at him, then dragged herself to her feet, groaning, and staggered over to the wash unit. Uncaring of his presence, she pulled her khaki shirt over her head. Braxiatel spun away from her, but not quite quickly enough to avoid a side view of her plump left breast and its pert, peach-coloured nipple.

'Nasty cough you've got there, Braxiatel,' she said. 'Not that I care. Why did you do it?'

Braxiatel risked a look back round at her, and was relieved to see that she'd put on a silk dressing gown in a sky blue that complemented her eyes rather nicely. 'It was John's suggestion,' he said carefully.

Renée frowned, opened her mouth, then shut it again. Her expression became slightly less irate. 'He said the same thing to me,' she said. 'I'd forgotten. Although what possible good either of you think it can do, I can't imagine. All this new morality rubbish will soon blow over; these things always do. Unless you both thought I could do with the exercise.' She bent to massage her thighs through the blue silk, affording Braxiatel another fine view down the gaping front of the gown. 'I must say,' she continued, 'exercising hitherto unused muscles is usually a rather more pleasurable experience for me.'

Braxiatel decided that he could now safely ignore her goading. He clasped his hands in front of him. 'You would have had to join up pretty soon, anyway,' he said. 'The Sultan's making it obligatory for all members of registered faiths.'

'Really?' Renée frowned. 'I don't like this. And I suppose you want me to keep you abreast of developments from the inside, as it were.'

He studied her face, but it was devoid of its usual mockery. 'John told me the armies of light could defeat the armies of darkness. I have to assume this was what he meant.'

'How much do you know about the Church of the Grey?' Renée asked curiously.

Braxiatel looked at her sharply. 'Absolutely nothing. Why?'

Renée smiled. 'I'm just wondering why you assume that I'll be fighting for the Armies of Light, that's all.'

Clarence floated on his back, gazing unblinkingly at the sun. Here in the sea off iSanti Jeni, he could have been alone in the universe. 'Do you think I'm good looking?' he asked.

Sara!qava laughed, and there was a splash as he righted himself in the water beside Clarence. Clarence flipped upright too, so that they both stood facing each other, waist-deep in the clear azure sea. 'You're very good looking,' Sara!qava said.

'Even more importantly, you're unique. Everyone who has ever met you wants to have sex with you.'

Clarence blushed, the red stain extending right down his naked chest.

'But you never have, have you?' Sara!qava said. 'Had sex with anyone, I mean.'

Clarence studied the distorted wobble of his feet with fierce intensity. 'No. It's just . . . it would be the most biological thing I could do, like a final admission of defeat. And –' his blush deepened '– I'm not sure I'd really know how to go about it. I did kiss Bernice once,' he added defensively.

'Ah, Bernice,' Sara!qava said, as if that answered everything. Maybe it did.

'Do you think I'm her type?'

This time, it was Sara!qava who lowered his eyes. 'You're not the only person to have asked yourself that,' he said with quiet humour.

Clarence was surprised. He knew that Sara!qava and Bernice were friends, and that they had met on Bernice's first visit to the Worldsphere; but he hadn't realized it was that kind of friendship.

Sara!qava seemed to sense what he was thinking. 'Oh, no,' he said. 'Some of us have realized that the answer is "no".'

Clarence breathed out a relieved sigh, then blushed again at Sara!qava's knowing smile. 'That's not exactly what I meant,' he said.

'I seem to be getting everything wrong today,' Sara!qava said, gently mocking.

'What I meant was: do you think God made me this way to be attractive to Bernice?'

Sara!qava grinned. 'I don't know. Is it working?'

'Not conspicuously, no,' Clarence admitted.

'Probably not, then. At least when God's manipulative, he usually gets it right.'

'Not where Bernice is concerned,' Clarence said fondly, thinking of God's mental simulacrum of her, which had proved to be as stubborn as the real thing. 'I was planning to keep on trying, though,' he said, brushing dripping black ringlets of hair out of his eyes. 'And now God's made sure that I can't.'

A gull shrieked and dived for the sea. A second before it hit the surface, there was a surge of water and a scaly head reared up and snatched the bird between wickedly sharp jaws. The head turned to look at them, then snapped back and swallowed the bird whole. Clarence could see the lump sliding all the way down inside the long, serpentine neck.

The sea-creature looked at them again. 'It all comes back to Operation Ragnarok,' it said.

Sara!qava blinked. 'Do I know you?' he asked.

'This is my friend, the *B-Aaron*,' Clarence said. 'We met recently, and realized we had some mutual interests. He's been hanging around making sure our conversation stays –' he flicked his eyes up to Whynot '– private. Nice remote drone, by the way.'

'Thank you,' *B-Aaron* said. 'It came in very handy during the War.'

Sara!qava was looking between them in puzzlement. 'So I'm not the only one you've been talking to about these thoughts of yours,' he said, with just a hint of suspicion.

'I've been thinking a lot recently,' said Clarence. 'About a lot of things. The evacuation of Bernice's galaxy. Never seeing her again.' He began to wade back towards shore and, after a moment's hesitation, Sara!qava joined him. The *B-Aaron*'s sea-creature remote drone sank once more beneath the waves.

Clarence turned to stare into the sun, wishing it could blind him as it would an ordinary human. 'I once chose not to risk death to rescue Bernice because I had a long life ahead of me,' he said. 'A lot of time to give up for one short-lived woman. Now I'm beginning to wonder if all I had to gain was a long life of missing her.'

Extract from the diary of Bernice Summerfield

Night falls in the mountains. Billy No Mates here wedged between some rocks on a rather narrow ledge. I seem to have fallen behind James and the others, all except faithful Shemda, the unusual Grel. Tan'a wanted to walk with her father (probably scared of the unbeliever) so now it's just Shemda and me. What a team. He keeps trying to force his spare dataxe on me, but there is just no way I am going to carry one of those ludicrous things. I feel silly enough with weapons as it is, let alone one that keeps bleeping and giving the weather reports while you're hitting someone over the head with it. I'd rather wear one of those huge retro multifunction sports watches. Honest.

Later.

Weird dream. Maa'lon led us into battle and I was right near the front, hacking away at the darkness. It was the darkness itself we were fighting, forming itself into blades and waves of searing heat. As I hacked away, I could see Maa'lon's smile and it gave me an insane strength. I was like a berserker. Then I heard one word, echoing through my mind. 'Shiva!' Then I woke up. Must stop eating cheese.

Extract ends

'Query: what is Shiva?' asked Shemda as they slid their way down the steep mountain path. Bernice grabbed a bush to steady herself before answering.

'A friend of mine was looking into it a while ago. Then the mysterious man in the bar piqued my interest further. It's an old myth about the destruction of worlds. Worlds destroyed by something called the Shiva: a threat without substance that exists within. It's often perceived to be female, but that may just be a reflection of some patriarchal societies. I never found anything concrete on it though, bar a link with Dellah, and that's not unusual for this sector. I would have thought the Grel would have a great deal of information on such a myth.'

Talking at such a high altitude left Benny feeling rather breathless, so she sat back on her haunches and looked out the canteen in her rucksack.

'The Grel have very little interest in gods and myths. Such catalogues are not deemed useful enough for direct access from the standard dataxe. All information available is censored and tailored for each particular mission; we do not wish access to core files to fall into the hands of others because of a captured dataxe.' As he spoke, Shemda pressed a series of buttons on the side of his own weapon, and two screens came to light. His large eyes danced across both multi-coloured panels, and the tentacles around his mouth twirled around each other in what Bernice assumed to be a look of concentration.

'Query: why do you not believe in Maa'lon, Professor?' he said suddenly, as if it was something he'd been thinking about for some time. His large grey face came round to look directly at her; the maroon splash over his eye giving him the look of a faithful hound.

'I don't know. I feel I ought to; I can see the good in him, the compassion. It's back to proof and faith again, I think. Or perhaps I'm just not a believer. Never one to be one of the herd, you might say.'

'I was unaware that humans had a herd instinct, Professor, but this gathering does seem to back up your assertion.' He looked at those passing them by, a uniform look of determination on their dark Hut'eri faces. Bright eyes shining, then disappearing into the mist. Bernice gave him a withering look, but decided not to labour the point.

She looked down at her own dataxe, a spare from the landcruiser that she had finally tired of refusing to let Shemda give her. 'So which files does this give me access to, then?'

'Essentially, only those pertaining to our mission on Dellah. Religious texts and histories that give us a working knowledge of the local situation and the requirements of local divinities. You would find much of interest there, if you could read Grel.' With that he gave another snuffling chortle and stood up. He grabbed Benny's arm, lifted her to her feet easily, and then they set off again.

'Why aren't you with Demka and Grenke anyway? Surely

your place is by your master? And he appears to be in a far better position to judge the divinity of Maa'lon: he's right by his side after all. You'll learn very little at the back with the reluctant soldier. Ow!' Bernice caught herself on another of the evil shrubs. Blood began to drip from the gash in her hand.

Shemda immediately came to her aid. He sat her down, washed the wound with a stinging antiseptic fluid from his pack, and then seared it with a small heat-lance. He bound it up and then sat down next to her, pulled his own canteen out and opened it in his mouth. After a long noisy drink he set it down by his side and turned to her.

'I must admit, I find them all a bit dull.'

'I've seen that writing before,' Elspeth said.

'What?' Emile stared at her with a mixture of disbelief and annoyance.

Elspeth held up his holo-screen, so that he could see the picture she had been studying, one of the snapshots of the death ship's walls. 'It's Tyleran, I'm sure,' she said.

When, after days of fruitless searching in St Oscar's archives, desperation had driven Emile to asking Elspeth for her opinion on the case, he hadn't for one moment imagined that she'd be able to help. He'd just wanted her to sympathize with him about how impossible it was. In fact, he realized, he was slightly irked that she seemed to understand more than he did.

'I suppose it could be,' he allowed grudgingly. 'I mean, the writing seems to come from all over the place.' He looked round the Witch and Whirlwind again, checking that no one was within earshot. But, at ten in the morning, they had it pretty much to themselves. Bernice's absence seemed to have put a definite damper on the spirit of the place. He'd have to tell her when she got back. 'So it came from Tyler's,' he said. He pulled the screen back from her and checked the passenger manifest. He was right. He showed it to her. 'One of the passengers came from the Folly. No big deal.'

Elspeth sighed, as if he was being rather slow on the uptake.

'Yes, but didn't you reckon it was the writing on the walls that mattered, because everything else was done by the victims? Well, I'm telling you that that writing came from Tyler's Folly.'

'Why didn't the linguistic search program pick it up, then?' Emile asked, then instantly wished he could ask it again, this time attempting not to sound like a sulky five-year-old.

Elspeth grinned at him affectionately, apparently both understanding and forgiving his ill-humour. He didn't deserve a friend like her, he thought.

'It's ancient stuff,' she explained. 'Nothing current, it's from some of the indigenous ruins. I did it for my fourth-form humanities course.' She paused to go and fetch them another round from the surly barcreature, obviously aware of the dramatic potential of keeping him waiting. Or possibly just desperate for a pint.

A few moments later, she set the glasses down in front of him with a clunk. 'I remembered it,' she continued, 'because they reckoned it was so unusual: not linked to any other known writing in this sector. A bit like the Basque language back on Earth.'

Emile looked at the passenger manifest again. 'But it doesn't make any sense,' he said. 'All the people on the ship died: fifteen of them on board, and fifteen DNA patterns in the goop.'

Elspeth winced at his phrasing. 'Could anyone else have stowed away on board?' she asked. 'When they stopped at the Folly to pick up that other passenger, maybe.'

'No . . . no, I really don't think so,' Emile said. 'I've seen plans and pictures of the inside of the ship. There just wouldn't have been room. And Captain Wantman was a notoriously wily old sod: I can't see anyone slipping that kind of stunt past him.'

They stared at each other, stumped. 'I assume you've checked out all the people who have been IDed?' Elspeth asked half-heartedly.

'Yep. Nothing too suspicious about any of them. Student

116

customs official. A bit of a twat, by all accounts.' Emile, suddenly realizing he'd spoken ill of the dead, felt a sharp stab of guilt. 'But, you know, probably an all right guy,' he added hastily. 'The captain I've already mentioned: a dodgy dealer, but I can't honestly see homicide being his scene. The bloke from Tyler's was a policeman, so no chance there.'

'The police always being paragons of legality and decency,' Elspeth said dryly.

Emile laughed. 'Yeah, I know, but he just seemed like a normal grunt from everything I could find out. There was some depression recently, which is why he was taking this holiday, but . . .'

'It would be more unusual to find a policeman on Tyler's who wasn't depressed,' Elspeth supplied.

'And finally there's the Dellahan local. Devoted wife and mother of two, absolutely no visible skeletons in the closet.'

'You've spoken to the family?' Elspeth queried.

Emile cleared his throat. 'Erm, not directly. I thought it would be a bit ghoulish – and they've been so hassled by all the media, I reckoned I'd be the last thing they needed.' Elspeth glanced up disapprovingly at him from beneath her brows. 'I know, I know,' he said. 'So I'm no Sherlock Holmes. Or even Dr Watson. But I really have checked them out and they're squeaky clean.'

Elspeth sighed and leant back in her chair. 'Well, I can't explain it. But the writing's definitely from Tyler's. Maybe it just isn't important.'

Emile shook his head. 'No, I think it's actually extremely important, I just can't work out why.' He glanced at the retro twenties novelty wall clock, then jumped up in alarm. 'Oh God, I've got to get back to my room. Adnan's lot are coming over in twenty minutes.'

'Adnan? I thought you were going to steer clear of him.' Elspeth looked genuinely disturbed.

'It's all right, I know what I'm doing.'

'Do you?' she asked disbelievingly.

'Nope. But I'm afraid I have to do it anyway.'

* * *

Fec's finding the ointment was a real boon. It leeched out the heat in his shoulders and allowed Kalten to think of something beyond his pain.

Fec continued to rub it into the red-raw skin.

'Feeling any more spiritual?' he asked quietly. Kalten knew he was smiling behind him.

'Spookily, no. In fact, during the whole process, I swung rather heavily towards the camp of the profane.' He chuckled to himself and then winced when his friend's hands hit an open wound.

'Know what you mean, man. Didn't feel the touch of god myself. Just that psycho drill sergeant's lash. He really enjoyed it, you know.'

'Yeah, didn't look too much like religious zeal. The loon was getting off on it.'

'Army life does strange things to strange people. He's true military, and that's even scarier than the religious.'

'Apart from that beardy-weirdy in prayer class: the one with no ears.'

'Oh yeah, apart from him.' Kalten felt the young Cham'di shiver as he spoke.

James knew they were nearly there. The mists were starting to clear and breathing became much easier. The granite-like stone gave way to more and more plants as they moved on, and he could feel his anxiety rise with that of all those around him. All except Maa'lon.

His God travelled effortlessly. He did not feel the fatigue of His Followers, but He did respond to it. He called a halt more often than was necessary. He clearly hated the pain He was putting them through. Each time they came across more of the gutted, skinned trophies of twisted N'a'm'thuli, the column came to a stop. Blessings were given; the bodies laid to rest. Maa'lon called for calm, for control. The time would soon come; anger would not hasten the end of this abhorrence. He alone would see into their hearts and condemn them for their crimes. Then would His Followers do His bidding.

He hadn't seen Benny for a day or so; she was lurking at the back of the column, clearly afraid of Maa'lon's judgement. Somehow she was unable to grasp the gravity of the situation. She couldn't see how lucky they all were to be alive at the time of the Return. To walk with the Lord and please Him.

He looked round at Kor'no beside him. The smiling child with the dazzling eyes of his master jogged excitedly, thrilled by the Hut'eri honour guard, each with a shining gl'ai, surrounding them and Maa'lon. He kept jumping on to the back of the Grel Master when the going became difficult, and the huge grey figure struggled down each ravine anxious to protect his charge. Even the Grel knew what Bernice denied. Even these creatures, that only a few days before had terrified him, were closer to him now than Bernice. Incapable of belief, despite all the evidence before her. Stubborn to the last. One to avoid.

'She will understand soon, James. Never abandon your hope for her soul. I will not.' Maa'lon offered him some fruit which he took gratefully and with a smile.

'As you wish, Lord.'

Emile was frantically clearing up his room, removing all traces of his recent obsession. He was hampered by his unusable right hand, which he kept lightly clenched to protect the still tender cut across it. When he'd agreed to join the cult three days ago, Adnan had made him swear what he called 'the blood oath of fealty and secrecy'. Adnan had kept his eyes fixed intently on Emile's as he drew the knife across his flesh, turning the wounding into an oddly intimate, almost sexual experience.

One-handed, Emile removed the last of the gory holograms from his desk. Without the pictures of carnage on the walls, he found that his room looked strangely bland: just a normal student's square grey box. It didn't feel like his any more.

Adnan's friends were due round in – Emile checked his watch – five minutes. Adnan had suggested they meet in

Emile's room because Emile would feel more comfortable there. Then he'd joked that, of course, he might be planning to murder Emile, since killers usually avoided doing that in their own homes. All that mess to clear up, you know.

Emile had smiled tentatively, fairly certain by now that this really was just a joke. He suspected that the real reason for hosting the meeting in his room was to avoid giving him too much information. Adnan's cultists seemed pretty secretive, and they had no reason to trust him all that much. In fact, they had no reason to trust him at all. Adnan had explained that they were very reluctant to allow anyone else into the sect, but that Emile's having taken the oath would mollify them. Now Emile knew that the price of betrayal was death. Emile hadn't smiled as Adnan said that. This time, he could tell that he wasn't joking.

He let his mind wander back over the one evening he'd spent with Adnan, and the two days since that he'd spent thinking about it, wondering when he'd next see Adnan. It had been so ordinary: just a meal, some drinks, a lot of talking. It almost seemed possible that Adnan was genuinely interested in him, that this was the reason he'd pursued Emile for his group.

Emile studied himself in the small mirror over the wash unit. Stocky, podgy if you were being unkind, round-faced and soft featured. He didn't even have a sparkling personality to compensate. 'Maybe he likes you for yourself,' he told his reflection.

His reflection didn't believe him. Unlike him, his reflection was living in the real world.

Bernice could feel the anticipation among the troops as they crested the final ridge. She tried to look as if she knew what she was doing with her dataxe and smiled at those around her. She received many smiles in response and a couple of the Hut'eri excitedly raised their gl'ai to catch the sun. They began the final descent.

Before them, clear now from any mist, lay the great plain of the N'a'm'thuli. The mountain's grassy foothills slid gently down into the even greener plain a few kilometres distant. She looked down the slope in front of them where the forces of Maa'lon, all bright eyes and shining webbing and blades, massed in their thousands in the hastily constructed camp. Shemda had said that their initial number had been nearly fifty-seven thousand, but Benny could tell that it had now swelled to easily two or three times that. Many of the mountain Hut'eri had joined the column on the march and hundreds of off-worlders had alighted from swiftly abandoned flitters as they began the descent.

It seemed that Maa'lon's cause was a popular one, and who could blame them? This was a righteous fight, and all who thought differently needed only to look at the edge of the plain, at the N'a'm'thuli's border with the rest of Dellah. It was a wall of flesh. Or rather a fence. Not a physical barrier as such, but a mental one. Stretching away to the east and west, as far as the eye could see, were hundreds of bodies, young and old, Hut'eri and many others, impaled on spikes and skinned like so many they had seen before.

The smell alone was enough to deter any passing traveller. The sight of this fresh barrier of death, so incongruous on the lush plains of Dellah, brought tears to her eyes. 'How can this be allowed? It's like something from another age, like nothing that should be on Dellah! I think it's time this got sorted.' She could feel the thick anger almost choking her as she spoke.

Shemda, with a curious wave of his tentacles, put one of his huge arms around her, and they headed down into the camp.

There were twelve of them. Thirteen, if you counted Emile, and Emile rather thought that whoever was counting did. They barely fitted inside the room, let alone around the perimeter of the chalk circle which Adnan had drawn on Emile's floor soon after he arrived.

The room was lit by candlelight, naturally, and was filled with a steady monotonous hum as the gathered students muttered their incantations. Emile, as a novice, had been spared the duty of joining in. Instead he'd watched as Adnan read aloud from the massive leather-bound book he'd brought with him. It looked like a prop from a comedy horror film, but Adnan treated it with careful reverence. No one else was allowed to touch it.

It should all have seemed very silly indeed. And it certainly would have done, if only it hadn't been working.

Emile stared mesmerized at the image which had formed in the centre of the chalk circle. The others seemed less fascinated than him. They'd probably seen it all before, although Emile couldn't believe he was seeing it even once.

He wasn't quite sure what it was; it was still fuzzy, like a badly tuned holo-screen. He'd thought at first that this was precisely what it was, but now he was positive that it wasn't. There was a feeling, something in the air, like undischarged static electricity, just waiting to give someone the greatest shock of their life. Magic, Emile thought, rolling the absurd word round on his tongue.

As he watched, fascinated, the image gradually cleared. Emile blinked. Then he blinked again, but the newly sharp image remained the same. It was a tiny imp.

There were shocked gasps from many of the gathered cultists, and Emile guessed that this level of success was a bit of a novelty for them. He wondered if they'd ever actually got past the badly tuned holo-screen stage before.

The imp smiled round at the surrounding students. Emile realized that it was wearing a little green hat set at a jaunty angle.

Adnan grinned triumphantly at Emile. 'Yes,' he hissed. 'I knew that the thirteenth person would be the key.'

'I can't believe it,' said one of the other students, a sallow, stooped Oolian. Most of the rest seemed too shellshocked to speak.

'You'd better believe it, buddy,' the imp said, in a high-pitched but still rather menacing voice. Emile jerked in shock. Several of the other cultists had actually backed against the door.

Only Adnan seemed unperturbed, still radiating pleasure at the success of his experiment. 'Greetings,' he intoned, in the kind of voice Emile imagined he'd heard used in holos of similar events.

'Yeah, yeah,' the imp said. 'What d'ya want?'

Adnan frowned. 'Oh, I don't think I shall be asking you for anything in particular,' he said in his normal voice. 'We're just trying things out.'

The imp hopped from foot to foot. 'I'm a busy guy,' he said. 'Any chance of freeing me up to see people who did summon me for a good reason?'

Adnan flushed. There were some muffled giggles from the other students, several of whom had overcome their fear sufficiently to gather round the tiny, impossible apparition. 'Of course, you're free to –' he said.

'No, wait a moment,' Emile said. Every eye in the room instantly swivelled to watch him. He shrank into himself but persevered. 'You can tell us things, right?' he asked the imp.

It put its tiny fists on its hips. 'I'm the guy who knows stuff, yeah. What's it to ya?'

Emile swallowed. If he was wrong about Adnan, he was about to make a terrible mistake. 'Can you tell me who killed those people on the ship?' he asked tremulously.

'Of course. That a formal request?' the imp said uninterestedly.

Emile sensed a trap. 'Why?' he asked.

The imp shrugged. ''Cause if it's formal, I gotta ask you what you're willing to do for me in return.'

Everyone was now staring at them in fascination. Emile felt like a character in an early folk-tale, gambling with the devil for a golden violin. As he recalled, the wager in that case had been the man's soul. He felt his stomach clench with fear as he realized that the analogy might not be that far off the mark. 'What do you want in return?' he asked cautiously, desperate not to say anything that might be construed as committing himself.

'Make an offer, and if I like it I'll take it,' the imp said. 'If not . . .' It shrugged, and Emile knew that it wasn't going to tell him what the consequences of making the wrong offer might be.

'So there's no chance of you telling me something for nothing?' he ventured. 'Kind of a free trial offer.'

The imp laughed unkindly. 'I wasn't born yesterday, bud,' it said. 'All knowledge comes with a price. Don't they teach you kids that any more?'

'I . . .' Emile looked round at the cultists, now clustered so close to the chalk circle that they were in danger of crossing it. Adnan noticed it too, and roughly pushed them back, an expression of alarm on his face. When he looked over at Emile, it had been replaced by one of avid curiosity. Emile suddenly felt like a lab rat in a very unhealthy experiment. 'I . . .'

The imp leant forward. 'You gonna reach a decision some time this century, kid?' it asked.

'I . . .' Emile clasped his arms around himself. 'No. You can go,' he said. 'I don't think I'm willing to pay the price.'

The little creature grinned ferally at him. 'Yeah, no one is till they're desperate enough. Be seeing ya, then.'

There was a small, clear pop, and the chalk circle was empty.

After that there was a moment's stillness, as everyone seemed to ask themselves if they'd really just seen what they thought they'd just seen. Then the gathered students dissolved into frantic talking and the too-loud laughter of frightened relief.

Adnan continued staring at the circle for a long moment, a look of disappointment on his face. 'I wonder what he would have told you,' he said.

'You could always call him back and ask him yourself,' Emile ventured.

Adnan stared at him, as if he'd said something very stupid or very insulting. 'This isn't a game,' he said. 'This stuff . . . it changes everything. With these powers we can do anything.' Then he flashed his signature broad smile. 'If we're willing to pay the price.'

Extract from the diary of Bernice Summerfield

It's always right to get things down before going into battle;

and, believe me, I am going into battle. This is a sickness that has no place here, no place in my world, my century. It mustn't be allowed, and, conviction or not, I am not going to watch. Maa'lon is right: we need to be flexible. I like to think I am, then suddenly I'm closed off again. Barriers up; none shall pass. Well, not this time.

Black and white is easy. I may not be entirely sure about Maa'lon, but I am sure about the N'a'm'thuli. The pleasure they take in what they do is sick; what they do is twisted; they are beyond redemption, and I will do my part.

Though I probably won't be right near the front. I'm sure there are others far better than me at this, and I'd hate to get in their way.

Extract ends

6

LIGHT AND SHADE

At dawn, James felt exhilarated. Maa'lon had chosen him to lead His faithful, the Army of God, into battle. He would be in the vanguard, bearing the weapon given to him by Maa'lon, leading a host of His children against the forces of evil.

He stepped out of the simple woollen tent that had been erected as a makeshift base for Maa'lon. Before him, like a purple tide, were the faithful. Their blades and steel webbing gleamed in the sun; their bright eyes shone with hope and excitement. Only a few looked scared, and they all seemed to be gazing up at Maa'lon, drawing strength from their God.

Maa'lon waved to the thousands seated before Him and smiled. All fell silent, and waited for His words.

'My children.' Maa'lon's voice seemed to boom across the foothills of the mountain. 'I have longed to be among you once more and to end the time of tests. This I have done, and it brings me great joy. But in this time of joy there is also a great sadness, a cancer on the Hut'eri nation. For too long I have allowed the evil that is at the heart of the N'a'm'thuli to walk the same mountains as my children, to use my children for the sport of one whom I myself should bring low. I can allow it no longer.'

A great cheer rose among the assembled Hut'eri.

'The time has come for the Code to be clarified, expanded. Death can be the only answer for these crimes. Those you will fight are without soul, compassion, or any regard for life. As such, they forfeit their right to live in my world. Now, my children, it pains me that I cannot merely remove them from my sight and yours, for all are my children. What I have given to all, I can take from none. I cannot bring myself to give these animals, and their corrupter, the gift of death. For this you are my instrument, my arms. You will strike them down, and each blow will be a blow from my own hand along with yours. I will be with you, protecting you all, throughout the ordeal ahead.

'So, my children, will you be my arms, and let me guide you to my bidding? Will you be the surgeons who cut the disease from my heart? Will you bear my banner and find the Way yourselves this day?'

The answering roar was deafening. Cries of 'Maa'lon!' and screams of 'Yes, Lord!' came in wave after wave that unsettled Harker by their vehemence. He steeled himself to the task before him, took several deep breaths, and raised the gl'ai as high as he could.

'Those who follow Maa'lon, follow me. Down to the plains and the task before us!' With that the reverend whirled round, his purple cloak flaring out behind him, and led the Children of Maa'lon into battle.

'Christ Almighty! Or rather not,' Elspeth said.

Emile stared at the proclamation which had been pinned to the door of the Witch and Whirlwind, straining up on his toes to see over the heads of the other students who surrounded it. 'I don't believe it!' he said.

One of the students turned to frown unfriendlily at him. 'You're all right, aren't you, mate,' he said. 'You already belong. The rest of us have to find one, or get out.' He looked at Emile more closely. 'I've got to finish my degree, or my family will never have me back. I don't suppose your lot are looking for new members?'

Emile shifted uncomfortably. 'Erm, I don't think they, you know, take just anybody,' he said, lowering his eyes.

The student's expression darkened further. 'Yeah, just the

real cream like you,' he said sarcastically. He pushed past Emile and headed away from the bar. 'Roman Catholicism, here I come,' he announced to no one in particular.

'It's mad,' Elspeth said to Emile as they walked away from the cluster of puzzled, irate students. 'What's the Sultan playing at? I mean, if he was forcing us to join his own religion, I could just about understand it. But what the hell's the point of making everyone join some religion, but not saying which one? He's lost it, big time.'

'So which religion takes your fancy?' he asked her, trying in vain to imagine his mercurial friend taking part in any sort of organized worship.

Elspeth stared at him as if he had gone quite mad himself. 'I'm not going to join any,' she said.

Emile reached out and clasped her arm firmly. 'I don't think that's a good idea,' he told her. 'I don't think the Sultan is kidding. And it isn't join or leave like that guy said. It's –' his voice rose incredulously as he repeated the words they had just read '– join or face ultimate sanction.'

'Yeah, right,' Elspeth said dismissively. She still seemed in an unaccountably good mood. 'It's rubbish, Emile; the university authorities will never allow it. And, in the meantime, I am not going to give in to this sort of bullying. I'm not an atheist because I don't believe anything. Atheism is what I believe. It's the principle of the thing.'

Before Emile could reply, she had gone, black mop-top bobbing as she ran to her next lecture. He hoped she was right.

Bernice was quite near the back of the host, still on the mountain slopes rather than the plain before them. In the distance, a few kilometres away, lay the great forest that made up most of the N'a'm'thuli lands: their foe would emerge from those trees. She was strangely glad Shemda was with her, his maroon eye-patch making him look somehow more at home in the purple-clad mass.

For the first time since they had set off on the trek through the mountains, Benny began to feel scared. She looked around at the thousands of Hut'eri, who were preparing to swarm down through the impaled corpses and right an ancient wrong. Some were so young: adolescents excited by the thought of battle. They smiled, while the older combatants closed their eyes and grasped their medallions: they knew what the N'a'm'thuli could do. Even the presence of their God could not wash away all their fear.

In the distance, across the plain, Bernice could hear a low rhythmic sound. The N'a'm'thuli were coming to make their guests welcome. They were still out of sight, the trees hiding their progress, but she could tell they were drawing nearer; their drums grew louder. She licked suddenly dry lips, and forced her mind away from what she knew was coming.

After about an hour of anxious waiting, two figures emerged from the woodland and stood stock-still. Fascinated by their behaviour, Benny grabbed the enhancer that Shemda had lent her and zoomed in for a closer look.

The two figures differed widely in height. One was clearly Hut'eri in origin, short and dark, with broad blue and ochre tiger-stripes across his almost naked body. On his head was a bizarre arrangement of horns and teeth, set into some form of dark fur-like helmet. In his left hand he carried a bright spike of metal, about three metres high, tipped with a lethal collection of golden barbs.

The figure next to him was nearly as tall as the barbed spike. He wore a long cloak with a cowl, which fanned out behind him and which partially covered a rather gaunt face. The face looked particularly pale set against the bright scarlet cloak. He carried nothing, his hands appearing to be linked beneath his robe, but it was clear he was in command. The shorter figure with the spike looked up to him and nodded; Bernice caught a glimpse of a black smile within the scarlet cowl; and then the Hut'eri's spike was thrust into the ground in one swift movement.

The N'a'm'thuli broke from the trees as one. Thousands of blue-stained, near-naked figures carrying spikes, blades, and energy weapons ran screaming at the forces of Maa'lon. Bernice could feel the unease in herself mirrored by the host, but then she saw James raise his blade above his head and call for the assault. In seconds they were rushing headlong at the forces of evil.

The spaceport was crowded, well beyond its safety parameters. Most of the people there didn't have tickets, but they were willing to wait around on the off-chance of a stand-by becoming available. They'd sensed which way the wind was blowing, and it didn't seem to be blowing anyone any good.

Safety Officer Hay smiled and flicked to the next page of *The Pronouncements of FoJal*. Like many others, he'd joined the sect when he realized that his job might be under threat if he didn't. Only recently had the words of the book begun to make sense to him; to speak to him in a way that nothing else in his life ever had. The other FoJa had said that it was because the Lord was preparing to pierce his heart with faith. They were right.

Last night his God had come to him. Since then, he'd had no doubts, no uncertainties.

He reached inside his trouser leg to stroke the butt of the knife that he'd strapped against his thigh. In all this crowd, he was sure he'd find another Holy Sacrifice. They wouldn't be missed. And it was what his God wanted.

Bernice knew she would never forget the sound the two armies made when they came together. A crash that became a scream that would last for hours.

She had hung back with Shemda when the main assault began. Somehow she still couldn't get the hang of blindly following, despite the passions of those around her. Caution in such situations was often wiser, and for once she decided to learn from herself and her mistakes. Shemda seemed happy enough with the decision, though he did look as if he wouldn't mind having a go with his dataxe.

'Your time will come, lad, believe you me.' She said as she dragged him towards the flanks of the battle. 'Now let's see if we can get round to those trees on the other side. I fancy a look at the man in red.'

'Why?'

'Because I admire his flamboyant style and casual good looks, of course!' Shemda fixed her with a penetrating stare.

'What?'

'I just think this probably isn't the best place for irony, Professor. If you look around, you will notice a remarkably high mortality rate in the battle at present.'

Bernice stopped for a moment and took in her surroundings again. Shemda was right: it was carnage. Both sides appeared to have opted out of using energy weapons and decided to hack each other apart. The Hut'eri gl'ai appeared to be able to make an awful mess of whatever it hit, and the guard blade saved countless lives, but it was the barbed spikes of the N'a'm'thuli that really caught her attention. The small blue-stained warriors seemed to have no conception of a clean kill; they sought out lingering, painful deaths and maimings.

Their barbs drew out intestines and organs, looped through eyes and ripped off ears. All the while the blood-spattered N'a'm'thuli laughed hysterically and revelled in the gore before them.

But the followers of Maa'lon were learning from their foe. Bernice saw many blades and spikes wreaking their own havoc as the fighting became more intense and more primal. She saw a Hut'eri woman bite the ear off a N'a'm'thuli warrior and then spit it back into his face before shattering his skull with a gl'ai. Some of the younger Hut'eri followed their fathers and mothers and poked small blades into the N'a'm'thuli dead as they passed and cut out those eyes that remained. It was a sea of blood haunted by weeping and the cries of the wounded, all to the rhythm of the N'a'm'thuli drums beating their relentless tattoo.

Bernice could feel the tears on her cheek, and brushed her eyes clear. Now was not the time to be caught unawares. As if to illustrate this thought, a screaming blue warrior, his body covered in deep crisscrossed wounds that looked deliberate, sprang at her out of the mêlée. All she could do was stare; panic took hold of her limbs; she took root. Her eyes fixed on the triple blood-soaked barb that he held before him, lunging towards her innards.

Before the steel could reach and tear into her, the N'a'm'thuli's head exploded in a shower of blood, brain, and bone fragment. The headless body staggered on for a pace or two before collapsing at her feet. Blood splashed across her bare feet, as she choked back a sob. She looked down at the body and then away to her right. There Shemda stood, brandishing his dataxe and looking warily into the crowded battlefield. After a moment, he looked back at her. The patch over his eye seemed to emphasize his sadness; he lowered his weapon and put his arm round her.

'I don't think we should stay here, Bernice,' he said, as he led her towards the distant trees. She gave him a grim smile and allowed him to take the lead.

It was only later on that she realized it was the first time he had actually used her name.

The parents came to Joe in his office in the Anthropology Department. Their child was terribly sick, but Joe was sure he could save her. His God had been a healer, and now he had that power too.

He laid his hand over the little girl's heart, and lifted up a prayer to heaven.

No one was surprised when she rose and walked, cured, from the room. There were demons abroad, but by the Grace of God they could be defeated.

James could feel the presence of Maa'lon, His blessing, all around him. The blade he had been given by his Lord did His bidding. He cut a swathe through the N'a'm'thuli as he sought his target. Demka, at his right side, hacked away mercilessly at the soulless devils that assailed them. The Grel Master was among the chosen; Harker could see the light of Maa'lon in his eyes. They were all His tools now, vessels of His retribution.

Images of the murdered women and children, their twisted, violated bodies, spurred him on. Outrage gave him strength, and another N'a'm'thuli, a young woman, split beneath his blade. These were beasts, no more than animals; they needed to be culled. Only their blood would wash the plain clean of the crimes committed there against the faithful.

Before him lay the prize. Hidden behind the blue mass of the N'a'm'thuli was their leader and the false god that had warped their lives. That was the target. The craven demon that dared stand against Maa'lon and the might of the faithful. Today that demon would be brought low by the one true God.

His Lord had not spoken as such, but James knew what was required of him. He was the instrument of His vengeance. He was the fire that evil could not endure. This was his time. An epiphany of blood. He brought his medallion up to his mouth and kissed it: a further blessing.

Then with a single blow he caved in the ribcage of a screaming warrior and continued his progress.

The first stoning took place an hour after the decree. It was for apostasy: a second-year student who had professed faith, but then recanted. One of his fellow worshippers had overheard him in his college bar, mocking the very religion to which he had just sworn undying allegiance.

The old Sultan watched, smiling, as the faithful threw fist-sized rocks at him until his screaming ended and he didn't move any more, even when they thrust a pin into his eye.

After that, membership reached an all-time high. The Sultan felt sure he'd done the right thing.

Bernice started to feel more like herself when she reached the trees. The huge dense firs provided shade, and the massive trunk absorbed some of the screams from the battlefield. She found a comfortable mossy patch and sat with her back to the smooth bark of a tree. Shemda handed her the canteen and then took up the enhancers.

'Thanks,' she said, after a long drink. 'I don't think that is really my scene, somehow. It's so animal: the N'a'm'thuli, I mean. I just didn't expect anything like that; I can't see where it comes from, why they do it. I can't find that place in myself, thank god.'

'Which one?' Shemda seemed suddenly very interested in her words.

'Sorry? What?' Bernice tried to read something into the agitated movements of his tentacles. His eyes never left her.

'I wondered which god you were thanking, Bernice.'

'Oh – well, I suppose, if I had to choose, I'd say Maa'lon. Compassion is more my bag than violence, after all. But I remain unconvinced of his godhood, though.'

'Query: why would a god smile at the slaughter of his followers? Is it not more usual for this to cause distress?'

'What do you mean, Shemda?'

The Grel silently handed her the enhancers and pointed back across the clear section of the plain towards the foothills.

It took her a while to find him, a few kilometres distant, but when she did her blood ran cold. In front of his small purple tent, high enough on the slope to have a good view of the whole battle, stood Maa'lon. His white robe shone in the sunlight, as did his eyes, but her eyes were drawn elsewhere: to the huge grin that dominated his dark features. Maa'lon was enjoying the battle, the carnage.

Suddenly, he looked away from the battle. His face swung round and the dazzling jade eyes looked straight through the enhancers at her. His smile grew even broader, and a cold chill ran down her spine.

'I think we should get out of here now,' she said as she dropped the enhancers.

James could feel the demon near him, and knew he would be able to strike soon. Demka stood strong at his side, laying low the beasts that threw themselves in their path in a vain effort to delay the inevitable. He knew they would be there soon.

Demka shattered another head and roared, his tentacles flaring wildly and his huge arms raised. Two more N'a'm'thuli tried to rush him, their screams trying to instil fear, but both were clubbed down almost casually by the Grel Master. James had a sudden flash of admiration for the raw power of faith. They were invincible; God would protect them throughout this ordeal, then He would reward the faithful and the Way would be clear.

He struggled on, stabbing and slashing away with the gl'ai. As he grew nearer his target, he felt the blade lighten, and looked down to see a blue nimbus begin to form around the burnished, blood-spattered steel. Faith preserves, and he was the right arm of God. He swung the blade round to deflect a blow from a vicious barb and felt the N'a'm'thuli steel splinter. He rejoiced as he ripped out the warrior's innards with the burning blade. He was chosen. Nothing could stop him.

He smiled as, with one clean stroke, he sliced the head off a wild-eyed female warrior who leapt into his path. The headless corpse gently smoked around the wound.

Bernice was starting to have a very bad feeling about the whole situation, and she knew the best course of action under those circumstances was to run, her favourite plan right now being to 'give it legs'. But Shemda was being stubborn.

'I cannot just leave the Master here. If there is danger, it is my duty to make sure he is all right. We must discuss this with him.' Shemka avoided her eyes but seemed resolute.

'But you've seen him out there. He is revelling in it all. He believes in Maa'lon; I heard your argument. He thinks he has found proof of divinity, an opinion unlikely to be changed by the revelation that his god smiles at inopportune moments. We don't have anything that will shake their belief, only our own. That's why I think we should slope off, leave them to their bloodbath, and see what Emile and Irving have discovered; it must all be linked.' Bernice gave Shemda her best imploring look, but could tell by his set features that it wasn't going to work.

'I understand the logic of your words, Bernice, but this is an obligation. I am a Grel servitor and I must protect the Master if I possibly can.'

'I personally think you're a lot more than that, Shemda, but, if you've got to go, fine. But I'm coming with you, and we'll use the trees for cover. We observe first and then decide whether to act. And we keep clear of the fighting, OK?'

'That will fulfil my obligation, I think.' Shemda put the enhancers back in his pack, picked up his dataxe and set off between the trees towards the fighting. Bernice took another swig on the canteen and followed.

Within a few minutes they were in the trees directly behind the battle. Maa'lon stood on the slopes opposite, and in between tens of thousands fought and countless numbers screamed and died. The tears returned to Bernice's cheeks once more.

A hundred metres away, a tall, scarlet-clad figure stood watching the blood-letting. Beside the figure a much smaller N'a'm'thuli warrior bearing a huge spike and a particularly ludicrous head-dress bounced up and down and shouted harsh, guttural words at those before him. 'The chief, I presume,' whispered Bernice, as she crouched behind a tree next to Shemda.

'It would appear so, but what of the non-Hut'eri next to him? None of these people grow to that height: it must be of another species.'

Bernice shifted round the tree to get a better look at the figure. As she did so, the red robe swung round, and she saw the face beneath the cowl. It was deathly pale, emaciated, and housed a huge black grin. The eyes were dark, no colour within them, and they were looking directly at her.

Bernice's heart began to race. The cowled figure's grin broadened.

'I don't know what species that might be, but it definitely gives me the creeps.' She couldn't drag her eyes away; the dark spheres seemed to grip her, draw her in. And then, just when terror was beginning to take a firm grip on her, James Harker came running out of the mass of the battle, a glowing blade held high above his head and a scream on his lips, and launched himself at the figure in red.

* * *

He had made it. Harker knew he would be remembered for this action. His God would be pleased with him as he brought His enemies low. The gl'ai shone and pulsed on his arm – Maa'lon was with him for this final act – and his heart nearly burst with power and joy.

The nameless one was before him. Clad in red, the brazen shade of the blood spilt for its pleasure, it covered its misshapen form so none would see its abhorrence and hear its lies for what they were: corruption, and affront to Maa'lon. Well, no more.

Demka cleared a path for him, a back slash from his dataxe leaving two N'a'm'thuli with open throats and empty eyes, then he was through. The nameless one was just standing there, its back turned as if awaiting that which it knew was coming. It couldn't even face its own end: craven to the last.

The N'a'm'thuli chieftain thrust a huge spike in his direction, in a vain effort to save his god, but Demka opened up a hole in his chest with a vivid blast from his weapon. The chieftain looked down at the hole before crumpling. Demka shot him in the head as he lay on the ground, then snatched the long spike from his lifeless hand.

The red-clad figure still had its back turned. Harker raised the glowing blade ready to strike and tensed his muscles for the killer blow. Then, just as he was about to strike down the false god, the gl'ai became heavier on his arm and lost its blue sheen. Its weight increased further and his arm dropped to his side. His whole body felt spent of energy; he felt drained, weak, on the brink of collapse.

'Stop, James: the test has gone on long enough.'

It was all James could do to look round at the source of the voice, but there, still clad in perfect white, stood Maa'lon. He smiled at the reverend and held out His arms in a gesture of welcome.

James Harker turned back to the figure in red, a ghoul who smiled back at him. He felt the waves of fatigue sweep his body, and then he collapsed.

Braxiatel looked round at his fellow academics, then at the kindly, implacable face of the old Sultan, and knew that they'd lost. The gloomy conference room was filled with discontented murmurs, but no voices were raised in outright protest. The university meeting called to counteract the Sultan's increasing authoritarianism was instead going to rubber-stamp it.

People were afraid. They'd seen that the Sultan was serious. He was surrounded now by an entourage of New Moral Army recruits who glared fiercely around the room, never letting their hands stray too far from their weapons. None of them looked older than twenty, but Braxiatel had no doubt that they'd use those weapons given the slightest excuse. He could see in their eyes how much they loved their new power and the fear it inspired in those around them.

Suddenly, the university was full of people like that. Or of people like Braxiatel's fellow academics: too cowed ever to take a stand. Everyone else was booking tickets off-world.

No one seemed ready to stay and fight. Even Braxiatel was having his doubts. The trouble was, he didn't know which side he was supposed to be fighting for. Still standing on the sidelines, he mocked himself, remembering John's words. But the sidelines didn't feel all that safe any more.

Benny knew something was seriously wrong. The fighting had stopped; the blood-red plain was silent save for the moans of the dying. N'a'm'thuli and Hut'eri alike stood and watched Maa'lon as he helped James Harker to his feet.

The reverend's eyes were wild when they eventually opened, and he looked up to his god in confusion. The red-clad figure walked slowly over to the pair and placed his hand on the human's head. James let out a short sob and a sigh.

'James, you have done very well,' said Maa'lon, a broad smile filling his dark features. 'I am very proud of you.'

The reverend looked around him, taking in the carnage, and returned the smile. 'You should have told me, Lord.'

'The test needed your ignorance to work, James. I needed to see what you were capable of, what lay deep inside. Now I know. And now it is free.' Maa'lon turned to the assembled survivors, thousands and thousands of blood-soaked warriors. 'You have all done very well today. You have performed the task I asked of you in my different ways.'

Maa'lon reached beyond James and grasped the shoulder of the gaunt figure in red. 'You'll learn that I have many aspects, faces, names. Today you have seen but two. But manifold are the names and faces of God. It is belief that matters, belief at the very core, the heart. And all here have shown their worth today. All save three. Grenke, come to me.'

The crowd parted to let the Grel servitor through. He kept his eyes low and his tentacles tightly wound as he approached Maa'lon. His dataxe was clean and he didn't appear to have any blood on him.

'Grenke, you did not do as I asked today. You did not slay the N'a'm'thuli, though it was my express wish. You have disappointed your God. Why?' Maa'lon's words were quiet and calm, but Bernice could sense real menace in them.

'I do not see how you can be Maa'lon if you are not the one true god. You have shown us evidence of the divine, then you have changed the tenets of your own faith. My own reading on the subject suggests that constancy is one of the key aspects of deity. My people are not very good at belief, and I chose not to believe in you, or that.' Grenke pointed to the red-robed figure.

'You disappoint me again, Grenke. And you offend this aspect of my intent.' Maa'lon gently stroked the red cowl. 'Brother, I think you should deal with this unbeliever yourself; I think you will enjoy it.' With that, Maa'lon drew Harker aside and turned his back on the Grel servitor.

The figure in red advanced on Grenke. Bernice could see the fear in the Grel's eyes. The cowl was drawn back and the pale hairless head, crisscrossed with what looked like scars, came into view. Long spindly arms were raised to Grenke's head and a low chuckle was heard.

Grenke began screaming when it happened, a deep hooting scream that had Shemda leaping to his feet. Bernice held him down with difficulty, then turned back to the screaming Grel.

She watched in fascination as the tentacles at his mouth peeled back and kept on peeling. The thick, leathery grey skin revealed deep red tissue that glistened in the sun.

The figure in red kept his bony hands tight to the side of Grenke's head as his clothes began to split apart. Soon he held a quivering mass of screaming exposed flesh. Then, with a sickening popping sound, the Grel's eyes burst and he was allowed to sink into a mound of his own flesh. He lay still. Another low chuckle was heard.

'There are two more here, my children.' Maa'lon's voice cut through a long silence.

'Time to give it legs,' was all Benny needed to say as she dragged Shemda to his feet.

Emile and Elspeth had decided that the grassy hillock over-looking the university was the safest place to talk freely.

Talk freely, Emile thought disgustedly. It wasn't a phrase he'd ever imagined using in relation to St Oscar's University.

That afternoon, Elspeth had joined the Church of Ahriman the Great. She had been lucky. The trooper from the New Moral Army who had come to arrest her for her failure to comply with the Sultan's decree had been a member. He'd been willing to let her join on the spot rather than carry out his duties. From what Emile had heard, most of the others would have been much less understanding.

He had never seen Elspeth look so miserable. She couldn't seem to meet his eye, choosing instead to look out over the open, flower-filled quads and dull red walls of the university buildings below them. He realized that she was ashamed of herself: ashamed that, when push came to shove, she'd been too frightened to stick to what she believed.

He was just glad that she'd done what was needed to save herself. There had been five more stonings since the first.

'It smells fresh and clean up here,' Elspeth suddenly said, as if it was the worst thing in the world. She finally looked over at Emile. 'You wouldn't even know the university existed, if you just had your nose to go by.'

Emile laughed. He couldn't help himself: somehow that

just said it all. After a moment, Elspeth joined in.

'Tell me about Adnan,' she said, when their chuckles had died down. 'Is he really the man of your dreams?'

'I don't know,' Emile said, tracing a path through the grass with his finger. He pictured the fair-haired, chocolate-skinned young man smiling in triumph when everyone else was terrified out of their wits. 'Actually, I think he is quite mad.' He heard Elspeth grunt inquisitively, but continued watching his finger's wormlike movement through the grass. 'He scares me, but that doesn't stop me being attracted to him. Does that make me mad, too?'

He looked up to find that Elspeth was studying him carefully. 'Would you have joined a religion?' she asked. 'I mean, I know you joined because of your investigation, but if you hadn't already?'

Below them, the university looked almost empty. It was just after seven in the evening, the time for work to end and partying to begin, but only the soldiers of the NMA could be seen on the streets. 'I don't know,' he said. 'Probably not, because I was too afraid of what joining would do to me. Almost more afraid of that than of dying, I suppose.'

'But less afraid of dying than of disappointing Bernice,' Elspeth said caustically. 'Where has she got to, anyway? She's in for a shock when she gets back.'

Emile frowned. 'Actually, I think this is what I was supposed to be investigating all along. Don't you feel like the killings on the ship were somehow the beginning of all this?'

'I don't know,' Elspeth said wearily, lying back in the freshly cut grass. Emile lay back too, and they rested in companionable silence as the sky tried out all the shades of blue between azure and black.

As the first stars began to show, Elsepth said, 'At least I could leave, if it got that bad. Poor old Kerri is two weeks off giving birth, and no ship's captain will take her. She's been trying to find a berth for days. Says she doesn't want to bring a child into the world on this world.'

Emile's heart lurched so strongly, it felt as if it had physically moved in his chest. Zombie-like, he stood up. He felt his hands clench into fists and, inside his boots, his toes doing the same. He imagined for one moment that this was what genius felt like: this sudden flash of absolute understanding.

Elspeth had rolled on to her side and was regarding him curiously. 'Something the matter?' she asked.

Emile shook his head, more to clear it than to answer her. 'I'm so stupid,' he said. 'It's so obvious. One of them was pregnant.'

And, because she always had been very bright, Elspeth understood. She too clambered to her feet, as if this level of inspiration required a certain stature. 'Fifteen DNA traces,' she said. 'But one of them wasn't quite a person yet, or at least not an independent one. Only fourteen of the passengers actually died. One of them really did do it.'

The grin on Emile's face was probably a bit manic, but he didn't care. 'The policeman from Tyler's,' he said. 'It has to be.' He hastily pulled on his jacket. 'I have to find him.'

At his determination, Elspeth seemed to deflate. 'Why?' she asked. 'Does it really matter any more?'

'Yes,' Emile said with absolute certainty. 'All this –' he looked down at the empty quads of the place he'd come to consider home '– all this crap started when he arrived. And, if I find him, maybe I can stop it.'

Extract from the diary of Bernice Summerfield

That was a close one. Thank god for the natural cover of trees and shrubs, and for the adrenaline that seeing incredibly unpleasant deaths provides. I think that was particularly true of Shemda. He saw one of his own kind peeled like an orange. Has to make it more immediate. Once he got started it was all I could do to keep up with him. The Grel certainly have an excellent turn of speed.

I think we only ran for an hour or so, though it felt like days and nearly burst my lungs, but it got us away and clear. At least for the moment. Our pursuers didn't seem to have it in them: knackered after the slaughter probably. Fortunately, we were fresh. We walked further into the forest and then decided we ought to work out a plan. The university is back the way we came, and we didn't fancy seeing Maa'lon and co. again, so we decided to push on, using Shemda's dataxe uplink for a global fix. It may be the wrong way, but it has got to be better than the way we came. And at least the forest seems empty; the N'a'm'thuli obviously hate to miss a bit of bloodshed.

Extract ends

Renée sat beside the camp-fire, sewing. She was so tired, her hands kept slipping, and her fingers were beaded with droplets of blood where she had pricked herself with the needle. She was determined to persevere, though. After nearly a week's training in the dreadful khaki uniform, during which she'd barely attracted any attention at all, she'd decided that something had to be done. She was currently pulling the material in more snugly around the bust area. When she was next allowed back to her room, she'd see what she could do about dyeing it a slightly more flattering shade of green; nothing too drastic, just something that didn't clash so terribly with her eyes.

At least all this exercise was helping her to lose some weight. She sighed, and stretched out her aching limbs.

She was currently in the middle of the New Moral Army's boot camp, about a mile from the main body of the university. The air was sultry and still; the camp sprawled as far as the eye could see, littered with canvas, small bright fires, and exhausted recruits. Renée didn't think she was the only one who'd been less than thrilled to discover that all the newest troopers were going to be obliged to attend a two-day outdoor training and 'bonding' session. Tonight, for the first time since she'd come to Dellah, Renée was going to have to sleep in a tent. She probably wouldn't even get to share it with anyone.

Renée studied her fellow recruits unenthusiastically. Most of them were immersed in studying their various religious texts. This was, officially, the 'solitary contemplation of one's faith' period of the day. Her unit were an unprepossessing lot, she couldn't help thinking: mostly first- and second-year students who looked as if adolescence was much more than a dim memory. The most interesting men among them were a pair of suspiciously stoned-looking paramedics.

Renée had tried to strike up conversations with some of them, but had elicited only monosyllabic answers. It wasn't just her they were avoiding, though; no one was speaking to anyone else. No one wanted to stand out from the crowd, or say anything incriminating. Three recruits had already been flogged for 'inappropriate utterances'. They'd been reported by their fellow recruits. Now, everyone was a potential informer.

Annoyingly, Renée found that she was missing Braxiatel; she had to keep reminding herself that he was the one who'd got her into this in the first place. But at least he always had something to say for himself, even if it was the last thing you wanted to hear. Braxiatel, she realized, was one of the few people in her life who actually challenged her. Not just his perverse refusal to respond to her flirting – for goodness' sake, would it *hurt* him to sleep with her? – but the fact that she couldn't really figure him out. He kept surprising her. Most people were so disappointingly predictable. She wondered when she'd next get a chance to see him.

She was so distracted by her musings, that she almost didn't notice the blue-skinned lieutenant approaching her until it was too late. Just in time, she dropped her half-stitched shirt and picked up her COG Uplink. Jabbing a button at random, she found herself presented with a passage from Corinthians which, last week, she had been debating including in her own *Book of the Grey*:

'God hath chosen the foolish things of the world to confound the wise; and God hath chosen the weak things of the world to confound the things which are mighty . . .'

As she read on with single-minded intensity, doing her best to pretend that she hadn't noticed the officer now leaning over her shoulder, she mused that this, too, for some reason reminded her of Braxiatel.

'You're not registered as a Christian,' the blue-skinned lieutenant said suddenly, and Renée didn't have to fake a start of surprise.

'No. I'm a member of the Church of the Grey,' she said.

The thin alien moved round until he was facing her, crouching down on his haunches so that their eyes were on the same level. 'Then why are you reading a Christian text?' he asked. There seemed to be more genuine curiosity than accusation in his voice. He was delicate-featured and probably no older than nineteen. He didn't look like the sort who'd condemn a woman for heresy.

But Renée wasn't willing to bet her life on it. 'It's an inclusive religion,' she said carefully, then added a hasty 'sir' when he frowned at her. He continued staring, as if expecting more. 'Would you like me to tell you about it?' she asked half-heartedly.

The rest of the recruits were now watching while trying to seem as if they weren't, shooting short, darting glances at them from lowered heads. Several had put aside their own religious texts with obvious relief.

The lieutenant settled in front of her, legs knotted into a position that would have been impossible with a human anatomy. 'Yes, I'd like that,' he said. 'Tell me everything.'

Renée looked into his cherry-coloured eyes. All she could read there was genuine interest. Some of the other members of the unit were now openly following the conversation. Several of them had moved closer.

She took a deep breath. She felt like a woman who'd just been offered a nice bit of rope: just the right length to hang herself by. But it was not as if she had much choice, and she so rarely did get a chance to talk about her beliefs. Braxiatel was not the only one who'd never evinced the slightest interest in discussing her religion with her.

'Well,' she began, 'the Church of the Grey was founded early in the twenty-first century. It was born on the Internet, out of the anarchy and paranoia that thrived there . . .'

* * *

Back in his room, Emile's optimism was quickly crushed. He'd sent a query to the communications' net for the policeman's whereabouts, but he'd been denied access. Only authorized New Moral Army personnel, it had told him, could now use the net for such things. He briefly considered asking one of them for help, but instantly dismissed it as far too risky.

Then he thought of a solution that was much, much riskier.

He sat on his bed for fifteen minutes, trying to come up with alternatives. When he couldn't think of any, he changed into some dark clothing, checked his palmscreen for the room number, which he had never quite brought himself to delete, and headed off.

Bernice threw some more wood on the fire and continued rubbing her feet. She moved closer to the fire and drew the small emergency blanket closer around her. Perhaps it was her fear that made her feel colder. The canopy of the trees should have made it warmer than the mountains.

It was damp and musty everywhere except near the fire, and she moved closer still. She nibbled on some more of the Grel field rations and wondered what, besides those and the blankets, Shemda kept in his compact silver pack. She decided to let him have his secrets.

'Query: how can more than one god exist if one of them claims to be the one true god?' It was the first thing Shemda had said since they made camp nearly two hours before.

'I think you can drop the "query", Shemda. There's more to you than queries, suppositions, and facts. You are more than just the sum of your Grel parts.' Shemda looked embarrassed but nodded his acquiescence.

'Your query is a good one, though. You would think they were mutually exclusive. If you're going to believe in that type of thing, then you usually go the whole hog. Even when societies believe in a pantheon of many disparate gods, individuals tend to worship just one. Though I suppose it's sensible if you want to hedge your bets. Do you have any information regarding a link between the god of the N'a'm'thuli and Maa'lon?'

Shemda hunched over his dataxe. The coloured screens lent his face a demonic aspect in the blanket darkness of the woods.

'The nameless god of the N'a'm'thuli is linked only with the deity of the Morkai who were destroyed by the northern Hut'eri. There is no link with Maa'lon. Do you wish me to try links with all the religions of Dellah?'

'How many are there?'

'One thousand and thirty-six are recognized by the Great Act of Toleration of 2528. Many are sects of the more major galactic creeds but five hundred and twelve are indigenous.'

'Five hundred and twelve? Isn't that a bit like overkill? How many of those are subsets of major Dellahan faiths like the Church of Maa'lon?' Bernice wished she'd paid more attention to local history.

'Only twenty-six. None of them linked with the Church of Maa'lon.'

Bernice was having trouble getting her head round it all. How could so many still exist, even allowing for Dellah's peculiarly multi-ethnic nature? 'Are there any broad themes to Dellahan religion that you can extrapolate from the information you have there?'

'I'll see what the interpretative engines can do.' Doing what he was born to, processing knowledge, seemed to be shaking Shemda out of his earlier malaise.

After about thirty seconds, Shemda gave a sigh of disappointment. 'There are only two broad correlations, neither of which seem useful, Professor.'

'Don't start calling me that again, Shemda. Bernice or Benny only. Now, what are they?'

'The first is a uniform belief in all indigenous faiths that divinity is linked to the earth, rather than the skies or heavens. All faiths preach paradise, the home of the gods, to be beneath the feet. Possibly the origin of the barefoot tenet of the faith of Maa'lon. The second is the comparatively recent sea-change in the style of indigenous religion.'

'What does that mean?'

'Well, it would seem that, for millennia of parallel cultural development, all the Dellahan races worshipped the inanimate fabric of their planet: trees, seas, and mountains. Three thousand years ago this began to change. Now all the indigenous religions prevalent have strong elements of personification or similar animal-spirit worship. None of the early religions survived.'

Shemda didn't look up from his dataxe. 'Before you ask why such a transition is unusual, it is because all the new wave of religions were founded within one hundred years of each other. And a planet that had been a remarkably peaceful multicultural preindustrial society then suffered two hundred years of religious wars.'

Bernice sat back and digested some of her rations. 'I have a strong feeling that this could be incredibly important, but for now I have no idea why.'

Adnan lived in one of the trendier areas of campus. Well, he would. Emile had been watching his window for half an hour, and it had remained dark and silent. Unless Adnan had gone to bed (which didn't seem likely at nine-thirty at night) his room was unoccupied.

Even if he wasn't there, there was nothing to say he mightn't return at any moment. Emile gently traced the barely healed cut on his hand with a finger. He didn't need to ask himself whether the cultists would consider this a violation of his oath. It occurred to him that they wouldn't even have to kill him themselves now; the New Moral Army would quite happily do it for them. If this didn't constitute apostasy, he didn't know what did.

Emile took a deep breath; he collapsed, choking, as his lungs were filled with the unpleasant aroma of burnt meat. When he'd recovered, he allowed himself a slight, nervous smile; someone wouldn't be enjoying their dinner tonight. It was only when he saw the unmistakable red tinge of flames above the central quad that he thought to wonder what precisely it was that was burning.

He shivered, and realized that he didn't actually want to know. Before he could think better of it, he slipped inside the hall of residence, and pressed the all-key Bernice had given him against Adnan's door.

Inside, he paused, shutting the door gently behind him and letting his eyes adjust to the near darkness. He knew that he couldn't afford to chance a light being seen from the outside.

Adnan's room was bigger than his: almost three times the size. Shadowy lumps of furniture sat scattered throughout it. They looked solid, expensive, not the usual student tat. He could make out frames set at regular intervals on the walls, but the pictures within kept their identities hidden in the dark.

He could see the bookshelf, though. Placing every foot carefully, he crept through the thick-pile carpet towards it. When he reached it, he risked taking out his pencil torch, holding it close to the books as he scanned along the shelves. Adnan had quite a collection, from ancient economics texts dating back to the nineteenth century, to limited-edition copies of modern novels.

But there was no sign of the book Emile was looking for. He crouched down and switched the torch off. The book was large: a huge leather-bound volume that Adnan had handled with obsessive care when he brought it round to Emile's room for the ceremony: *The Grimoire of Atheron the Mage*. But in the dark, it could have been sitting on one of the chairs and Emile wouldn't have been able to see it.

He hung his head. He didn't have time to look through every possible hiding place for the book. He had to think where Adnan might have concealed it. Think . . .

There was a sudden noise outside. Emile jerked his head up in alarm. He heard the sound again, recognized it this time: it was a chesty laugh, muffled by the door, but still clearly approaching.

He looked frantically around the room, but it only confirmed what he already knew. There was nowhere to hide. If they came in, they'd find him; it was as simple as that.

He felt that he ought to face whatever was coming on his

feet, but his legs felt too weak to support him. Instead, he slipped backwards on to his buttocks, jarring his coccyx painfully as he did so. He stared at the door through his raised knees. His mind began working at twice the speed of light, oil-slick thoughts flashing across it. He wondered if he could possibly have chosen a less dignified position in which to meet his fate. He thought about Elspeth, and how right they would have been for each other, and how silly it seemed that as simple a thing as sexual attraction meant that they'd never settle down and raise kids and live the life that he'd always imagined for himself when he was nine and the world still seemed easy.

He thought that he was just being hysterical, that the people he could hear approaching were almost certainly heading for another room in the hall. They weren't coming to get him.

But they were. As Emile gazed, transfixed, Adnan opened the door.

'So you can believe anything you want?' a skinny, ginger-haired trooper asked.

Another trooper leapt in before Renée could reply. 'No! Han't you been listening?' he said in a strong Arcturan accent. 'It's the Church of the Grey, ain't it? They're waiting for them grey aliens that everyone was on about back before space flight. Waiting for them to turn up and make everything all right. Peace and brotherhood, and all that.' He stopped, and shut his mouth with a snap, as if rather surprised at everything that had come out of it.

'But while you wait for them to turn up,' the ginger-haired boy persevered, 'you can make up your own rules, right? There isn't one *Book of the Grey*, you all make up your own. Right?'

Renée nodded. 'Absolutely right,' she said. 'Except . . .' Her audience leant forward, and she realized that she rather liked having a bunch of people hanging on her every word. Even this bunch of people. 'Except for the "all" bit. The trouble with a religion that tells you you ought to study all the alternatives and make up your own mind, is that lots of people do.' Her audience didn't look like they were following her. 'They convert to other religions,' she elaborated. 'The Church of the Grey has always had a bit of a problem hanging on to its membership.'

'So how many members of the Church are there?' the Arcturan asked.

'At this precise moment, I'd say, approximately, one.' Renée pushed a stray lock of hair out of her eyes. 'But I'm a very committed member,' she added, flicking her eyes at the blue-skinned officer.

He had been studying her in intent silence throughout her explanation. Now, finally, he asked, 'Couldn't numbers be increased through conversion *to* the Church?' and Renée felt like the jaws of a trap had closed around her.

'But I wasn't, I mean I only told you . . . I was only explaining what I was asked to explain.' She tugged down her khaki vest and attempted to regroup. 'I hope that you're not suggesting I was evangelizing, sir,' she said more steadily. 'I'm sure the NMA would frown on my trying to tempt its troops away from their own religions.'

The alien leant forward, until his long, sharp nose was almost pressed against hers. 'But your religion does allow you to convert new members, doesn't it?' he said.

Defeated, Renée shrugged. 'The Church is open to anyone. And it's in our creed to encourage people to think for themselves. So in a way, yes, I suppose you're right.'

He smiled, revealing pointed, jet-black teeth. 'In that case, there are now two members of the Church of the Grey.'

'What are you doing?' Adnan asked. His voice was quiet, almost friendly. Emile thought it was the most frightening thing he'd ever heard.

Emile just stared at him, and the eleven other cultists crowded into the doorway behind him. Three of them were now wearing the uniform of the New Moral Army.

Adnan crossed to the bookshelf and removed one of the larger volumes from it: *The Protestant Ethic and the Spirit of Capitalism.* As Emile watched, mesmerized, he traced each of the letters of the word 'Spirit' with his finger. When he'd finished, the outline of the book began to blur, then resolved into the familiar leather-bound form of *The Grimoire of Atheron the Mage*.

'Is this what you were looking for?' Adnan asked softly.

Emile nodded up at him from the floor. He cleared his painfully dry throat. 'But I would never have worked out how to find it,' he said.

The other cultists had surrounded him. Two of them were holding ritually carved but still lethally sharp daggers.

'You want to find the killer from that ship, don't you?' Adnan sounded mildly interested, as if he were asking whether Emile took one or two sugars in his coffee.

Emile nodded again. Adnan nodded, too. 'Yes, that's probably why you joined us in the first place.' He rolled up his sleeves until all the harsh red scars on his arms were exposed. 'I bet you even thought we might have done it.'

'No,' Emile said, desperately trying to keep the tremor out of his voice. 'Not really. I didn't believe you were involved.'

Adnan smiled, brushing back the blond hair from his face. 'Or you didn't want to believe it,' he said.

Emile realized that his hands were visibly shaking. He quickly clasped them together, and struggled up into a kneeling position. He wasn't sure if he had chosen it because it looked more dignified or because it was the traditional posture for begging.

'You swore the oath,' Adnan continued, 'and I'm sure you understood it. I'm sure you know this attempted robbery is a rather serious violation of it. But you were prepared to risk death for this knowledge.'

'Yes,' Emile whispered. 'It's important.'

Adnan knelt down beside him, and Emile lowered his head and braced himself for the killing blow.

The seconds passed with agonizing slowness.

'Well, take it,' Adnan said.

Emile looked up at Adnan in shock. He was holding out the grimoire towards him. Adnan smiled. 'The book's yours,' he said. 'You've earned it.'

'I don't understand,' Emile said.

One of the other cultists clapped him companionably on the back. Another two hauled him to his feet, then grasped hold of his arms when it looked as if he'd collapse back to the floor again. The room was suddenly filled with the low buzz of conversation. Several people called out congratulations to him.

'When you turned down the chance at knowledge before, I thought we'd made a mistake,' Adnan said. 'But now you've proved that you'll pay the highest price for knowledge. That's all we ask. That's all we are: people who want to know. The augury told us that you were supposed to be our thirteenth member. Then when I first saw you –' Adnan gestured dismissively at Emile's shorter form, as if the reasons for his reservation were so obvious they weren't worth stating '– I thought it must be mistaken. But you've proven the augury right.'

Emile felt realization like a stone in his gut. He wasn't entirely sure that having his life spared was worth the revelation of Adnan's exact feelings about him. 'So I can take it,' he said expressionlessly. 'You're giving it to me, because I was willing to risk my life to get it. And that's what you believe.'

Adnan smiled. 'That's our religion.'

There didn't seem to be anything else to say. Wordlessly, he took the grimoire from Adnan's hands and left the room.

7

FLIGHT BEGETS UNDERSTANDING

The N'a'm'thuli drums woke Bernice in the morning. She struggled to her feet and, after rubbing the sleep from her eyes, saw that Shemda had already begun to break camp. She tossed him the blanket to pack and reached for her canteen.

'What I wouldn't give for some coffee right now,' she said as she replaced it in her small canvas pack.

'I don't think we would have time, Bernice. They appear to be rather nearer than we would have hoped.' Shemda finished packing and pulled the pack on. He then ripped open some rations and crammed them into his mouth with the aid of his tentacles. The Grel wouldn't be first on the list next time she had a sophisticated dinner party. If she decided to start having sophisticated dinner parties.

'We'd better move, then,' she said. 'I just wish I'd had the foresight to pack my boots. You'd think that after the life I've led, I would have learnt not to let solid running footwear get too far away from me.'

Shemda consulted his dataxe and pointed away into the trees. 'It would be sensible to suppose that our pursuers will expect us to keep our previous course. They probably hope to create terror with the sound of their pursuit.'

'It seems to be working with me,' muttered Benny as she looked back the way they had come, searching for a sign of those following.

'Indeed. I would suggest we head east at speed and attempt

to circumvent their search. This would also mean that, once clear, we can emerge from the forest and head across the eastern plains north of the mountains and back round to the university. If we continue as before, we would spend at least three days in the forest before we encountered the Lake of Ortule. We would then need to find some kind of vessel, a task that could take valuable time.'

'Anywhere in the direction of home is fine by me.'

As they headed out of the clearing, the N'a'm'thuli drums stopped for a moment. Bernice could hear the shouts and shrieks of their pursuers. They began to run.

Kalten shook Fec awake excitedly.

'Come on, wake up, man!'

The Cham'di rubbed his huge eyes and stared blankly back at his friend's. 'What's up? You now joined the ranks of those desperate to make my life shitty? Starting with sleep deprivation.'

Kalten knew he always woke grumpy, even more so these days, so he let it slide. 'Shut up, Fec. I think I solved our Ahriman problem.'

'What Ahriman problem?' Fec was now fully awake.

'The one relating to it being bollocks.'

'Oh, that.' Fec nodded sagely.

'Yes. And the fact that any day now we're supposed to be meeting our God. Do you want to meet Ahriman the Great?'

'Fuck, no. You never know where you stand with that guy.'

'Right.' Kalten grabbed his friend by the shoulder. 'But I think it's time to move on. Away from those happy clappies and on to a far more manageable proposition.'

'What are you talking about, Kal?'

Kalten swept back his dark hair and sat down. 'I was over at the showers, talking to Jekker from B Company, and he's just had a sly drink with Hansen from A-squad.' Fec's eyes started to glaze over. 'Well, anyway, Hansen had met this fox, woman, over there who was spouting all this really weird shit about personal religion and stuff, about believing what you want to believe, and no one seemed to mind. Some of the others even went for it.'

Fec was on his feet in a second, pulling up his fatigues.

'Time to chat to the fox with the plan, matey,' he said as he ran out of the tent.

Braxiatel looked out of his office and realized that he simply had to do something. For the first time it was occurring to him that he, personally, might be in danger.

He looked again at the smouldering fire below. The charred remains staked in its centre had once been Emeritus Professor Solomon Merrick, Fellow of All Souls and Chair of the University Cross-Cultural Council. As a Jew, he had been put to death for working on a Saturday. The other Jews on campus had attempted to point out to the Sultan that this wasn't, according to their scriptures, the correct punishment for his crime, but the Sultan had smiled and done it anyway.

Merrick was the first senior staff member to be executed. Braxiatel was quite sure that he wouldn't be the last. After that initial visit from the New Moral Army trooper, Braxiatel hadn't been bothered again. Now he found that he was in a constant state of nervous tension, waiting for the soldiers to come back. Every knock on the door caused his pulse to speed up and sweat to prickle on his palms.

He was rather surprised to learn that he was afraid of dying. He'd always imagined that he'd regard it with the same calm dispassion with which he'd conducted the rest of his life.

He let his gaze drift once again to the pyre outside. He felt almost dizzy with all the emotions flowing through him, in danger of being washed away on a tide of feeling. He looked down at his hands, and saw that they were both clenched into fists, the knuckles white with pressure. Vaguely, he experienced the discomfort of nails digging into his palms. It was anger, he realized. More than the fear, or the confusion, he was absolutely furious.

How dare they do this to St Oscar's? How dare they do this to his university?

The rage was more frightening than the fear itself. It felt so vast and powerful, he wasn't sure what the consequences of letting it out would be.

There was a group of students who had watched the execution, he saw, carefully monitored by a division of the New Moral Army. Now one of them turned to her friends and laughed. For just one moment, Braxiatel wanted to kill her. He pounded his fist against the desk, then again, harder, until the pain was all he could think about.

Then, very carefully, he unclenched each of his hands and used them to push himself up from his desk. If he couldn't control his anger, he could at least direct it at the right target.

It was a close-run thing, but they got by. Bernice's ears were filled with drumming, counterpointed by her own racing heartbeat. Shemda could move much faster than her, but the Grel stayed close, urging her on and helping her through some of the denser foliage. Despite her terror she was struck by how chivalrously he behaved.

The N'a'm'thuli screamed and wailed in their pursuit; she heard them hacking their way through the forest. Suddenly visions of them hacking through her own body swamped her mind. She kept running, fighting her way across the line, knowing that they couldn't be more than a hundred metres away.

Shemda grabbed her arm and almost pulled her off her feet. She kept silent with difficulty as the Grel dragged her through the trees. Ahead, the undergrowth seemed to thicken and sprout around the great trunks. In one swift movement she was hurled low through the air and into the foliage. Shemda dived in after her.

As they lay on the ground, holding closed the gap they had made in the shrubs and looking back the way they had come, they saw the N'a'm'thuli. The blue-stained warriors almost skipped between the trees, dancing madly and slashing with their lethal barbs. One headed towards them and scythed downward with his length of thin steel. Bernice stifled a cry as the barb flashed past her face. She scrambled backward and nearly screamed as the ground gave beneath her. Shemda grabbed her arm.

Then, as quickly as they had appeared, the N'a'm'thuli moved on through the trees. In the distance, skipping along with the scarred and stained warriors, Bernice thought she saw the young Hut'eri, Tan'a. The girl seemed to be laughing as she danced between the firs.

'Well, we've learnt some more about our pursuers and their deities, Shemda,' said Benny once she was sure the woods were clear around them. 'They are not great trackers, nor are they omniscient.' She looked down curiously. Her legs had disappeared down a rather regular-looking hole that had clearly been covered with grasses and leaves.

'Indeed.' The Grel's eyes swept around him once more, then he began to get to his feet. He dusted himself down and offered to help Bernice up. 'I apologize for my roughness, but I'm sure you will acknowledge the need for speed under the circumstances, Professor.'

'Indeed I do, servitor.' Shemda looked at her quizzically. 'Two can play at the formality game, you know,' she said, with a raised eyebrow. 'Anyway, said roughness may prove to be extremely useful. Now, give me a torch so I can see what's down the rabbit-hole.'

'Indeed.'

Bernice sighed, snatched the offered light, and dropped down through the hole. She only dropped a couple of metres but still managed to sprain her ankle slightly. 'Typical,' she muttered, as she swept the torch about her, then the breath caught in her throat.

A skeleton lay prone before her, the head resting on what looked like a primitive altar. Two dull bronze candlesticks must once have illuminated the chamber.

The skeleton looked too tall to be Hut'eri, and the skull too long, and Bernice wondered whether it could be one of the mysterious Morkai. But, if it was, they must have gone in for ritual suicide, for the skinless, age-old hands still held the two blades that the penitent must have thrust into its own sides, and chips on the ribcage told of the force of the action.

Bernice stared for a while and wondered what could make someone act in such a way, then decided the thought was probably not too helpful given their current situation. She looked up through the hole that formed the only entrance to the macabre temple.

'Get down here, big guy,' she called quietly. 'It's time to hole up.'

Braxiatel took great satisfaction in kicking down the door. He had rarely used his superior physical strength in his long life, and now seemed like an opportune moment to start.

It was even more satisfying to see the expression of surprise on his nemesis's face, staring at him across the echoing expanse of his ridiculous villain's lair. John twisted round from the bag he had been packing, looking just like a little child who had been caught with his hand in the cookie jar.

'How very macho,' he said. 'Feel better now?'

Braxiatel strode briskly across the floor towards him. He inspected the room as he walked, noticing that it had been stripped nearly bare, with just John's desk and the chair in front of it remaining. It was only when he was nearly upon it that he realized they weren't alone. 'Captain Stewart,' he said coldly to the middle-aged woman perched on the edge of the high-backed ivory chair. 'What are you doing here?'

Captain Stewart, with whom he'd done a fair bit of business in the past, didn't seem to know quite how to deal with him in this unusual mood. 'Professor Braxiatel,' she said, with careful diplomacy, 'I was –'

'That will be all, Lorna,' John interrupted hurriedly. 'Unless you have any problems.' He didn't make it a question.

Lorna Stewart stood, obviously understanding that she wasn't welcome. 'No, it's all in order; you will have the ships you want.' She nodded brusquely at Braxiatel and marched stiff-backed from the room, clearly glad to leave the tense atmosphere behind.

As soon as she had gone, Braxiatel snapped, sweeping all the occult paraphernalia from John's desk in one brutal gesture. 'Stop it!' he shouted. The objects clattered and shattered on the floor around him. Braxiatel fixed his eyes on one delicate crystal ball as it bounced once, twice, then split neatly in half, releasing a translucent silver fluid on to the marble floor. He looked up into an impassive pair of alien yellow eyes. 'Just . . . stop this.' Braxiatel found that all the anger had drained out of him, leaving only a terrible weariness, and an aching worry that nothing would ease. 'Tell me how to make this stop. Please.'

John reached out one bony hand and gently touched a fingertip to Braxiatel's flushed cheek. It seemed to be a gesture of reconciliation, or maybe comfort. Then he crouched down and began carefully clearing away the objects that Braxiatel had scattered on his floor. 'Something's been released,' he said quietly. 'It's very –' he laughed abruptly, self-mockingly '– it's very serious.' He raised his head to look at Braxiatel, and it was Braxiatel who dropped his eyes first. 'If I seem to be manipulating you, believe me that it's for your own good.'

Braxiatel managed a slight smile. 'Isn't that my line?'

John stood again, and Braxiatel noticed for the first time the dark shadows in the yellow of his face. 'Speaking of which,' John said casually, 'I'm surprised you haven't sent Bernice to see me. Where is she?'

'We decided she should investigate the second coming of Maa'lon – in the mountains,' Braxiatel replied. 'Why?'

The remaining colour drained from John's face. 'You what?'

Braxiatel cleared his throat, unaccountably feeling as if he had to justify himself. 'Right when this all began,' he elaborated. 'She's been gone for days.'

'Are you absolutely out of your mind?' John was shouting at him now, his earlier calm vanished. 'Bernice is much too important to send into danger like that. You complete cretin! What on earth were you thinking of?'

The tirade was so unexpected that Braxiatel found himself more alarmed than offended. 'I didn't know . . .' He gathered himself. 'How *could* I know what you wanted, when you wouldn't tell me anything?'

But John was already heading for the door, somehow having managed to stuff his bag with all the remaining bits of equipment in the room along the way.

'What –' Braxiatel said.

'No time for that,' John said, holding the door open. 'It's up to you now. I think you have a personal stake in seeing that things don't get any worse. Do what you think is right, Braxiatel. Your feelings will tell you what to do, if you'll just listen to them.'

'But –' The door slammed behind John. Braxiatel shut his mouth. He felt as if he had just been caught in the path of a small whirlwind. 'I used to be so good at this sort of thing,' he muttered, as he followed John from the room.

The work was well underway. His compatriots were freed, and already they had found themselves some followers. They were enjoying their newfound freedom. He carefully arranged the features of his borrowed face into a smile. They had suggested a further task for him, and he had been happy to comply. Too many of their potential followers were leaving. Leaving before they had seen the light, and given of themselves. The route back to the spaceport was long, but his will would carry him there. He would ensure that his compatriots had all the followers they needed.

8

NEW DEALS

There were now seventy-six members of the Church of the Grey. Throughout the course of the second day's training, Renée had found herself surreptitiously approached by soldier after soldier, asking her to explain her religion to them, and then asking if they could convert.

The fourth time it had happened, she'd been unable to stop herself asking why.

'I need something to believe,' the young Earth Reptile had replied.

Renée had been puzzled. 'I thought you joined up because you already believed in something.'

The Earth Reptile had laughed humourlessly. 'I joined up because my room-mate was killed by NMA soldiers,' she'd said flatly. 'I reckoned I was safer in than out. And I know I'm not the only one. But they're sending the sergeants round, questioning everyone about their faith.' She placed a clawed hand on Renée's shoulder. 'If they asked me ten questions about the Cult of G'na, they'd get ten wrong answers. But in the Church of the Grey there are no wrong answers. So they can't catch me out.'

Renée had watched the Earth Reptile march happily away to rejoin her unit. It was at that point she realized she was on to a winner.

* * *

Clarence pushed his way impatiently through the crowds of the market. He'd already managed to lumber himself with a dragon-skin leather jacket, an earring in the shape of a turtle made out of dwarf-star alloy, and – his latest acquisition – an ivory cutlery set made out of the shopkeeper's own cloned tusks. None of them were things he had the slightest interest in owning.

The *B-Aaron* stared at his latest purchase with undisguised distaste. 'You have to learn how to say no,' it said.

Clarence shook his pinions into place. 'If I knew how to say no, I wouldn't be here with you today,' he pointed out.

The *B-Aaron*'s remote drone shrugged. Clarence studied it as he clipped the turtle earring into place. 'Anyway,' Clarence said, 'if anyone's the fashion victim around here, it's you. Just how many different remote drones do you have?'

'I needed them for espionage work during the War,' the *B-Aaron* said defensively, but it seemed to know when it had lost an argument, and shut up.

The remote it was using today was a particularly absurd example. It looked like a very primitive robot from a just post-silicate world. No, actually, it looked like the robots imagined by a just pre-silicate world. It was only about two feet high, silver with gold dressing, and an abundance of flashing (and utterly pointless) lights. One especially annoying one on its chest flashed in time to its speech. It moved as if its joints needed oiling. Only its face didn't fit: fully flexible, it was capable of showing the full range of human expressions. The *B-Aaron*, Clarence thought, was not a being which was prepared to limit its ability to show what it felt, even for the sake of maintaining a consistent illusion.

They walked on in silence through the bustling, happy, smelly market of Lefteye on Whynot. Anywhere else on the Worldsphere, a pair like them might have attracted some attention. Here on Whynot, they were among the more normal People on the streets. The planet floating within the sphere was God's, and People lived there on his sufferance. He liked the company, of course, but if he decided he felt like a bit of redecorating – shifting a continent here or there, or raising the sea-level a few feet – he didn't feel he had to ask their permission first. The People who chose to live on Whynot liked unpredictability.

They liked God, too, which was why Clarence and the *B-Aaron* didn't discuss their reason for being there as they walked through the crowded streets. Only when they reached a deserted alleyway, overhung with beamed buildings in a self-conscious imitation of medieval cities on Earth, did they speak.

'This is your last chance to pull out,' the *B-Aaron* said.

'No, I want to know,' Clarence said. 'Let's do it.'

The *B-Aaron* dropped to its knees with a musical metallic clunk. It plunged its blunt silver fingers into the pavement.

The cobbles melted away like butter. In front of them, a flight of perfectly symmetrical mat-black steps led down into infinity.

The *B-Aaron* smiled. 'Best infiltration drone in the quadrant,' it said. It gestured at the bottomless hole in front of them. 'Welcome to the Mind of God.'

It was also on the second day that Renée was told she would not be returning to her job at the university. Ever.

As she stood ranked with the other recruits – a great, muddy, miserable field full of all two thousand of them – General Watt told them that they were now full-time soldiers in the New Moral Army, ready to devote their lives to the furtherance of the cause. Congratulations.

Ten soldiers to the right of Renée, someone sent up a cheer. There was an almost imperceptible pause, then a massed chorus of voices joined it. Renée's was one of them. A week in the army had already taught her that discretion was the better part of valour.

After that, the sergeants marched among the ranks, handing out a fully charged assault rifle, an ammunition belt, a copy of the *Coda of the Army of the Gods*, and a pair of dog tags to each of them. Renée saw that hers were printed with the figure 1397. It was nice to see the army recognized something unique about her, even if it was only a number.

Then they all sang a rousing hymn (Renée had been taught the words during her first training exercise) before being told that they were dismissed.

It was as Renée was trudging back towards her tent that the adjutant stopped her. 'The General wants to talk to you about the Church of the Grey,' he said. 'She's heard what you've been up to.'

'At ease, Private Thalia,' the general grated. Her voice was deep and rough, like a newly excavated hole.

At ease was about the last thing Renée felt. Her uniform was stuck to her body with clammy sweat, and her primitive rifle felt like a lump of lead on her shoulder. She had never thought she would come to miss the weight of her cello.

'Four hundred and ninety-seven converts,' General Watt said. She squinted at Renée from under her close-cropped brown hair.

Renée's last hope that this wasn't about what she thought it was about died. 'I think someone's been exaggerating,' she said. 'Sir.' It seemed like the day had lasted forever. She knew she ought to be afraid. Somewhere buried deep inside her, a shrill voice was screaming that this was the end. But she'd just found out that she was going to spend the rest of her life in the army. She couldn't entirely bring herself to care how short that life might be.

General Watt shook her head, sending out a spray of fine droplets of sweat. Several of them landed on Renée's cheek, and she fought down the urge to wipe them off. 'Don't contradict me, soldier,' the general said. 'Are you trying to tell me you haven't been evangelizing for the Church of the Grey?'

For a second, Renée considered pointing out that it was she who'd been approached by the converts, not the other way round. Then she realized that saying this might possibly save her own skin, but would almost certainly condemn all those who'd converted. The needs of the many outweigh the needs of the few, she thought. Which was all well and good, unless you were one of the few. 'I've only personally converted a hundred and twelve,' she said. 'But, yes, I have been evangelizing.'

Surprisingly, the general smiled, a big toothy grin that looked strangely goofy on her hard-bitten nut-brown face. 'Well, soldier, I'm telling you that your converts have been converting. The word is spreading.' She glanced across at her adjutant, who gazed back at her expressionlessly. 'Hoping to convert the whole army, were you?'

'Only half of it,' Renée said dryly.

The general let out a quick bark of laughter. 'That's the attitude, soldier.' She nodded brusquely. 'The New Moral Army needs more like you.'

For a moment, Renée assumed the general was joking. But then she realized that it all made a twisted sort of sense. The one thing no soldier would ever be punished for was following the dictates of their religion. No wonder the blue-skinned lieutenant had been so careful to check that evangelizing was encouraged in the Church of the Grey.

'There is too little faith in my ranks,' the general continued. 'We could all learn a lesson from your fervour.'

Renée ventured a small relieved smile. 'We all have to do our part,' she said.

'Indeed,' the general agreed. She reached forward and grasped the neck of Renée's newly tight-fitting shirt in one hand, frowning slightly at the lack of give in the material. Then, as Renée looked down, she pinned a small golden badge to the collar. 'Carry on the good work, *Captain* Thalia.'

They had descended for hours, and the view had remained unchanged. Just a flight of black, black stairs, leading down forever. 'You're sure he can't see us?' Clarence asked for the fourth time.

The *B-Aaron* sighed. 'He's blind inside his own Mind,' it said. 'It's his Achilles' heel, to use a mythological analogy. The Awfully Clever Hacking Interest Group told me about it.' Without warning, the robot stopped, and Clarence found himself pressed up against the cold metal of its back. 'We're here.'

It touched the wall beside it. Once more, the apparently solid surface melted away. In its place appeared an open doorway, leading through into a wood-panelled Victorian study. At its centre stood a solid oak table, on which was perched a bowl of suspicious yellow dip.

The *B-Aaron* pursed its lips disparagingly. 'Nice to see God's sense of humour even extends to the decor inside his own head.'

'Where exactly are we?' Clarence asked.

They both walked through into the room. 'Not inside normal space any more,' the drone said casually. 'If you were a genuine organic, you'd be dead by now. Haven't you noticed that you aren't breathing?'

Clarence realized that he hadn't been ever since they stepped on to the black stairway. He felt foolish for not realizing earlier.

'Right,' the *B-Aaron* said. It had moved over to the bookcase on the far wall and was studying a collection of volumes, all of which had the word 'Dellah' written in gold cursive script on their spines. 'Hmm . . . where to start?'

Its too-human face was set in an expression of carefully controlled calm. It occurred to Clarence that the drone's excessive self-confidence was an act. The *B-Aaron* was not at all sure that God wouldn't catch them. Clarence swallowed nervously. 'How about religion?' he suggested.

'Religion?'

Clarence spread his wings in a great white fan behind him. 'Operation Ragnarok,' he said. 'Me. You. Don't you think that's what this is all about?'

The *B-Aaron* looked at him intently for a moment, then picked out a volume two-thirds of the way along the shelf and set it down on the reading table between them. 'God couldn't make this easy,' it muttered. 'I suppose info-cubes would have been too last year for him.'

As Clarence watched over the drone's shoulder, it opened the book. Clarence looked at the page, and then immediately wished he hadn't as he felt a horrible wrenching sensation in his eyes. He screwed them shut in pain. When he opened them again, he wasn't in the wood-panelled study.

He and the *B-Aaron* were standing on a fluffy white cloud, facing a craggy-faced, white-bearded old man. 'The religions of Dellah,' the old man said.

'Yes?' Clarence said.

The old man remained silent.

'I think we need to ask him a question,' the drone suggested. 'What's significant about the religions of Dellah?' it ventured.

The old man unrolled a scroll which he was suddenly holding in his hand. 'Dellah was chosen from among the alternatives for two primary reasons. Firstly: the unique diversity of its religious faiths,' he said, his voice deep and terribly cultured. 'Secondly: the fact that each religion worshipped an inanimate object, to which very few powers were ascribed.' He re-rolled the scroll with a dry snap, and lapsed into silence, his eyes devoid of expression.

Clarence and the *B-Aaron* exchanged a look. 'Um,' Clarence said. 'But the Dellahans worship all sorts of gods. With all sorts of powers.'

The old man nodded. 'It wasn't anticipated that the imprisoned forces would be able to influence the indigenous population in that way. If this outcome had been foreseen, Dellah would not have been chosen.'

A gentle breeze blew through their cloud world. One of Clarence's feathers detached from his wing and drifted to land at the old man's feet. Clarence watched the old man watching it. For some reason, he felt reluctant to ask the obvious question.

The *B-Aaron* asked it for him. 'Chosen for what?'

All the lights went out.

'I think you've found out quite enough for one day, don't you?' said the disembodied voice of God. 'If you don't mind, I'd like you to get out of my head.'

There was a brief, tearing sense of dislocation, and Clarence's mind curled inward like a flower at night. When he woke again, he was lying on a cobbled pavement. His naked buttocks were unpleasantly immersed in a muddy puddle.

Beside him, the *B-Aaron* was resting supine in an enormous, and very pungent, animal dropping. It struggled into an upright position, vainly brushing clinging clods of dung from its now rather tarnished legs. 'The bastard did that deliberately,' it said. 'Oh well, back to the drawing board.'

The tents seemed to be scattered for miles in every direction, like khaki pimples on the brown landscape. Small khaki-clad figures occasionally scurried between them, like . . . no, Braxiatel realized, that was where the simile broke down.

Renée, a gruff Pakhar sergeant had reluctantly told him, would be found in tent 402. Braxiatel couldn't quite get his head round that. He'd never really considered Renée to be part of anything else; he resented the idea that someone might think of her that way, reducing her uniqueness to a three-digit number.

He realized that he was attracting curious glances as he strode through the camp, his normally sombre clothing seeming like a riot of colour and individuality in this shrine to conformity. Some of the looks were overtly hostile. He felt like a virus in the army's bloodstream; his shape didn't fit and soon the regimental antibodies would cluster around him, surrounding him till nothing of himself was visible, and the threatening foreignness was hidden from sight.

He realized that he was lost. Tent 402 – fifth row, twentieth column – had been easy enough to spot as he had looked down on the camp from the hills surrounding it, but here in the thick of things he had lost his perspective.

A blue-skinned Maryan in a lieutenant's uniform seemed to sense his confusion. 'You're looking for Captain Thalia, aren't you?' the Maryan said, flashing Braxiatel glimpses of his sharp black teeth as he spoke.

'I am, yes,' Braxiatel confirmed. 'I'm looking for her to get her out of this mess I've got her into. I'm wondering if she's going to forgive me.'

'You must be Braxiatel,' the Maryan said.

Braxiatel raised a curious eyebrow. 'My reputation obviously precedes me,' he said. He wasn't sure this was necessarily a good thing.

The blue-skinned alien grinned, displaying the complete mouthful of his coal-black teeth. 'Renée's told us about you,' he said.

Only good things, I hope, Braxiatel thought, but he didn't bother saying it. Given the mood Renée had been in when he'd last seen her, they almost certainly hadn't been.

The Maryan lieutenant pointed back the way Braxiatel had come. 'Three rows back, tenth tent on your left,' he said. 'You can't miss it.'

He left before Braxiatel could ask him what exactly he meant by that.

A few minutes later, he knew.

Renée's tent was surrounded by concentric circles of seated soldiers. It looked like a stone that had been thrown into a puddle of muddy humanity. Braxiatel's hearts jerked momentarily into overdrive, thinking that she was in some sort of trouble. Then he noticed the woman herself, sitting at the centre of the ring, Buddha-calm. She was, he could hear, reading aloud from a screen cradled between her thighs.

When he was still twenty paces away, she noticed him. She glanced up briefly, a spark of some nameless emotion in her eyes. Then she bent her head again and continued reading from the screen. Only when most of her listeners had themselves noticed Braxiatel, craning round from her to stare at him, did she acknowledge his presence.

'Irving,' she said coolly. 'Thinking of joining up?'

Several of her audience giggled. Braxiatel found himself mildly offended. Did he look that unlikely a candidate for the army? 'I was hoping to speak to you,' he said, struggling to keep the note of irritation out of his voice. 'Somewhere private,' he added.

Renée pursed her lips and raised her eyebrow at him. There were a few half-hearted wolf-whistles from the crowd.

'Well, I've never been a woman to turn down that kind of invitation,' she said. She stood up, waving away her audience as she did. 'The meeting will resume in half an hour,' she told them, and, glancing askance at Braxiatel, concluded, 'This won't take long.' That elicited more ribald comments, as she'd certainly intended. Braxiatel was annoyed to realize that he was blushing.

When the crowd had dispersed, many of them blatantly pausing to stare at Braxiatel, she ushered him into her tent.

Inside, he was amazed to see an almost exact re-creation of her college room. Down to the items of questionable equipment.

'Rank hath its privileges,' she said.

'Is it safe to talk?' Braxiatel asked softly, still loitering uncomfortably by the entrance.

'Really, Irving, how terribly melodramatic of you.' She lounged back on one of her abundance of velvet-covered throw cushions. 'Do sit down,' she added, gesturing to a cushion beside her.

Braxiatel frowned, and settled on a wooden stall several feet away, perching uncomfortably on the very edge. He opened his mouth, then shut it again, no longer sure what he was going to say. 'I've come to take you away from all this' didn't really seem appropriate any more. In the end, he decided to say it anyway.

'What brought this on?' she asked, leaning forward until the distance between them was almost breached. Braxiatel couldn't help noticing that her uniform seemed rather more, well, snug than when he had first seen it. 'I thought you had forgotten about me.'

How could I forget about you? I've missed you, Renée. But those were things he couldn't say. 'I heard that the draft had been made permanent. I didn't anticipate that happening when I forced you to join. I felt that I owed it to you to find a way to get you out, if that's what you want. I'm organizing ships off-planet. You could be on one of them.'

'Has it really got that bad, Irving?' she said. There was a tone in her voice he'd never heard before; he realized that it was complete seriousness. He found that he didn't know how to respond to it.

There was a moment of silence. 'You couldn't find someone less suited to the army than me, could you?' she said wryly. 'But you know what? I'm going to stay.' There was a note of amazement in her voice, as if she couldn't quite believe what she was saying, either.

Braxiatel reached forward and grasped her hand in his own. After a surprised second she clasped her fingers firmly around his, so that he could feel the hard calluses of her cello-playing and the rougher abrasions of her more recent exertions pressing into the soft skin of his palm. 'I'm sorry, Renée,' he said. 'It's all gone much further than I imagined.' He looked into her forget-me-not eyes. 'Leave,' he said. 'For my sake. I hate feeling responsible for you. I can't concentrate on what I need to be concentrating on when I'm worried about you.'

Abruptly, Renée jerked her hand from his grasp and turned away from him. He saw her shoulders rise and fall as she took a deep breath, but when she turned back to him there was still a trace of anger in her expression. He pushed himself to his feet, not meeting her eyes again until he could once more look down on her from the vantage of his greater height.

'I'm needed here, Braxiatel,' she said hotly. 'I have a purpose: that's not something I've been able to say very often in my life. And I'm not leaving just to stop you feeling guilty. Believe it or not, my whole existence doesn't revolve around your needs.' She seemed to read an expression in his face that he wasn't aware was there. Her own softened slightly. 'But thank you for caring, as much as you're able.'

Braxiatel looked at her for a long moment before turning and leaving the tent. He knew that she'd just said good-bye.

Emile sat in his bare grey room, clutching the grimoire to his chest. He'd got what he wanted. He had thought he was willing to pay the price, but now he wasn't so sure.

He bowed his head until it was resting against the hard

leather spine of the book, and its unmistakable musty scent filled his nostrils. It smelt of secrets and age. He squeezed his eyes shut painfully, and felt the delicate trickle of tears playing join-the-dots with the freckles on his cheeks.

Why is this bothering me so much? he wondered. I never thought that Adnan was really interested in me. And, if it had all been what it appeared to be, I'd probably be dead by now.

These are tears of relief, he told himself. He almost believed it.

After ten minutes, he opened *The Grimoire of Atheron the Mage* and set it on his chair. The words 'blood is the hardest currency in the spirit world' stared accusingly at him from the title page.

Turning the greasy parchment pages with gentle care, he flicked past spells of healing, and cursing, and projection of emotion. He stopped for a moment at the ingredients for a love potion, but he didn't have a ready supply of frogs' tongues, and he was not sure that Adnan was capable of love, anyway.

The spell for summoning an elemental spirit was on page fifty-seven. It even had a little picture of the imp etched in green pen into the illuminated 'W' at the top. It didn't look very much like him.

Emile read it carefully.

'Shit,' he muttered.

With his usual lack of foresight, he'd failed to supply himself with any of the ingredients necessary for the enchantment. And foxglove and sparrows' eyes weren't available in the college shop.

He laughed, inexplicably feeling a little better. Boy, did Bernice ever choose the wrong man for this job.

Then he thought about Elspeth, too ashamed to look him in the eye after joining the Church of Ahriman the Great. And he thought about a strange woman he'd never met from a world he'd never seen, butchered with her unborn child still inside her.

He set his mouth in a grim line. He wasn't good for much, but he'd be damned if he'd give up now. He'd already faced

Adnan's mad cultists; this ought to be the easy part.

Blood is the hardest currency in the spirit world. It didn't say what the exchange rate was, but Emile suspected that if he spilt enough he would get what he wanted. Maybe, he thought with sudden insight, that was the principle on which the murderer had worked. It comforted him somewhat to think that he might be using the killer's own methods to catch him.

It took three passes with a blunt bread knife to open the vein in his arm deeply enough. The blood spilt out in a viscous stream. Walking widdershins as he'd learnt he should, he drew a wobbly scarlet circle on the plasti-crete floor. The wound was almost sealed by the time he'd finished, and the initial numbness of shock had given way to a throbbing agony that spread upward to his shoulder and through his chest.

Cradling the arm against his chest, smearing his beige shirt with red, he recited the words of the spell.

There was no period of fuzzy uncertainty this time. The imp was simply there.

It smiled cruelly. 'We meet again,' it said. 'Ready to make a deal this time, buddy?'

Extract from the diary of Bernice Summerfield

I think I shall go mad soon. So small and airless. Sitting in the darkness most of the time to avoid looking at the remains. All the while the N'a'm'thuli moving noisily about, shouting guttural challenges and screaming defiance.

It's been days. I'm sick of Grel rations. Shemda too seems to be suffering in this atmosphere: he hasn't spoken for hours. I'm starting to understand what makes someone stab themselves in the side. Twice, just to make sure.

I really need to get out of here.

Extract ends

Emile sat down heavily on his bed. He felt as if all the energy had been drained out of him. He knew that this was the point of no return. 'Yes, I will make a deal,' he said. 'But the question has changed. I've found out who the killer is. Now I need to know how to catch him.'

There was an extended silence.

'I'm waiting,' the imp said. 'You gotta make me an offer, remember?'

Emile swallowed, then made him an offer he couldn't refuse.

The imp laughed. 'That's one I ain't gonna turn down. You got yourself a bargain.'

'I'm still waiting for an answer,' Emile said in a dusty voice.

'Yeah, yeah.' The imp scowled, as if he'd been hoping Emile might forget. 'He's in the spaceport. You're gonna have to hurry if you wanna catch him.'

Now that he'd actually gone through with it, Emile was feeling a sort of light-headed relief. He'd committed himself; all the tough business of making choices was over. Everything became inevitable after that. 'What's he doing at the spaceport?' he asked with almost casual curiosity, already heading for the door.

There was no reply, and he turned round to see that the imp was fading out of existence like a rainbow after the rain. 'Only one question,' it said, its voice a memory of an echo. 'Don't worry: you're heading for an appointment you won't be able to miss.'

And it was gone. Suddenly feeling a formless dread, Emile rushed out of the door. Then he rushed back in again and grabbed the grimoire. It was the one thing in the last few days that hadn't let him down. Clutching it painfully to his chest with his uninjured arm, he ran as fast as he could towards the spaceport.

9

DEPARTURES

They were nearly clear of the forest when they began to hear the drums again. The N'a'm'thuli hadn't been as far off as they'd thought. Bernice's lungs were bursting, but they were bursting with fresh, open air, so she still drove her legs on. Shemda, a little way ahead, remained apparently indefatigable. She wondered whether she'd ever had need of that word before.

'We're going to have to stop for a minute,' she gasped. 'My left arm's beginning to feel odd, and I'd hate to foil my own escape with an ill-timed heart attack.'

Shemda turned and jogged back to her. He settled her down by a tree and brought some water to her lips.

'I strongly recommend you regain your breath and strength quickly, Bernice: I would find it much more convenient.'

The smile around his eyes showed the humour in his words. Bernice drank in silence.

'They appear to have worked out your cunning plan, Shemda,' she said once she had emptied the canteen.

'Indeed. I shall have to work on being more cunning, Benny. While I am doing that, you could possibly be working on your fitness.' He helped her back to her feet.

'Don't push it, squid-mouth, or I'll unleash my devastating wit!' She slapped him across the buttocks and ran past him towards the edge of the forest. 'It's a foot-race now, so let's get on with it.'

Within three or four strides Shemda overtook her, but once more he didn't race away, but kept time with her. She hated to be the weak link, but was thankful for his kindness. After a few minutes they cleared the trees and were out in the open of the eastern plain.

It was open savannah as far as the eye could see, save for the Hut mountains to the south. There was no cover, only the knee-high grass. Once they were seen, their pursuers would have them. Benny's heart sank, but Shemda suddenly hooted excitedly and grabbed her arm.

About half a kilometre away, slightly to the north, she could see a distinctive hump in the grass. A shape that could be an off-roader. She stared at the transport for a few long moments in stunned silence. The gods, whoever they were, had smiled on them.

It took them a few minutes to work out how the off-roader worked, time which was made more unpleasant by the state of the vehicle. The two ribbed bucket-seats were covered in blood, caked dry in the blazing sunlight of the savannah. Small rips in the woven upholstery and cuts through the safety harnesses showed where weapons had cut through the occupants. Bernice was in no doubt that the previous owners had come across the N'a'm'thuli and not lived to regret it.

Benny sat gingerly in the driver's seat, sinking down to almost grass height. She grasped the steering column and cautiously depressed some of the built-in trigger switches; nothing happened. Next to her, Shemda struggled to fit himself into the vehicle. The light four-wheeler was clearly built for smaller humanoids; even Bernice filled all the available room. After trying all angles of entry, Shemda gave a resigned snort, ripped out the passenger seat, and settled down on the clear plastene floor. It creaked a little as it took his weight, but did not give.

Bernice, furious, pressed the bank of switches across the simple dashboard, but still nothing happened; she swore. She looked round the tiny vehicle; there were no other switches near her. The simple poly-bonded frame contained only the two seats and the see-through bubble body with its cut-out roof. It was clearly a sports model, low-tech and seat-of-the-pants.

She turned when Shemda tapped her on the shoulder. He pointed down to the floor between them. There, almost beneath her seat, were two sliding switches, red and blue. One of the Grel's large hands came down and slid both towards the rear. As he did so, ikons flashed within their translucent surface, and the vehicle sparked into life. The gas turbine whined and screamed for action. Loud industrial surf rhythms blared out of speakers hidden under the dashboard.

Benny flicked all the switches again before she found the one controlling the sound system. In the relative quiet of the turbine ticking over she turned to the Grel and raised an eyebrow.

'Enablers,' he answered innocently, returning her look.

'Smart-ass,' was all she said before pulling back the column and gunning the off-roader into action.

She swung it round in a broad arc before the trees and headed off eastwards, just as their pursuers emerged. The vehicle raced away, accelerating rapidly as Benny hauled back on the stick, its turbine pitch rising, and suspension failing to deal with the rough terrain. As they bounced wildly away, some of those hunting them opened fire with energy weapons. Pulses ignited grasses nearby and one scorched the plastene bubble.

Benny realized that while the forces of Maa'lon clearly preferred primitive weapons, they were no Luddites: they used whatever served their purpose. Fortunately, with the vehicle screaming through the savannah, they were soon out of range.

Braxiatel looked at the raggle-taggle group of people before him, trying not to think too much about the person who was missing from it. 'Remember that your exit visas are faked,' he told them, 'so try not to draw too much attention to yourselves.'

His room felt horribly crowded with twenty-three people

in it. Especially twenty-three terminally frightened academics. Braxiatel eyed some of the more elderly members of the party, seriously wondering if they'd make it to the spaceport.

'If we're all here,' Professor Travis said, a high, nervous note of impatience in his voice, 'can't we just go?'

'We can't go yet. Kerish Taan isn't here,' Dr Jalal replied softly. The short, furry Pakhar was actually standing on Braxiatel's desk to make more space for the others in the room.

'Professor Taan isn't coming,' Dr Curtis said with numb finality. Her eyes slid away from the enquiring gazes around the room, and no one bothered to ask where Kerish Taan was.

'So there's no one missing,' Travis persevered. 'Is there?'

Braxiatel drew in a deep breath, then let it out again. 'No, everyone's here that's coming,' he said. 'We can head for the spaceport.' Looking around the eccentric, scared band of academics, he knew it was a useless request, but he made it anyway. 'As far as anyone knows, we're all just on a junket, so do try to act naturally.'

Jalal huffed a short laugh, clearly having formed the same opinion as Braxiatel of his fellow academics, but he was too polite to vocalize it. 'Will you be joining us on the ship?' he asked Braxiatel.

Braxiatel took a last look around his wood-panelled, leather-upholstered, book-lined office. He felt like a hermit crab abandoning its old shell without having found another one to move to. 'There's nothing for me to stay for,' he said quietly.

The off-roader packed up after an hour.

'Out of gas,' said Bernice. She hit the dashboard and then immediately grasped her hand to her chest. She rubbed it for a while before looking across at Shemda.

His eyes looked rather wild, and his tentacles had flattened down across his cheeks and chin, leaving his mouth exposed. He had clearly not enjoyed the ride. Benny tapped him on the shoulder and smiled at him. 'Time to walk once more, and try not to look too relieved.'

The Grel didn't speak as he struggled to extricate his large body from the machine. When he finally succeeded, he sank to his knees in silence and bent his head down through the grass to the ground. He let out a small choked sob and seemed to grip the grass around him. After a moment he rose once more, untied his pack from between the back wheels, and headed east. Benny ran to catch up with him.

'Oh, come on. I mean, I know I'm not the galaxy's greatest driver, but it did the job. We got away. We must have come at least two hundred K. They'll never overhaul that on foot.' As she spoke she pulled on her own pack and looked back the way they had come.

'Indeed, Bernice. We have covered a great deal of distance in a very short time.' Shemda's tentacles seemed still to have some rigidity in them. 'Just do not ask me to do it again. I am trying to decide whether it is preferable to facing Maa'lon and his cohorts.'

'Oh, don't be such a baby. Take your mind off it. Whip out your dataxe and do something useful with it. Tell us who we might come across once we clear the plain.'

The Grel unhooked the dataxe from the front of his suit and tapped away at it. It bleeped discreetly and he looked back at Bernice. 'We are now in the Arcarnate of Hedra, which controls the territories north of the Sultanate and beyond the Hut'eri homeland. The savannah belongs to them but has never been developed; they were nomadic and have maintained their ancestral lands despite their adoption of city culture. The plains are now apparently the home of a sport called freak-speeding, popular in your university, and at which you appear to be naturally adept.'

'Less of the sarcasm, Shemda, and more concentration on the salient facts: i.e. local religious beliefs.'

Shemda returned his gaze to the dataxe. 'Three sects, all aspects of the triple-god Anoouki, master of the plain. Belief states that Anoouki inhabits the plain by day, guarding his (or their) children, and then returns to the palace beneath the earth at sunset to revel with his faithful servants.'

'Beneath the earth again. I'm sure I'm missing something.

What's Anoouki like? Triple-headed, or some such?' Bernice turned and saw that Shemda had stopped to consult his dataxe more closely. She wandered back towards him.

'Anoouki represents the three paths of the Hedrai: warrior, farmer, and healer. Each is distinct and part of the whole. Each inhabits the savannah around us. Each is approximately forty centimetres tall.'

Bernice stared at the Grel and then began to laugh. 'Now that's the kind of god I wouldn't mind being chased by.'

James Harker saw Bernice laugh and then turn and head back through the grasslands. He put down the enhancers, stared for a moment at his bony, bloodstained hands, and then smiled at Maa'lon beside him.

'They're just where you said they would be, Lord. And they have left their transport.'

Maa'lon stood up in the back of the Grel landcruiser and swept the plains with His bright jade eyes. James wondered whether He could see that far from the mountains, and then caught himself.

'Indeed I can, James. You know I can do whatever I wish. Now, Demka, head down to the plain; we should keep an appointment I've arranged.' Maa'lon smiled at James and touched him on the shoulder. 'Don't worry yourself. You'll get used to me, James. All I want is your belief, and you do believe, don't you?'

Maa'lon cradled James's chin with one hand and looked deep into his eyes. The jade stones seemed to burn into him. The fatigue in his bones seemed to dissipate. 'Of course, Lord, with all my heart. I would do anything for you, you know that; you know my heart.' He struggled to open his heart to Maa'lon to let Him know how free he now felt; how sure he felt of his own destiny.

Maa'lon's answering smile filled him with a joy that made him light-headed. His heart almost burst. He was right. He had chosen the right path. He was a believer and he would serve the many aspects of Maa'lon and spread their creed.

In front of him, the former Grel Master started the engine,

and they headed swiftly down through the foothills. Behind them ran hundreds of Hut'eri, still stained with the holy blood of Maa'lon's crusade, but eyes bright and showing no fatigue. They swept downward, eager to meet their brothers and serve their lord. Behind them, lying still on the hillside, were the empty vessels of those who were not worthy: those whose faith had lacked the necessary strength.

Emile hid behind a pillar, wondering why he was bothering. In all this seething mass of desperate humanity, would anyone notice one podgy, pasty-faced young man? And if his prey did spot him, what could he do about it in front of all of these people? His mind was filled with an unwelcome image of gore, and unrecognizably mutilated bodies. He realized that, far from protecting him, his presence here might endanger those around him. Heart beating wildly, he remained in concealment behind the pillar, darting occasional terrified glances in the direction of his quarry, before pulling his head back into cover.

The man he was pursuing, the policeman from Tyler's Folly, had been remarkably easy to find. The words of the imp kept echoing through his mind: 'You're heading for an appointment you won't be able to miss.' It was as if he was meant to find the man, and the forces controlling his destiny hadn't let the improbability of tracking one person down in a crowded spaceport prevent him.

He had spotted the man almost as soon as he entered the building. The policeman hadn't been attempting to disguise himself; well, why should he? No one but Emile knew who he was, what he was responsible for. It occurred to Emile that perhaps he should have disseminated the information more widely than Bernice's data banks. But, under the Sultan's new regime, would the man's actions even be considered a crime? It was quite possible that he'd done what he'd done under the guidance of religious conviction. Emile had a sudden mental image of the Sultan presenting the murderer with a medal, for services in the furtherance of his faith.

So Emile couldn't tell anyone else. He could just follow

the man, and . . . He didn't know. At least following him had proven easy enough.

The policeman didn't appear to be going anywhere in particular. As far as Emile could tell, he hadn't booked a ticket aboard any of the departing shuttles, which was just as well, because Emile certainly couldn't afford the fare to follow him.

The man didn't buy a ticket. He didn't talk to anyone. He just stood there, calm in the middle of the chaos, watching the increasing hordes of people flooding into the spaceport, with a blank, almost bored expression on his face. His stillness was the most remarkable thing about him; in every other respect he was one of the most nondescript people Emile had ever seen. He didn't look capable of murder. He didn't look capable of the passions which would inspire it.

Then, suddenly, he wasn't there any more.

Panicked, Emile scrambled from behind the pillar, desperately scanning the multitude of faces in front of him. He almost didn't spot his quarry, but, this time, it was the man's speed which gave him away, flittering almost ghost-like towards one of the far doors.

Emile ran to follow, already panting by the time he had taken ten strides, the huge leather-bound volume of *The Grimoire of Atheron the Mage* clutched uncomfortably in the crook of his armpit. He was attracting lots of attention himself: intrigued stares from passers-by and grunts of annoyance from the people he had to shove out of his way. Flushing with embarrassment, he tucked his chin into his chest and jogged doggedly on.

It didn't do any good. He reached the door through which the man had been heading, but when he burst through it, into a maze of dingy brown service tunnels, there was no sign of him. He ran a little further, down one of the forking branches, then halted, realizing it was hopeless. If he wasn't careful, he'd just end up further away from his quarry.

Slowing to an exhausted hobble, he carefully headed back out of the door, then looked at the sign above it: MAINTENANCE AND POWER AREAS – STRICTLY NO ACCESS TO PUBLIC, in large yellow holo-script.

Emile frowned, trying to work out what the man could want there. He spotted a public information point, and used it to call up a map of the port, but the area the man had entered was represented as a blank mass covered by the words 'Danger, No Entry'. Here Be Dragons, Emile thought.

Think, he told himself. The man had been waiting for something. He'd been watching the crowd, waiting for . . . whoever. And then he'd seen them, and he'd gone into the Maintenance area to . . . do whatever.

Great, he thought bitterly. Well done, Emile. Go to the head of the class.

The man was a killer. Who could he have been waiting for as he stood, watching more and more people rush into the already overcrowded spaceport, looking like they might soon reach some terrible critical mass, then –

Oh God, Emile thought, that was it.

The man wasn't waiting for anyone. He was waiting for everyone. Waiting until there were enough people to make whatever he was planning to do in the Maintenance Section worth doing.

The man was a murderer. It didn't take much imagination to work out what he was planning to do again.

Bernice had wanted to stop for a rest before Shemda had pointed out the N'a'm'thuli behind them. They must have been running continuously for hours, and sprinting. She had to admire their stamina, but chose to do so at a distance. She broke into a run, once more trying to keep pace with the Grel. She could hear the drums again and wondered who had the time or the energy to run and drum at the same time: clearly not her.

She cleared her mind and ran faster, briefly overtaking Shemda as she did so. They had to move fast, couldn't stop. She wondered how long she would last for. An hour? Minutes? She knew they would catch her, that they would be overrun. Then it would all end rather unpleasantly in the middle of an enormous field on a not particularly important planet.

Just as she was about to look once more at their pursuers, the grass before them erupted into life. Hundreds of dark-skinned, reptilian humanoids, all mounted on short, stunted pony-like creatures, blocked their way. Their skin was dark, green, and leathery, and their eyes were yellow and black vertical slits. They seemed to have no noses, just small, horned, beak-like mouths. All of them wore simple overlapping armour made of dried animal hide, and none of them said a word.

Bernice and Shemda stopped running.

Without conscious thought, Emile's feet had taken him to the security desk.

'Everyone out,' he gabbled breathlessly. 'You have to. Everyone must leave.' The official, whose lapel badge identified him as Officer Colin Hay, stared at him blankly. 'Now,' Emile finished desperately.

'You'll have to slow down, son,' Officer Hay said, his voice not unkindly, but with an edge of impatience to it. 'Whatever it is can't be more urgent than breathing.' The officer beside him snickered.

Emile stared at him, unable to comprehend how he couldn't feel the same desperate sense of urgency that Emile did. 'You have to evacuate the port,' he said, forcing himself to speak more carefully. It felt like the slow-motion running in nightmares, when the menace is right behind you, and you know it's about to catch you.

The officers were still regarding him with polite scepticism.

'There's terrible danger,' Emile said forcefully. 'I think someone's about to blow up the building.' It was only as he said it that he realized that this probably was the policeman's plan. His heart rate sped up still further.

But the officers continued to regard him with infuriating unconcern. Officer Hay smiled. 'Nice try, son,' he said. 'You're the fourth one we've had today.'

'What?' Emile shouted. He felt a sudden urge to do to this man some of the things the Tyleran policeman had done to his victims.

'Oh, I understand,' Hay carried on obliviously. 'I don't like these infidels being allowed to leave any more than you do. But the Sultan's soft, he's given them all exit visas; we have to let them go.'

'I'm not . . . I don't . . .' Emile spluttered.

Officer Hay laid a fraternal hand on his shoulder. Emile could feel its clamminess through the material of his shirt. Hay leant in towards him, his breath moist in Emile's ear. 'It's your religion telling you to do these things, to keep them here,' he said, more excitement in his voice now. 'I know. I've felt the call, too. But you have to be discreet. You have to be clever.'

Emile pulled back and stared into his eyes. Officer Hay was never going to help him, he realized. No one was.

He felt as if he might actually seize up with fear. If they could all feel what he felt, he thought. If he could only make them feel his fear, then there'd be no question of their staying around like passive sacrificial victims to face their deaths.

Make them feel what you feel, a quiet, sensible voice in his head suddenly said. Spells of projection of emotion, pages 123 to 130.

Emile dropped to the floor, pulling the grimoire from under his arm and opening it before him. The tide of people parted reluctantly around him, tut-tutting away.

Desperately, he flicked through to page 123. 'Engendering those feelings of love that you yourself feel'. He groaned, and flicked forward again. And there it was: 'The spell of any projection of emotion felt by the caster, a thousandfold, upon those around him'.

Emile laughed hysterically. It was too good to be true. Then he looked at the section that listed the requirements of the spell. 'No materials being required outside of the human mind,' it said. Emile smiled. 'The mind of the caster, and the mind of one both strong and centred, through whom the emotions may be projected.'

His smile was beginning to fade when Irving Braxiatel tripped over him.

* * *

Braxiatel landed, sprawled forward on to his hands. He heard more than one of the academics in his party tittering. He rose and spun around to glare at them, then focused the full force of his annoyance on the person who had caused him to take his undignified tumble.

It was one of Bernice's students: Emile. Who was already on his feet, oblivious to Braxiatel's displeasure, moving forward to, unbelievably, clasp the sharply ironed lapels of Braxiatel's grey suit between his chubby hands.

Emile's face was slicked with sweat. It was trickling in runnels over his chin and through his mousy-brown hair. He was, Braxiatel realized, absolutely terrified.

'What's wrong, Emile?' he said softly.

The young man's face crumpled, and he sank downward, as if he'd suddenly been deflated. Braxiatel was alarmed to see that tears had begun to accompany the sweat tracking down his face.

'Someone is going to blow up the port,' Emile said, a hysterical note edging into his voice. 'No one will believe me, but they are. And I've got, I've got a spell that can get everyone out, but I need your help, Professor Braxiatel. I need your help.'

For the first time, Braxiatel noticed the strangely anachronistic leather-bound volume at the student's feet. 'How do you –' He broke off, and studied the young man's pale, panicked face. 'It doesn't matter,' he said. 'Damn it! Our only way off the planet!'

He turned to Dr Jalal. 'Get everyone out,' he said. 'Now.'

For a moment, it looked as if Jalal might argue with him. But then the little Pakhar bustled round and began herding his fellow academics in the direction from which they'd come.

Emile sagged to his knees in relief.

'A spell?' Braxiatel asked him.

The young man turned his face up towards him. Braxiatel couldn't help noticing the premature lines of tension which had been etched into it. He wondered if his own face was beginning to look that way, too.

'The security people won't evacuate. They don't believe me,' Emile said. 'I don't think they'll believe anyone. But I've got this spell: I can project my own fear. I can make people leave because they are so afraid. But I need another mind to project through. Your mind.'

Braxiatel nodded. 'And you're quite sure this will work,' he said neutrally, not quite a question.

Emile looked at him and, for a strange moment, Braxiatel felt like the child being studied by a member of an infinitely more ancient race. 'I think it will work if you believe it will,' Emile said. 'Do you believe?'

The Sultan made people join a religion, Braxiatel thought, but he didn't care which one. 'I can't tell you, because you might believe me,' John had told him.

With horror, Braxiatel realized that he knew the answer to the question. 'I do,' he said. 'I do believe.'

Bernice wondered why their pursuers stayed silent. They'd been caught, headed off at the pass. The N'a'm'thuli were closing in behind, and the Hedrai formed a barrier in front. There was nowhere to go. And somewhere else, she knew, was Maa'lon, waiting for her. Smiling the smile that had greeted the deaths of thousands. Panic rose within her.

'Bernice.' The Grel tapped her on the shoulder. She nearly jumped out of her skin. 'Look down there.'

Shemda was pointing to the ground in front of the most impressively armoured nomad. She looked down and saw movement. The grasses moved independently of the wind. The nearby ponies snorted nervously and shifted their feet. She saw a tiny spear rise up and disappear. Then the grasses began to glow.

Three distinct patches of light, deep red, blue, and a sickly green, appeared before them. At their heart, rising up supported by the lights, were what could only be Anoouki. The tiny figures took their colour from the lights around them. Each was identical physically. A thin, almost wasted, body supported a comparatively large head with no features save two bright yellow eyes. The eyes had no pupils; they were merely burning orbs, circles of light.

Each of the figures held a long, thin pole, subtly distinguished. On the right it was tipped with an arrow-head, in the centre a bell, and on the right the pole formed a sickle.

'Warrior; healer; farmer,' said Bernice in a hushed whisper.

'Indeed, Professor.' They spoke as one, the harmonics of their voices creating a depth that belied their size. They seemed now to be standing on the very tops of the grasses that made up the savannah. 'You come to Us in Our place. You allow Us to delight in your misfortune. The Hedrai have reclaimed the plains and they have brought you to Us, that We may continue the game begun by Our brothers. They will be here soon. They are anxious to be in your company once more. But they will not mind what condition they find you in, as long as you still have your eyes and breath in your bodies.'

The lights around them became more intense. Bernice could feel her breath shortening, her heart beating faster. Heat began to rise around her feet. She looked quickly along the line of the Hedrai: all had their narrow eyes cast down. None returned her gaze.

She smelt smoke, then let out a small scream as a flame licked at her bare feet. She jumped. Anoouki laughed a sing-song laugh, blazing eyes boring into her. Bernice hopped from foot to foot, and suddenly wondered how anyone could walk across hot coals. Or want to.

The heat rose; she could feel her feet starting to blister. Then, in one swift movement, Anoouki were knocked high into the air as the dataxe connected, and Bernice was jerked to her left. They were running again.

As Bernice and Shemda ran, the Hedrai held their position. Unmoved, eyes cast low. Benny, despite the need for speed, couldn't help looking at their sunken cheeks and grim expressions. The silence was truly unnerving. No one spoke or moved. The only sound was the distant harmonic shouting of Anoouki.

'I can't believe you did that,' she gasped in the direction of the Grel's back. 'I mean, it was so low-tech.'

'Bernice, there are certain things it crosses your mind to try, and which you will always regret not attempting.' She could hear the smile in his laboured speech. Even he was getting tired.

'Triple-god home run. Definitely one for the grandchildren.' With that she decided to shut up and concentrate on her running. Once more the N'a'm'thuli drums could be heard, getting louder as usual.

The Hedrai never sought to interrupt their progress. New mounted figures appeared constantly before them, shepherding them along the line. Directing them south along their ranks. Towards something.

The N'a'm'thuli arrived from the east and mimicked the nomads before them; they too formed a line. Soon Bernice and the Grel were running along a silent corridor; each side's eyes cast down, weapons held at ease. An honour guard for her terror.

Benny knew she should stop running, that she should call a halt to it all. Stop Shemda wasting his energy. They were caught. She knew where they were heading, who they were heading towards. But her terror drove her on. Fear kept rising and rising within her. Her breath grew shorter; she wanted to scream, had to scream. And then she stopped, and collapsed to her knees.

'Shemda,' she called to the fast-disappearing figure, 'stop.'

The Grel came to a halt and turned. He looked about himself nervously, but the N'a'm'thuli and Hedrai remained immobile. He started to walk back slowly, uncertainly, towards her, constantly looking at the assembled troops on either side. When he got to her, she could see the terror in his eyes too, and she knew she was right.

Bernice looked up at Shemda and smiled. She drew him down to the ground with her. Gently she cradled his head in her hands. His tentacles clung to her forearms, desperate; his wild eyes looked deep into hers. She smiled once more.

'Let go of the fear, Shemda. It's not yours; it's theirs.' She nodded across to the Hedrai and then back towards the

N'a'm'thuli. Shemda looked about him, and then closed his eyes. He gave a deep sigh and sank into Benny's embrace.

For some reason, Emile had imagined that he'd be immune from the effects of his own spell. But the fear which gripped him was almost suffocating in its intensity, like a great tidal wave trying to wash him out of the spaceport and as far as he could run. Braxiatel, he could see, was allowing himself to be carried by the tide, although his face showed only its usual slightly disdainful calm. Even as the stampede of panicked people dragged him away from Emile, he could see that Braxiatel was trying to control the exodus, to prevent people being crushed to death in the mad rush.

Emile alone wasn't going with the flow. He was fighting his way step by painful step towards the Maintenance area where he had last seen his quarry, fighting against his own fear as well as the physical obstruction of the people heading in the other direction.

He wasn't quite sure why he was going, except perhaps what Braxiatel had said about this being the only way off the planet. He had to try to stop it.

Eventually, he battled his way clear of the fleeing people. Remarkably, he had emerged very near his target. He pushed through the door, and found himself confronted by the same dingy, tangled mess of corridors.

Without pausing, he ran down one of them, suddenly quite sure that it was the right one. At each junction, he turned unerringly left or right, not pausing to wonder what was guiding him, just knowing that his prey was near.

And there he was, standing by one of the power generators, a great golden lump of metal. He was smiling. A smaller lump hung beside him. Its surface contained a little red LED which, as Emile watched, ticked down from 1:00 to 0:59.

There wasn't enough time left: he knew that instantly.

'I've been expecting you,' the man said.

Emile wasn't capable of feeling any more fear. Instead, he

felt a cold creeping horror consume him. 'Worried about dying alone?' he managed to croak. 'Everyone's escaped, you know,' he added, wanting this small victory at least.

The man shrugged. 'A shame. But now they're trapped here, my brethren will convert them eventually. It's inevitable.'

The LED clicked down to 0:35.

Emile couldn't tear his eyes away from it. He'd always imagined his death would be something he would be given a chance to come to terms with. Not like this. Not so, so fucking *unplanned*.

The man looked at the LED too. 'Twenty-five seconds,' he said. 'You made a bargain. Do you want to keep it?'

And Emile realized that he was being given one final chance to get out of the deal he had made with the imp. An escape from the price he had agreed to pay. He swallowed dryly. The price of escape was high, too.

The man seemed to sense his wavering. He smiled blandly. 'Do you really believe your soul will survive your death, anyway?' He glanced at the bomb. 'Fifteen seconds to decide.'

Emile switched his gaze from the little, ticking LED to the man's hollow eyes.

'All you have to do is believe,' the man said. 'Do you believe?'

The LED clicked down to 0:01.

Emile decided to keep his bargain.

Braxiatel didn't see the beginning of the explosion. He was standing with his back to the spaceport, still trying to herd the panicked hordes into some kind of order. He experienced it first as light, then sound, and soon afterwards force, driving him and those around him to their knees.

Only when it was over could he turn to regard the sooty husk of their only escape route from the planet. He was ashamed that this was his first thought. Emile was only his second. His shoulders slumped, and he buried his face in his hands. I've failed, he thought. I'm not in control any more. And I'm very much afraid that I've realized what is.

* * *

After a while, the silence of the troops on either side had ceased to unnerve them and they settled down to chat. Bernice had made it clear that, from now on, if someone, something, or some god wanted to talk to her, they would have to make the effort themselves; she was going nowhere.

'So they appeared as gods, have godlike abilities, and seemed to be winning the "who's got the most on their side" competition. But what are they?' Benny knew the question had been running through both of their minds for days, but she wanted the calming influence of the obvious. 'They can play with our own emotions, or implant different ones within us.'

Shemda sat cross-legged and toyed with his dataxe; he was clearly trying to lose himself in the pursuit of knowledge. 'The logical position, based on the facts, is that we appear to be living in a time of gods. That what we have seen is true. In each area we have travelled to, we have been confronted by the local deity. Each has conformed exactly with either religious texts or folklore. Each has been exactly what we would expect. Logical, but prosaic.'

Bernice looked up sharply at this last word. Something about it struck her. She knew Shemda had hit on something. 'Prosaic.' She let the word roll around her mind, allowed it to bounce off anything else that might be there. Then she had it. 'Time to run naked through the market-place, Shemda. I think I know which way to look at this.'

The Grel looked at her rather curiously, but by now knew when not to speak.

'You said it yourself. We have found exactly what we would expect to find. Text and folklore are true; and one thing that academia has taught me is that that can only mean one thing: it's bollocks. I feel a bit of a fuckwit actually: it has been staring us in the face for so long. It's so *prosaic*. Nothing can be that literal; time and bullshit combine to create a hybrid of nonsense, often contradictory, that sits around the kernel of truth. This is the opposite. Nonsense has coalesced into truth, and that is extremely silly.'

Shemda nodded as she spoke and then returned his gaze to

the dataxe. 'In which case, Bernice, we still need to know what they are. That must remain our primary concern. And we appear to have no idea.'

'You're right, Shemda. We need to work on that. But try to stay a bit more upbeat. We appear to have a bit of time on our hands for the moment, so let's think. We have a veritable surfeit of deities, all so far native Dellahan. Now what were the common links between all the indigenous faiths?'

'As I said before, Bernice: they were all propagated in a remarkably narrow historical window; they are all anthropomorphic or animal-spirit driven; and they all believe paradise lies beneath our feet.' Shemda continued to toy with the dataxe.

'Now, the key must lie in there somewhere. The timing could be coincidental, possibly affected by political or economic up-heaval. The styling of the gods is roughly in line with broad societal trends. It's the paradise thing that's really odd: too uniform. Some of them should look to the skies at least. Instead they all look down, within Dellah. Inside the planet itself.' With an almost jarring sound within her, it all clicked into place. 'Oh, my god,' she whispered, 'Tyler's Folly.'

'To which of us would you be referring, Bernice?' She looked up, and there before her stood Maa'lon, flanked by the crimson-clad god of the N'a'm'thuli and Anoouki, who were all staring straight at the rather startled Shemda.

10

PERFECT VICTIMS

Bernice refused to get up. She was knackered anyway, and it seemed sensible to stay comfy on the ground and let Maa'lon have his moment.

'You've led us a merry dance, Bernice. I should thank you for providing my brothers with most singular entertainment. Unfortunately, you have also shown considerable disrespect, greatly offending our children. You seem determined to deny the obvious, and it pains me that this leaves me no choice. The loss of a soul is beyond your understanding, but at such times it can be the only option. You have denied me. You set yourself above my children. And they are not happy about that.'

Bernice looked at the predominantly Hut'eri forces gathered behind Maa'lon. Most were bloodstained, all looked gaunt and shattered, but the gaze of each was unwavering. All their bright eyes stared straight back at her. She could see their hatred and contempt. Each breathed heavily, drawing air into a chest that seemed somehow hollow; obvious ribs rose and fell. They had pursued her without thought for their condition and now they wished to punish her. Bile rose in her throat.

'One of my children, Bernice, was especially distressed by your actions. His disappointment has closely mirrored my own. He begged me to deal with you, and you know I can deny my children so little. They are everything to me, so I have granted him his wish. I am sure you will appreciate the care he will go to to please the rest of my children. His devotion, in a way, honours you.' With that Maa'lon stepped aside, and James Harker, gaunt and pale beneath his purple robes, approached her, carrying a shiny ceremonial gl'ai.

Clarence flew towards the sun. He was tired of playing games. Or, rather, he was tired of playing a game to which he didn't know the rules with someone who'd learnt them millennia before he was born.

He was going to confront God. Demand some straight answers. The computer knew they'd been in its mind. He suspected God knew an awful lot more about what he and the *B-Aaron* had been up to than he was letting on. He'd probably only let them think they were getting away with spying on him, Clarence thought angrily, to spare their feelings. That would be absolutely bloody typical.

Well, enough. Clarence wasn't going to be led around by the nose any more. He was going to the source.

Of course, he knew that God didn't live in the sun. But it seemed somehow symbolically right. And he knew God would stop him before he got close enough to hurt himself. And, if God didn't, who the hell was there to care?

Soon the heat began to singe even the super-strengthened feathers of his wings. His eyes, dazzled by a light brighter than they were ever meant to see, watered in pain. He closed them, but the ghost image of the sun persisted, a perfect yellow circle in his mind.

After a while, the sensations in his body became so extreme that a trip-switch in his nerve-circuits cut them out altogether. He felt like he was floating in nothingness, not even sure that he was moving forward any more. He realized that God was actually going to let him die. Oh well. Only the yellow sphere behind his eyelids remained to mock him.

The yellow sphere now appeared to have developed two black-dot eyes and a wide, downturned mouth. 'What in the world do you think you're doing?' it asked.

Clarence's eyes snapped open, but the sphere remained, frowning gently at him. He realized that the pain wasn't being blanked out; it was gone. He was floating much nearer to the surface of the Worldsphere, God's bright yellow drone floating beside him.

'I want to know what's going on,' Clarence told the drone. 'I want to know . . . everything.'

God chuckled warmly. 'Don't we all?' It circled round him, gradually spiralling downward towards the world's surface. 'I'm sorry. I should have realized you'd be worried about Bernice.'

Clarence felt a strange prickling behind his eyes, and realized with shock that he was about to cry. Had that really been all this was about? 'Yes,' he whispered. 'I want to know if she's going to be OK.'

The yellow drone looked sympathetic. 'I can't lie to you,' God said. 'My calculations show her current chances of survival are negligible.' The drone's cartoon face brightened. 'But I still have the mental simulacrum of her, if you feel in need of a chat now and again.'

An intense jolt of fury shot through Clarence. He realized he had lunged for the drone, which nimbly darted out of the way, an expression of puzzlement on its face. They were almost at the world's surface now; they'd make their landing in a field of grass and daisies.

'That's not . . .' Clarence blazed. 'How could you?'

The drone frowned, as if God really didn't understand. 'It's indistinguishable from the real thing,' it said apologetically.

Clarence sighed, and settled lightly on his toes in the grass. 'I don't just love her for her mind,' he told God.

At last she lay before him, ready to make amends for her crimes. For her disloyalty. James Harker looked down on her and could see the emptiness within her; her eyes knew not the love of her god. He pitied her, but he knew there was only one thing he could do for her. She was lost: it was for him to end her misery.

'You can't see it, can you, Bernice? You are untouched by it. You will never know the joys and certainty of our Lord's love. You have no place for the Lord. Do you not see yourself as incomplete? Do you not wish for His love?' He walked over to the abomination and looked down into her eyes. 'Do you not wish to believe?'

Bernice shuffled uncomfortably, unused to the look of the righteous. She tried to move away but he held her gently around the neck. The beast beside her sought to come to her aid, but the professor wisely stayed its hand. She knew all their efforts were now in vain. Only faith could save her now, and that was beyond her; or was it? He looked once more into her eyes and thought he caught a glimpse of certainty, of belief. Even such an abomination could perhaps be saved; nothing was beyond Maa'lon.

He looked back to his Lord, and he saw agreement in His eyes. There was a chance, a hope. And he had the honour of the attempt. Maa'lon had allowed him to try to save a soul.

He touched her cheek gently with the blade of the gl'ai, drawing only a little blood. Sharpening her mind and senses to the choice before her.

'What do you believe, Bernice?' he said quietly into her ear.

Bernice couldn't believe the change in James. His casual smile was gone; his mouth was now bent in a rictus of joy. His eyes were glazed, his dilated pupils making them almost black. Sweat glistened on his pale cheeks and rolled down the dark hollows that had recently appeared. He must have lost ten or twenty kilos. He looked like an animated husk swathed in purple and brandishing the lethal gl'ai.

'What do you believe, Professor?' When the question came again, she still had no idea how to answer. She felt struck dumb by the appalling sight before her, by James's transformation. She tried not to think of the blood running down her cheek.

'We all need to believe, Benny.' His voice was deeper, warmer now. 'Without my faith I would be nothing. It makes me whole. It gives me purpose. We all need that purpose. You're no different to the rest of us. We are blessed. Maa'lon is here among us, in all His aspects. He has given you a chance to divine your own purpose, and to realize it is His.'

Benny stumbled backwards, anxious to be out of the reverend's reach.

'There's a god-shaped hole within each of us, Benny. He put it there. It is His place, the place where we can all welcome Him. Without Him, we would be empty. In the way you are empty now. You're searching in the wrong place; the answers are all within you. You just have to allow yourself to see them, open yourself to them. Without those answers you are nothing, less than nothing.'

He touched her face with the gl'ai again. The cold metal caressed her hot cheek. Her heart beat faster still.

'You've seen what I have seen, what we all have seen. It's time to make that leap. It's not even a leap of faith any more: you have proof. You have seen Him before you. You know what He can do for us all when we follow Him.'

He was so close to her now, his thin frame doubled over, that she felt his breath on her face, and turned away. He grabbed her head once more and turned it back towards him. His eyes shone with zeal. His breath stank.

'You know you want to believe, Benny. Open yourself to the place within. Let the worries ebb away; usher in a time of certainty. It's what you want.'

Benny knew she had to say something, wanted to say something.

'I'm one of the lucky ones, Benny. I have been blessed by Maa'lon. He is love within us all. Look upon Him. You can be blessed too; His love is without measure and embraces all.'

Bernice looked beyond him at the smiling face of Maa'lon, his god. The tall Hut'eri still seemed to radiate innocence from his piercing jade eyes; his arms were spread wide in a gesture of welcome and love. She knew it would be so easy to agree. To embrace Maa'lon and get James out of her face. She knew what she had to say.

'What about his love for the thousands that died on the plains, for those that fought in a pointless bloodbath that only

199

seemed to give Him pleasure?' She held her head defiantly high and met the jade gaze.

James's grip on her head tightened; the gl'ai came nearer. Bernice was waiting for the fatal stroke, stretching her senses to feel the cold metal. The reverend turned to his god.

Maa'lon no longer smiled at her. His beautiful face was now set in a pained frown.

'James, my child, bring the professor to me, that I might end the distress in her heart.' With that, she was dragged to her feet – James showing surprising strength considering his emaciated condition – and brought before the god of the Hut'eri.

Renée read her orders. Then she read them again. Then she smiled. She was going to take a certain perverse satisfaction in seeing these through, she realized.

'Men!' she shouted. 'And, well, all the rest of you.'

Over four hundred pairs of eyes looked up at her. All of them belonging to bona fide members of the Church of the Grey. Renée wondered for a moment if the history books would remember her as the great saviour of her faith, just at the point of its extinction. She knew that many of her troops were incorporating her own words into their personal *Books of the Grey*. It made her feel like a terrible fraud, but it was undeniably flattering.

'I've got a job for us,' she said.

Her troops groaned theatrically. The adjutant who'd delivered the general's orders glared at them disapprovingly, but Renée hadn't been one for enforcing discipline in her unit. Or at least not that sort of discipline.

'Some of the infidels who've refused to embrace any religion are attempting to flee the planet,' she said, enjoying rolling the word 'infidel' around on her tongue.

Her words were greeted by silence. Her troops – who, frankly, weren't the most wholehearted believers themselves – weren't quite sure what to make of this. She suspected that quite a few felt 'infidel' might equally well apply to them.

It didn't matter. Orders were orders, and she'd ensured that their life in the army wasn't so grim that they were willing to risk the consequences of disobeying them. 'Well,' she told the soldiers, 'we're going to see that the filthy disbelievers don't get away with it!' The adjutant smiled approvingly. The troops let out a feeble cheer. 'We're going to round them up, slay their godless leader, a man known as Irving Braxiatel, and convert the rest by the sword. Or, more accurately, the standard-issue laser-rifle.'

For the first time, she realized she was actually looking forward to carrying out one of her duties. It certainly beat digging latrine pits. She couldn't wait to see Braxiatel's face when she arrested him. Couldn't wait to see that expressionless façade finally crack.

'One final thing,' the adjutant said to her softly.

She quirked an enquiring eyebrow.

'I didn't want to share this with the troops, didn't want to get them too excited, but I think you'll find there's a bit of a treat in store for you.'

Renée's mind was suddenly filled with a very vivid image of a boudoir full of rich food and naked young men. 'Oh yes?' she said blandly.

The adjutant grinned, displaying the sickly pink of his gums. 'The Sultan has received a message from your god.' He looked at her expectantly, and she pasted a suitably overjoyed expression on to her face. 'He is pleased with your work,' the adjutant continued, 'and he wishes to reward you. The Sultan has asked me to promise you that, when your task is completed, your god will come to you. After six hundred years of waiting, the Grey will finally show Itself.'

Renée very carefully maintained the same expression of rapt pleasure.

Shemda tried to control himself. He knew the professor, Bernice, didn't want him to interfere. It had taken all his willpower not to deal with that diseased reverend. He had seemed weak-minded before they set out to find his god, but now his reason seemed to have completely collapsed, along with his body.

The way Harker had touched Bernice with a weapon made his blood boil; he wanted to hoot with rage and teach him a simple and final lesson with his dataxe. But he had to control himself, allow the facts to become clear before him and Bernice. He knew she had started to understand the madness that surrounded them.

He looked along the assembled gods: Maa'lon smiling once more and looking down on Bernice; the nameless crimson cadaver also grinning; and the silent, ridiculous figures of Anoouki glowing in front of their people. This couldn't be right. Bernice had known all along it wasn't right.

'You disappoint me, Bernice. You have such potential, such belief.' Maa'lon's words snapped Shemda's eyes back from Anoouki. 'Such a believer with nothing to believe. A waste. I dislike waste, as do my brothers.' He gestured to the other gods and they all nodded back to Him. 'But sometimes waste is inevitable, Bernice. Sometimes it is necessary. I must think of the greater good. Therefore your contamination cannot be allowed to spread. I hate to carry out such tasks myself, but fortunately James is perfectly happy to perform the surgery.'

The reverend advanced on Bernice, holding the lethal gl'ai out before him.

'No!' Shemda only realized he had spoken when everyone turned round to look at him.

Bernice snapped round when she heard the strength in the Grel's voice. Shemda was staring at her. He held his dataxe before him, aiming it at Maa'lon. Despite the weapon, the dark patch over his eye made him look vulnerable, and his hands seemed to be shaking. She knew he wanted to help, and she was certain he knew this wouldn't.

'Ah, Shemda. It's always the quiet ones, isn't it?' Bernice could hear the sneer in Maa'lon's voice. 'I'm afraid you won't be able to save the professor: I won't allow you. Indeed, you won't allow yourself.'

Shemda grew even more uncertain. He tightened his grip on the dataxe.

'You see, I know you, my child; I know your people, what they want. Demka here wanted to believe, just as you do. You have to believe, Shemda. I can feel it within you. Your race above all has to believe in me, and my brothers, because we offer you proof.'

As Maa'lon spoke, Bernice turned and saw Demka emerge from the bloodstained crowd. He looked older; his skin was more leathery, hanging off his huge frame in loose folds. But there was fire in his eyes, and he held two N'a'm'thuli barbs in place of his dataxe. His tentacles folded back to reveal rather vicious yellow teeth.

'Shemda,' the Grel Master said quietly, 'don't disappoint me. Everything we have done, everything we have searched for has been leading towards this. We have found the ultimate fact. The truth at the heart of all knowledge. You were always an intelligent servitor; your queries and suppositions sharper than those of others. Grenke was unable to understand, to see the truth in his belief. He believed, but he didn't trust in that belief as I do, as you can do. Maa'lon can forgive as well as punish.'

Bernice, no longer the centre of attention, got to her feet. Beside her, James was watching the interplay between the Grel and had lowered the gl'ai. No one moved.

Shemda looked at the Grel Master and then down to his dataxe. The tentacles at his mouth fluttered gently. He took a deep breath. When he looked up once more he seemed more sure of himself. He stared straight at Maa'lon.

'I will not believe in you.'

Maa'lon chuckled quietly, and then whispered, 'Go to him, my brother, and let him feel our final embrace.'

With that, the crimson-clad god of the N'a'm'thuli advanced on Shemda. The Grel tried to raise his dataxe, but his arms appeared to be locked. He struggled vainly.

The thin, pale arms came up to his cheeks.

'Go on, my brother, admonish this wayward child.' Maa'lon's voice had real steel in it. Bernice wanted to turn to him, to scream at him, deny him, but she couldn't turn away from Shemda.

She knew what was going to happen. The tentacles at his mouth began to fold back, lying pale and flush against his face. Then they stopped. Time passed in silence.

'I can feel your belief. You know what I can do. Accept it. The flesh will fall away.' The deep, breathy voice of the nameless god carried easily. Bernice shuddered.

'Your belief will set you free, Shemda. Embrace it,' urged Maa'lon.

'No,' gasped the Grel in response. Bernice could see that there was terrible stress beneath the god's touch. She started to go to him, but at that moment James drew the gl'ai along her back, reminding her of her own situation. She froze.

'This won't take long, Bernice. Maa'lon can feel his belief. It will soon be your turn again.' She could hear the anticipated pleasure in the reverend's voice.

More time passed, the only discernible movement Shemda's slight tremble. Demka broke the silence.

'Query: what do you believe?'

Shemda turned with difficulty to look straight at Bernice. She saw the pain in his eyes. 'I believe in her.'

Bernice didn't know whether to laugh or cry.

James had seen enough. The abominations had to die. Their defiance was an affront to Maa'lon. He looked to his Lord and received a nod in reply. The Grel first.

He walked across to Maa'lon's brother and the beast, still locked together. He touched a scarlet shoulder and the god moved aside, back to Maa'lon and away from the contamination.

The Grel drew its tentacles back around its mouth and turned to him. James drew the gl'ai back and prepared to dispatch the beast; it wouldn't have time to bring its own impure weapon to bear. He would be swift, which was more than the beast deserved, parading its own twisted beliefs before the Lord.

'Just one question before you do anything terminal, James. And this one is going to Maa'lon, Saviour of the Hut'eri and

Shower of the Way. I was wondering, been to any nice prisons recently?'

The professor just couldn't keep her prattling mouth shut.

Shemda only caught the end of Bernice's question. He was more concerned with the imminent arrival of the blade the reverend carried. But Harker stayed his arm and looked back to Maa'lon. The Grel took the opportunity to turn round too.

Maa'lon looked angry. His large green eyes were fixed on Bernice who stood gloriously defiant before him. He could see no fear in her, and he knew he was right to feel as he did.

The tall Hut'eri god struck her across the face and she fell to ground clutching her cheek.

'Touched a nerve, eh?' said Bernice, as she scrambled back to her feet.

Maa'lon struck her again. This time much harder: the loud slap of the blow carried across the assembled throng. Bernice didn't get up.

'You may think you know us, Bernice. You may think you're terribly clever. But I'm afraid it won't help you when you're terribly dead.'

Maa'lon nodded to Demka, who advanced on Bernice with his barbs. Knowing exactly what was about to happen, Shemda turned back to the reverend and saw him raise the blade once more.

11

WE MEET AGAIN

'I'm terribly sorry to interrupt all this, but I'm afraid I can't allow you to kill these two.'

Bernice wondered if she had misheard something, or if the blow had given her a concussion. She looked up.

There, standing casually before the assembled gods and Followers, hat in hand, was the man from the bar. He brought a cigarette to his lips, inhaled deeply, turned to her and smiled. She smiled back, then instantly regretted the effect it had on her loosened teeth.

Everyone was waiting for someone to say something. No one moved. Bernice suddenly realized the Grel Master was towering over her, holding his N'a'm'thuli barbs out before him. Motionless.

Maa'lon turned to the man in beige. He received a broad, yellow smile.

'John, isn't it?' he asked politely, apparently eager to be as genteel as the recent arrival.

'Apparently so. Indeed. So they say.' He took another deep drag on the cigarette.

The two continued to size each other up. The man from the bar, apparently John, came over to her and helped her to her feet. He offered her a cigarette with a yellowed smile and chuckled at her polite refusal. He made a more general offer, but none of the crowd saw the need for a smoke.

'What exactly were you planning to do to prevent

whatever we may have planned for Ms Summerfield and Servitor Shemda?' Maa'lon's smile had returned to his lips, as had the assurance in his speech.

'Oh, you know, stuff.' John put the hat back on his head and began rummaging through the pockets of his coat.

'Stuff?' The deep voice of the god in red seemed ill-suited to the word.

'Yes, you know, stuff. A little bit of this, a little bit of that. All essentially stuff.'

Bernice began to hope he was being deliberately surreal; otherwise, her situation had improved little since his arrival.

'Or, more accurately, knowledge. You see, I know what you are, who you are, and I don't fear you.'

Shemda was fascinated by the unusual human's behaviour, and by the reactions of Maa'lon and the other gods. They just stared at him, and seemed to visibly start when he came close. The tall figure in red didn't even do anything when a large cloud of the smoky vapour that he was producing was blown into his face. They were scared of the newcomer.

The Grel saw that the reverend had stayed his hand, and was equally fascinated by the man's behaviour, so he walked over to Bernice and gently laid a hand on her shoulder. She turned to face him, her smile quickly turning to a wince. Two large bruises, one just beneath her right eye, the other along her jaw line, ripened on a face that was pale beneath her tan. A tiny amount of blood escaped from the corner of her mouth.

She gave a gesture which he assumed meant she was fine, and turned back to the centre of attention.

'Indeed, knowledge. Knowledge of this planet, what makes it so unique. Of the provisions made for it in the most secret codicils of a treaty which itself was meant to be secret. A planet with a secret at its very core, if you will.' The man chuckled to himself, obviously finding his own words humorous.

'So you know who we are. Why we are here. What we are. You are indeed the man with all the information, John.' Maa'lon seemed to have regained His earlier poise and now appeared to be simply curious. 'In what way would this

207

information serve your purpose in coming here. Much as I am impressed by a man of knowledge, I do not fear him. Nor do my brothers.'

The triple god Anoouki nodded enthusiastically, and the tall red-clad figure inclined his head slowly, a smile creeping across his slim lips.

'But that's what it's all about, isn't it, Maa'lon? Fear. Fear as a route to belief and belief as a route to fear. The game you play. What you need. The nub of your gist, you might say. Though I don't know why you would: sometimes these things just happen.'

Shemda began to worry that, despite his good intentions, the man that had apparently come to save them was clearly a babbling maniac.

Bernice now knew she'd been right. She'd guessed correctly. It all fell into place: the People's withdrawal, Braxiatel's worries about his own people, Clarence's caginess. And the Dellahan religious obsession with the planet beneath their feet. Or with the People beneath their feet.

It explained God's interest in an academic backwater in a proscribed galaxy. You didn't need a brain the size of a planet to work that one out. She'd thought he was just curious about her, or liked her, when in fact she was just an excuse to keep an eye out. The strategic equivalent of a conversational gambit.

If she ever got out of this, she'd wipe the smile off his ikon.

The man from the bar continued to smoke, and be irreverent before the Lord. James felt the blood boil within his sinewy limbs, waiting for the word that he could halt his prattle.

'You see, you need people to fear you. God-fearing's probably a popular phrase round your way. You get off on it. Need it. And without it you are nothing. You can't touch those that won't believe. Well, from within that is. I'm sure your low-tech hordes would do something very sudden to an unbeliever in your sight. As you intended with these two here –' he pointed to the abominations '– before my timely arrival.'

James smoothed the blade of the gl'ai along his thigh, wiping the professor's blood on his purple robe. Soon he would be dirtying the blade with the impurities of the man before them. A man who would be silenced at Maa'lon's command – when the cleansing would begin. It was only a matter of time.

Shemda watched the curious man's progress. He continued to smoke. He still rummaged through his pockets. And he seemed unable to be quiet.

'But I don't fear you. And I don't believe in you. Must be a real pisser for you.' He circled round Maa'lon and his fellow gods and walked up to Bernice. 'Would you hold my hat for me a moment, dear. I'm afraid it's proving rather distracting.'

With that he removed the item from his head and gave it to her. She looked down at it curiously for a moment. The man blew his smoke politely away from her and turned back to Maa'lon.

'That name trick must do you rather well. Knowing I'm called John and I never told you etc., etc. Not that it's my real name: just something for everyone to get their teeth into. Must be a boon with the weak-minded, though. It's so easy. Names sit there like flags on the top of primitive minds, the type of minds that you like. Anyone with any skill can pluck them out. I bet even Sha'tah over there could do it, if she really put her mind to it. And if she still had a mind left to put to any use.'

Everyone turned to look at a pale, emaciated Hut'eri who seemed terrified to be brought so suddenly into the meandering conversation. Maa'lon walked over to her and gently touched her cheek. He smiled back at John.

'Indeed, some things can be done by many. I'm sure your own gifts are manifold. But you know nothing of faith, fear, and belief. For you it is an academic question, a philosophical discussion. For us it is the essence. You cannot conceive of the beauty within that we can free. Certainty and power and love, and devotion. Purpose. The gods lend meaning to miserable lives.' Maa'lon spread his arms widely as if to encompass all his flock.

'I see no beauty here. You and your kind are leeches. You always were. Draining strength from the credulous, manipulating synapses. Gutting those who believe. Look around you. I see no beauty here, only bodies on the verge of collapse. Spent fuel for extrovert insanities. Now, if you don't mind, I think we'll be off.'

Bernice had been waiting for John to cut to the chase. It was time. She grabbed hold of Shemda and clutched the hat close to her.

'We're heading that way,' she whispered in his ear. His expression looked somewhat confused, but he nodded almost imperceptibly and brought his dataxe up ready for use.

'I don't really think we can allow that, John. We've gone to so much effort to get Bernice and her charming Grel companion here. It would break everyone's heart if we abandoned the show now.'

Bernice was beginning to truly tire of the mock-pleasantries. She wanted Maa'lon to shout his defiance. Swear. Show some aggression. Just lose the sinister 'Englishman abroad' bit.

'Well, I'll be staying to keep you company for a while. My friends can go first; we can still chat.'

Bernice, readying herself to run, turned quickly back to John. 'Sorry? You're staying? That really isn't a good idea. This lot can get pretty twisted. You come too.'

'No.' It was the first time since his arrival he'd said anything succinct.

Bernice was taken aback by the curt response, but wasn't giving up. 'We all go, if we can. I'm rather dubious as to why they should let us go anywhere.'

'As am I.' Maa'lon walked slowly over to them and smiled. 'I fail to see the manner of your escape.'

John dipped his hand once more into the deep right-hand pocket of his coat. When it emerged, it held an opalescent black ovoid. He polished it quickly and then twisted something on its flat underside. A low beeping sound began and then shut off. A small red diode light started to flash slowly.

'I think you'll find this a convincing argument. I wonder if you can survive the heat at the heart of a sun. Can ideas exist outside of everything, or do you all need hosts, need the strength of others to realize yourselves? If you want to find out then try to stop them leaving. I suggest you let them go myself, as I'm not exactly over-anxious to vaporize myself. But needs must and all that.'

John tossed the ovoid lightly from one hand to the other, a broad smile on his face.

Maa'lon's brow creased into a deep frown and he looked quickly from the Anoouki to the tall figure in crimson by his side. He received nods from each.

'They can go.'

'Excellent. Now, please be off, Professor. Sorry I didn't have time to chat, Shemda. Go!'

Bernice wasn't going to give up. 'You've got to come with us. We all go together. That thing will work just as well on the move.' She tugged at his arm, but he wouldn't move. He just stared straight ahead at Maa'lon.

'No, you go first. I'll follow on when I'm sure you're away. It's vital you get away.'

'Why?'

'Because of who you are and who you touch. You're very important. You're very important to someone who's incredibly important. You're leaving, and I'm going to make sure you get away.'

Bernice didn't know what to say. She searched John's eyes for any hint of humour and then gave up. There was nothing to say.

She kissed him on the cheek, grabbed Shemda's hand, and headed south at a run.

Once they were clear of the troops, Shemda turned and asked where they were heading.

'A flitter, half a K to the south of here.' She held up the open end of the man's hat for him to see into as they ran.

'Nav-board ignition system: I've only ever seen them in flitters.'

Shemda looked down at the simple silicon-plastene wafer and saw the bright yellow note attached to it: '½ K South' written untidily but legibly. He lifted his head and scanned the grassland ahead for the transport.

After a moment he saw the low hump poking up above the grasses, and he steered Bernice towards it. She was starting to tire and was totally breathless when they arrived moments later at the flitter.

It was a simple black plastene shell, gently curved and essentially open to the elements. Two small seats, one with a flight column, filled the whole craft. A small comscreen sat in front of the column, with a channel already keyed in. Shemda looked at it nervously and began his attempt to get in.

In the end he had to abandon his pack, and he wedged the dataxe under the seat. Even then he was still half hanging out of the tiny craft.

Bernice slid the wafer into the base of the column and the pulse motors kicked in. They flew straight up in the air at astonishing g and then headed west at what must have been the flitter's top speed.

As Shemda struggled to stay in the craft and to control the tentacles which seemed desperate to escape his face, he gave a low hoot of fear in the wind.

'Don't think this is anything to do with me,' said Bernice. 'It's preprogrammed. On automatic. Totally out of my control. Hopefully, John chose somewhere nice, 'cause we've no choice in the matter.'

Shemda managed to get his head back inside the flitter and turned to his companion.

'And don't look at me like that either,' was all he heard before he nearly fell out again.

Braxiatel sat on a muddy hillock and examined the three thousand-odd people who had suddenly, somehow, become his responsibility.

Odd, he decided, was definitely the operative word. The

refugees from the spaceport were a mixed lot: academics, students, native Dellahans, support personnel, off-duty shuttle crews. The latter were in the worst shape. They had just seen their livelihoods literally blown up before their eyes.

Not that anyone was looking exactly cheerful, huddled together under the drizzly, slate-grey sky. They all knew what the destruction of the spaceport meant. At first, most of the people who had fled it in a blind panic had seemed willing to head meekly back to St Oscar's. It had taken Braxiatel to point out to them that it could well have been the Sultan himself who had ordered the destruction of their only escape route. If they went back to the university, they could face arrest and probable execution. It was, Braxiatel supposed dourly, at that point that he had inadvertantly elected himself their de facto leader.

In that capacity, he had led them as far away from both the spaceport and St Oscar's as he could manage. And now here they were, somewhere in the Dellahan hinterland, waiting for him to tell them what to do next.

As if he knew. Braxiatel had been many things in his life, but he had never been – had never wanted to be – a leader. I never intended to get involved, he thought, imagining the happy curves and planes of Renée's face. I don't want to fight in this war, especially now I think I know who I'd be fighting against. But, of course, he already was. He thought about what John had said to him, and realized he always had been. But, like a reserve in a peacetime army, he hadn't known he was committed until the call to battle came.

He suddenly realized that his pocket was beeping at him, had been for some time. Frowning, he reached inside it, and drew out a rather lumpy, old-fashioned communicator. His frown deepened. It wasn't his.

He flipped open the lid, and was surprised to find the elfin, but very tired, features of Bernice Summerfield staring up at him.

'Irving!' she exclaimed. 'So he did give you the other one. How marvellous!'

'Bernice?' he said, rather stupidly. He collected himself

with a powerful effort of will. 'Where are you?'

'It doesn't matter,' she said. Her image glanced over her shoulder, then back up at Braxiatel, looking even more worried. 'Our mutual friend left me a message for you.' He didn't have to ask who she meant. 'He wants you to get to these coordinates –' a string of numbers scrolled along the bottom of the screen '– and take everyone with you.'

Irving pinched his lower lip between thumb and forefinger. 'And you think I should trust him?' he asked.

Bernice scrubbed a hand across her eyes, and Braxiatel realized that she looked more than just tired. She looked on the point of collapse. 'He saved my life, Irving,' she said. 'And I suspect that you probably don't have much choice.'

The transmission cut out before he could reply. It didn't matter anyway; she was right. Sighing, Braxiatel rose to his feet and prepared to lead the refugees to the coordinates she had given him.

Harker had heard the craft take off, but didn't concern himself with the professor's flight. She would soon be brought back, laid low before Maa'lon and then cleansed.

His immediate, angry thoughts were aimed towards the man who had seen fit to interfere. Had gone against the will of Maa'lon. Standing there, holding the black device. Mocking them all and his Lord.

He would pay. He could feel the anger rise within him. The strength flowed through him, from him, to the Lord. He could feel the others straining to give of themselves, to allow Maa'lon further into their hearts. They too knew He needed their strength. As His love filled them, so their strength bound all together.

It was perfect symmetry. He could voice Maa'lon's love, hear His voice. And God sometimes needed him. Those were the special times, when he felt closer to Maa'lon. In those times they were bound tightly together and he couldn't tell where he ended and where His wisdom began. Now was such a time; he could feel it.

'I can sense your fear, John.' Maa'lon's voice was full of strength and certainty. 'You're not as certain as you might at first appear. I'll admit that threw me.'

Maa'lon walked towards the long-coated figure and looked down at the smoking cigarette in his hand.

'That'll kill you, you know, John.'

'So will this.' The man lifted the black ovoid in his left hand and held it near the Lord's face. He inhaled deeply on the cigarette.

'You claim to have no fear, John. No fear of us. You say you know what we are and where we came from, and you think that knowledge protects you. It doesn't.'

James saw a flash of anxiety cross John's face.

'My knowledge can control you; I can stop people believing in you.' John tried to sound confident but his voice had lost much of its assurance.

'Don't be silly, John. How can you stop others when you can't control yourself? I can feel your belief, and your fear. You know what we can do, what we have done before. You are scared of us, and that is your weakness.' James could feel the power rushing through him. 'And that is why you can no longer move your arms.'

The look of terror on John's face elated James. Now he would understand the power of God.

'As you can't move your arms, I think I will move this out of harm's way.' Maa'lon took the black device out of his hand and carefully handed it to a young Hut'eri child who immediately headed off with it out across the savannah.

'I think I should remove some other things as well, don't you? You really do have to be punished. Sight first.'

Harker laughed as the eyeballs exploded and the wretch's screams began.

'I wonder what you look like beneath all that skin. Let's find out, shall we?'

The tearing flesh erupted from beneath the long coat, spattering Maa'lon who simply smiled at the sight before Him. All around Harker were now laughing and rejoicing in the sight of the Lord.

Maa'lon gently ran His hands across John's open chest to cheers from the faithful.

'And those hearts look just fit to burst.'

Renée watched the straggling column of refugees through her binocs. The line extended back over a mile, and even the front of it wasn't moving at much more than two miles an hour. At the very head of the column, she could just see the upright grey needle of a man. It was, she was quite sure, Braxiatel.

She laughed; how typical of him to take control, and then make such a pig's ear of it. And where on earth did he think he was going? The refugees hadn't made any effort to cover their tracks, so their trail had been childishly easy to follow, but neither Renée nor any of her sergeants had been able to determine where it was they were heading in such a deter-mined straight line.

It didn't matter, anyway. Wherever they were going, Renée was about to make sure they didn't get there.

The flitter had settled down. It now merely travelled very fast in a straight line. Shemda felt a little more comfortable, though he was still glad their recent flight had precluded any form of large meal.

Beside him Bernice looked down at the nav-board and appeared to be trying to decipher the symbols there.

'I think we're heading almost due east: there's a site marked which looks to be just north of the university archipelago,' she said over the roaring wind.

'Do you know what's there?'

'Not a clue. We don't even know whether or not John had a proper plan. We could be heading anywhere. But I've told Irving to head that way too, so we'll just have to hope. This thing might not even be able to land on automatic.'

Shemda held on to the side of the craft tighter, and made soothing knots of his tentacles.

Maa'lon moved away from the heap of contaminated flesh. James offered his robe for the cleansing of the Lord's blood-soaked hands, an offer which was gratefully accepted by the master of all. Another smile lifted the reverend's spirits still further. There was no end to the blessings.

After his god had removed the stain of the damned, He turned to the Grel, Demka.

'My brothers tell me that Bernice is nearing the university. It would be preferable if her progress were permanently interrupted before she can join her friends. The situation there is a little . . . fluid at the moment.'

The Grel inclined his head to show the proper deference and then immediately began to operate his dataxe with a swiftness and dexterity that spoke of the animation of the Lord. The weapon made several beeping noises punctuated by a chime. After a few moments, Demka leant fully over the machine and muttered quietly a short phrase in what must have been his own tongue. His words were answered by another, deeper chime.

The Grel looked up from the dataxe and bared his yellow teeth to Maa'lon.

'It is done, Lord.'

Once more they basked in the beauty of Maa'lon's smile.

In geo-synchronous orbit above the savannah, the Grel datarunner came to life. Its sleek form shifted slightly as manoeuvring thrusters did their work. Two small apertures irised open to reveal the flame-orange tips of the smart interceptors.

Within the craft, auxiliary lighting, an attractive green in hue, was replaced by harsh analogue sunlight. The data-stream systems went off-line. There was no need for the link with Grellor now: the call had already gone out. Other ships would soon arrive to mine this rich vein of knowledge.

The surveillance interpreters logged into the weapons systems and calculated a strike resolution. They checked the standard thirteen times and then armed the system. The strike was simple: the only hot spot in scanning range, and travelling sub-sonic. The weapons systems screamed overkill, but the twin interceptor resolution was locked and coded.

The systems executed.

The twin interceptor pulse motors fired.

All in under 1.2 seconds.

They hit their target four seconds later.

Bernice could only remember the flash, and the sudden lurch. There was no sound. No explosion. Just their progress halted by a ball of light. And gravity.

She didn't feel the landing either. A very bad sign.

She should have felt something at that speed, from that height. It certainly wasn't soft. Some pain in her legs though: encouraging.

Shemda looked bad. His size hadn't helped him at all. Through the pink film in her eyes Bernice could see his head wound, and the tears in his tentacles. She was sure she shouldn't be able to see that much of his mouth. Another very bad sign.

It was his right hand that looked the worst though. Or rather looked the most absent. The flitter had clearly scraped along the rocky terrain before wedging beneath the boulder before them. His hand had been on the outside.

There was practically nothing below the wrist, except for the jutting fragments of two very yellow bones. Some deep red flesh clung to them, but the rest was gone. Bernice couldn't conceive how much it must hurt. Or why it wasn't bleeding more.

Then she saw the dataxe in his left hand, and the signs of clumsy cauterization on the huge wound. Benny wondered if she'd ever be able to do something like that, but she already knew she wouldn't.

Shemda came round after a light tap on the shoulder. His groan seemed the most natural thing in the world. Bernice told him not to move, though he didn't seem to have any such plans.

'I appear to be discovering a whole new arena of pain, Bernice. In many ways I should find it fascinating. It is after all a new experience. Unfortunately, I'm having trouble seeing it in that light.' His speech was strained and showed the suffering beneath the forced levity.

'Do you have any pain-killers?' Bernice wondered if they were going to regret the abandonment of the Grel's pack.

'Pocket at my left knee.' He was wheezing slightly now.

She leant forward to search for the pocket in his all-in-one suit. The blood splashed there seemed to have come from elsewhere, and she soon wiped it off without complaint from the Grel. She opened the seal and removed the bubble pack of what looked like huge tablets.

She offered them to Shemda with a quizzical look.

Despite his condition, he still managed to look sheepish.

'I get terrible headaches sometimes.'

It was then that she suddenly realized where the blood had come from, as agony exploded up through her legs.

Demka gave another toothy smile as his dataxe began to beep once more.

'It is done, Maa'lon.'

James felt his own joy mingle with that of his god. The abominations had been struck down from the heavens, as Maa'lon would smite all who dared to question His wisdom.

The professor and the deluded Grel would not be able to spread their lies. Dellah was safe and His purpose would soon spread to the stars.

'Do you wish to see their remains, Lord?' asked Harker.

'No, my child, there are others nearer than we. Let us save our energies for more fruitful purposes.'

Once more Maa'lon's smile lit a fire at the reverend's heart. He knew he could do anything, go anywhere, to spread the word of his god. He knew he would never again feel tired.

For just one second, Braxiatel was pleased to see Renée – more pleased than he had ever been to see anyone in his life. Then she continued pointing the rifle at him, and he knew that this wouldn't be the reunion he had imagined.

He couldn't take his eyes off her. But he could hear the high-pitched whine of laser-fire. And the screams. He thought he saw a flinch in her eyes at those.

'Hello, Irving,' she said. 'I've been sent to arrest you, for –' she glanced down at a small screen in her hand '– well, rather a lot of things, actually. Failure to comply with Sultanate Decree Number 193. That's the decree about joining a religion,' she added helpfully. 'Encouragement of others to flout the Sultan's decrees. Forgery of exit visas. Attempting to flee justice. I could go on. But I won't bother, because that's already four different capital offences.'

Now he did look away from her, at the people he was supposedly protecting. He was relieved to see that most of them were still standing, only the occasional body carelessly tossed here or there. But they were surrounded by the drab troops of the New Moral Army. There would be no escape. Many of the refugees had already raised their arms in the universal gesture for surrender.

Renée had noticed it too. He thought she seemed relieved, or maybe he just wanted to believe that she was glad to have avoided more killing.

'Don't do this, Renée,' he said to her. 'You're stronger than this. Resist them.'

She shook her head. 'You sent me to them, Braxiatel,' she said. 'You knew I was a believer, but you sent me anyway.'

He hung his head. 'He told me to do it,' he said, then realized what a truly pathetic excuse that was. He met her too-blue eyes, for the first time hiding nothing from her: neither what he felt nor who he was. He saw her eyes widen in shock and for a second she rocked forward on the balls of her feet, as if she was going to come to him. Then he saw her check herself. She centred the tip of her rifle until it was almost touching his hearts.

'I was a fool to trust him,' he said softly. 'I'm sorry, Renée. This isn't your fault.'

'They told me my god would come to meet me,' she said, and he couldn't stop himself shuddering. 'To witness this. Do you think it's true?'

'I'm very much afraid it is.'

'Then I have no choice,' she said.

* * *

And, on a hill not far away, her god watched her and was pleased. No one, it knew, was immune from belief. And it was willing to become whatever the believer wished it to be. It was a small price to pay, for everything it gained. Smiling, the Grey headed down to witness the sacrifice about to be made in its name.

12

DEUS EX MACHINA

Down thither, prone in flight
He speeds, and through the vast ethereal sky
Sails between worlds and worlds, with steady wing,
Now on the polar winds, then with quick fan
Winnows the buxom air; till within soar
Of towering eagles, to all the fowls he seems
A phoenix gazed by all

Milton, *Paradise Lost*, Book V

Extract from the diary of Bernice Summerfield

Well, I won't be going anywhere for a while.

Shcmda's analgesics have kicked in now, but the ache won't go away. I nearly screamed when he dragged me out of the flitter. I'm trying not to look down, though he doesn't think it's as bad as it looks. Just a shattered ankle and two crushed feet. Believe me, it looks a hell of a lot worse.

Starting to feel a bit woozy. Quite pleasant really.

It was his idea that I should write something. Keep my mind occupied. Keep my fuddled mind occupied that is. Seems to be working though. I may not have any boots, but you don't catch me without my diary. How my enemies must quail in fear at my readiness to mock them wittily for posterity. Be prepared was never my motto, though I think I might work on that one. Bringing my datapad might have been sensible, but no, I just leave it on a pile of clothes guarded by Wolsey back at the ranch. Behold Bernice the Wise.

We could have contacted someone then. If there is anyone to contact back home. I have a very bad feeling about that.

Shemda's all-singing all-dancing dataxe is practically out for the count. Low on power, and he thinks he's been locked out of the datarunner's systems. No help there.

It's so frustrating. He thinks we're only about ten kilometres from our destination, but we've no way of knowing for certain. And even if we knew that, how would we get there? He's on the edge of collapse, whacked off his mind and only just coping with shock. A hand down following his first and probably last adventure with Bernice Summerfield, Professor of Arse-Ups at the University of Dellah and holder of Regius Chair of Perennial Peril. I must take some time out if I ever have any to try and forgive myself. And yet he carries me out and looks after me: he must be seriously concussed.

Feeling a bit dizzy now. Better ride the wave.

Bit calmer. The bindings on my feet seem to lessen the pain. The ankle is still singing its monotonously painful melody though. One of those pains that keeps making the bile rise up and tears well in your eyes, as if it runs through your whole body. You know where it should be but you can't lock it down.

Could have been worse though: you should see the front of the flitter. On my side it looks like a boiled egg that someone tried to open with a sledge-hammer.

Looks like it's a week for miracles.

Can't really get away from the idea that I should have seen it coming sooner. I've been to Tyler's Folly. The links in religions should have been obvious to me. And I know God. I know he doesn't mess around, that his concerns are always on the big side of massive.

It's my own vanity that got in the way. I thought they were all interested in me. When in fact they just wanted an excuse to drop in on Dellah and make sure the chocolate egg hadn't revealed its surprise. Only it did. And they legged it.

I thought I'd gone beyond menaces from the dawn of time. Not my scene any more. Been there, done that. More of a nuts and bolts girl now; trying to stay on the human scale. Be more down to earth. I should have looked further down.

The People's legacy left for another galaxy to deal with. Their desire to preserve and imprison making victims of us all.

Just once let me find a highly advanced civilization that ties up its loose ends, rather than sweeping them under a carpet a billion light years away. Or something.

Best not to get maudlin though. And anyway, looks like we've got company.

'Frying-pan' and 'fire' are words that immediately leap to mind.

Extract ends

The stake to which he was tied was chafing Braxiatel's back. Before placing him there, they had removed his shirt and jacket, as if afraid that the flimsy material would somehow deflect the lasers from their intended course into his chest. His kind weren't easy to kill, but he was pretty certain this method would work. And, if it looked like he'd survived, they'd just line up and kill him again. And again. Until the job was really done.

There were eleven troops in the firing squad. Renée made it a round twelve. They were standing ten paces from him, quite close enough for him to see the expression on Renée's open, attractive face. She looked tense, her lower teeth lightly biting her lip, but otherwise OK. She didn't look like a woman in the thrall of some terrible power. She just looked like Renée.

Since she had told him that she had no choice, Braxiatel's head had been a muddle of imagined words: all the things he should have said to her and never did. All the conversations they should have held. He briefly thought of holding them now, but quickly dismissed the idea. There weren't many choices left to him, but he could at least choose to die with dignity.

He couldn't quite face the thought of dying with Renée's laughter echoing in his ears.

He saw that the firing squad had raised their rifles.

No more time for choices.

Braxiatel watched closely as one soldier, a young blond boy no older than seventeen, tightened his finger imperceptibly on the trigger. He told himself that he felt nothing.

'Stop!' Renée suddenly shouted.

The air left Braxiatel's lungs in a great whoosh of relief.

'Don't you think we should wait until our god can witness this?' Renée asked.

Braxiatel opened his mouth to reply, then realized that she wasn't addressing him.

There was a low murmur of assent from the soldiers facing him. Two of them lowered their rifles.

Renée dropped hers to the ground, and raised her arms in what Braxiatel imagined was a gesture of invocation. 'Show yourself, O Great Grey!' she called out. 'Reveal yourself to your followers that we might worship you!'

Despite the situation, despite the fact that nine rifles were still pointed at his hearts, Braxiatel couldn't shake the feeling that Renée was somehow taking the mickey.

And then her god appeared.

Shemda didn't recognize the uniforms, but the looks on the soldiers' faces didn't fill him with confidence. And he recognized the zeal on the face of the leader, a short human with a shaven head wearing a large silver pendant in the shape of a star.

Next to this uniformed woman stood a tall, pale creature that seemed to glow beneath its translucent skin. On its large forehead a golden sun pattern blazed away. Shemda wondered if the blow to his head was more serious than he previously thought. The light seemed impossibly bright, yet he could make out every detail.

'You're wasting an awful lot of energy on that effect, you

know.' Bernice's words carried the slight slur the pain-killers were bound to impart.

'Some things are rather expected,' said the being of light with a grin that almost filled its featureless face. The dark coals of its tiny eyes bore down on the professor.

'Haven't you led us all a merry dance, again.' It walked over to where she lay. 'And look where it got you.'

'It may seem technically impossible, but try to imagine me looking down on you,' she said to the bright, towering figure. 'You and your friends have no future, only a past you won't let go of.'

'How little you understand us, Bernice. We are timeless. We represent a need. A need which something else filled at home. But millions here still have use for us, need us. And billions more beyond. Thoughts, desires, and fears don't go away: they can only be banished for a while. And then they come back stronger. And this planet is making us strong.'

Despite the pain apparent in her face, Shemda was moved by the defiance of Bernice's reply.

'You're just parasites. Subverting, perverting people's minds. Lying your way in and then gutting them from the inside. Drawing the energy from their belief in something that you're not.'

'But we can be, Bernice. We can be whatever you want us to be for a while. And that will bring you joy. We can bring a joy that you cannot conceive and which is a fine reward for their exertions. And, when there are more, the drain will be less noticeable, the available energy that much greater, so that this regrettable suffering will lessen. And death will be by our choice alone.'

Bernice attempted to struggle to her feet, screamed, and then thought better of it.

'I could make your pain go away, Bernice. I could restore Shemda's hand for him. The hand he lost because of you.' Shemda could see the tears running down Bernice's face. He tried to go to her, but was restrained by three of the silent soldiers. 'I could make everything better and fill that hole within you. Would you like that?'

'You know exactly what I'm going to say, so why keep asking? This is all happening with monotonous regularity. Get it over with, quickly.'

'I asked only from the need to play a role. I, and my brothers, have no intention of allowing you to live any longer. However, I feel I should inform you that it will not be quick. You have been out in the provinces while our strength has grown in your backyard. Minds are stronger here, and so, in many ways, is the need for belief. And there is less of a need for subterfuge; our Dellahan forms are merely loose, possibly more palatable, analogues of an ancient pantheon that truly explored sensation and emotion. The big city is the place for us.'

Shemda began to wonder whether they were going to be ruthlessly talked to death, and then tried to think of other things, when the glowing figure suddenly turned his dark eyes on him.

'Your people too, Shemda, will fuel the fires that will light up a new order. Belief seems so important on your worlds, and your hearts and minds are so giving when you crave the ultimate reward. Still, time is getting on, and this is going to take a while.'

The figure approaching them looked absurdly like the dark-eyed, oval-headed alien abductor of twentieth-century Earth folklore. It was an image, Braxiatel knew, which had once adorned a thousand T-shirts.

But there was nothing funny about the power Braxiatel could feel radiating from the creature before him. It was a power, he now knew, born out of the belief of its followers. And not just the troops of the New Moral Army. He could see it in the faces of his own band of refugees: they believed this creature to be the god that Renée had claimed. They believed it was a god, and so it was.

Braxiatel realized with horror that his own understanding of the situation just added to the entity's power. He, in his own way, also believed.

Renée, he saw, was studying the Grey God with rapt

fascination. Then she turned back to regard Braxiatel. 'It came,' she said, her voice astonished. 'You were right.'

Braxiatel's throat was so dry that it took him two attempts to speak. 'Yes, but it's not what you think,' he said. 'It's using you, Renée.'

'Oh, no,' Renée said, her golden curls bobbing as she shook her head. 'It's exactly what I think.' She turned to the creature. 'Welcome, my lord.'

The creature graciously bowed its head in acknowledgement of her words. 'Proceed,' it said. Its voice was musical, otherworldly.

Renée stooped to pick up her rifle, swung it once more to centre on Braxiatel's chest. After a second, her troops followed suit.

Braxiatel lowered his head. He found that, now it had come, he couldn't face his death. Not if it took this form.

It was the collective gasp of those around him that caused him to raise his head once again. To find that Renée had swung her rifle round still further, until its barrel centred on the Grey God.

The God took a step forward, began another. Renée's finger tightened on the trigger. It stopped. 'Daughter of Earth, what are you doing?' it asked. Its voice was a little less musical now. 'Do you not know that the penalty for disobedience is death? Am I not your God?'

Renée smiled. Braxiatel couldn't take his eyes from her, but he could sense the uncertainty in her troops. He knew that some of them were milliseconds away from turning their own rifles on her. When she spoke, he knew it was them she was addressing.

'Didn't I get around to telling you about the Great Schism in the Church of the Grey?' she asked conversationally.

There was a confused silence. After a long moment, a lone voice called out, 'No, sir.'

Renée nodded, her rifle never wavering from its target. 'First contact, you know,' she said. 'A real alien race introduced itself to humanity, and suddenly the Church of the Grey faced rather a large dilemma. Half of us decided that this was it, these were the Grey our scriptures foretold, and we worshipped them.' She paused. 'And half of us decided they weren't. That any aliens we met couldn't, by definition, be the aliens we were waiting for.'

The creature took a step backwards, and Braxiatel knew that it had made a terrible mistake. Renée followed it. After a second's hesitation, some of her troops moved in behind the alien. Its fathomless gaze flicked between them and Renée, and it halted its retreat.

'But you see,' Renée continued, still in the same conversational tone, 'the aliens we'd met weren't gods. They were just aliens, who didn't want our worship and couldn't possibly live up to our expectations. And so that branch of the Church of the Grey died out.'

'You are mistaken,' the creature said finally. 'I am your God. And I will make you suffer for your blasphemy.'

Renée shook her head sadly. 'God must always be sought, but can never be found,' she said. 'It's the second paragraph in my *Book of the Grey*.' With startling suddenness, her finger tightened on the trigger, and a spear of light reached out and struck the Grey God in the centre of its chest. Then the creature was deluged in a fierce fountain of light as all the troops at Renée's back turned their guns on it too. When they'd finished, the charred corpse was barely recognizable.

Renée turned to Braxiatel. 'It's the second paragraph in all my troops' *Books of the Grey*, too,' she said. 'I do keep telling them they have to think for themselves, but the poor dears seem to hang on my every word.'

She approached him, and it was only when he saw her grin that he realized that his mouth was still hanging open in astonishment. He didn't feel like he had the energy to close it. 'I must say, Irving,' she said, 'the expression on your face is absolutely priceless.'

The length of Renée's body pressed up against Braxiatel's as she reached behind him to undo the ropes that bound him. He could feel her breasts squashing softly against his naked chest. He had never felt more human in his life.

'You really believed I was going to kill you,' she said quietly, her voice muffled against his shoulder.

He took a deep breath, and she pulled back a little to regard him, her full lips parted in a wistful smile. His hands were free now, but he kept them clutched behind him. It seemed like the safest place for them.

'You let me believe that,' he said. She opened her mouth to reply. He didn't give her the chance. 'No, I understand. You had to keep up the pretence.'

Renée frowned, but he could see that the familiar sparkle of mischief had returned to her eyes. 'Well, yes,' she said. 'But I quite enjoyed giving you a taste of your own medicine, too.'

She could obviously tell that he didn't understand. She smiled more widely, and reached out towards him, trailing her fingertips down his chest before letting her hand come to rest in its centre. He could feel his hearts beating violently beneath her palm. 'Why did you come to get me from the camp, Irving?' she asked.

'I . . .' Braxiatel couldn't seem to tear his eyes away from hers. 'I don't . . . I don't know. I don't think I understand myself any more.'

Renée shook her head slightly, then, before he could react, leant in to press her lips briefly against his cheek. When she leant back to look at him again, he was sure that he was blushing. 'If people can become gods through the power of belief, maybe gods can become people, too,' she said. She turned away from him, pausing only to call over her shoulder, 'You're welcome to come and see me when you work it out.'

Bernice's breath caught in her throat as Shemda was jerked off his feet. She thought the soldiers around him were holding him aloft until they withdrew. He spun gently and remained about a metre off the ground.

'Sorry, showboating again,' said the god.

A subtle movement of one thin, glowing arm halted the spin. A fist clench began to bend the Grel's spine further and

230

further back. The huge grin appeared on the translucent face again. Shemda started to scream.

'Why not me first?' shouted Bernice, desperate for any delay or excuse not to see the Grel snapped in two before her.

'Your time will come, Bernice. And I can feel your guilt for the fate of this ridiculous creature. I rather like guilt, you see. You could say it's my big thing. Now shut up and enjoy the show.'

Bernice felt her throat constrict; she couldn't breathe. She tried to gasp, clawed at her collar. She could feel herself going blue.

Then, just as suddenly, she could breathe again. The air came in in huge gulps.

'Believe me, my dear, it's not going to be that easy.'

The blood vessels in her temples began to throb. Capillaries in her eyes began to burst. Once more her vision ran red and distorted, but through it all she could still see Shemda hanging in the air. His back had arched further and his arms and legs were drawn back. She wondered how much he could take.

Then the tentacles began to peel back. One of the torn ones on the right of his mouth snapped off. Shemda screamed and Bernice cried out.

More capillaries burst, this time in her hands. She looked down at the source of this new agony and wondered why her vision seemed to darken. A slight movement of the darkness made her look up to see the source of the shadow.

'Clarence.' She wept the word as she stared up into the sun. Like Icarus her winged friend fell to earth from the sun. Only Clarence was going at a hell of a rate.

Soon all the troops were looking up too, gazing in silence. Shemda fell to the ground with a grunt. The being of light looked up at the falling angel.

Clarence hit the ground next to Bernice and quickly picked her up. The dark eyes of the god stared coldly at him. 'You have no place here.'

Clarence didn't even look at him, but gently stroked

Bernice's cheek. 'I'm taking my friend away from here, and I advise you not to get in my way. I'm liable to become very angry indeed.'

Bernice leant towards his ear and whispered, 'We've got to take Shemda, the Grel, too. Can you carry him?'

Clarence looked at his still form and frowned.

'I'll provide extra lift if you need it, Clarence. And shielding,' said a loud and rather excited voice from above.

Bernice looked up to see the unmistakable form of a People drone hovering overhead.

'Don't mind me, Benny. I'm just here to provide cover for old Clarence.' With that, it did a broad circuit of the flitter crash site, swooping low over the still-silent soldiers.

She hugged Clarence closer as he moved towards the injured Grel.

'I'm sorry to interrupt all this, but I can't allow you to leave. You've seen what we can do, Bernice; you're not going to get away that easily.' The glowing form raised both its arms and then stabbed them down in their direction. Bernice braced herself for a thunderbolt, for searing heat and tearing flesh. Nothing happened.

'Shooting blanks, eh?' laughed the drone overhead.

The would-be god looked around and stared at his uniformed troops. They all tried to avoid the blazing anger in his dark eyes. Some shuffled uncomfortably.

Clarence, still holding her around the waist, stooped down to his right and picked up Shemda with an ease that astonished Bernice, and soon they were airborne.

As they rose gently away from the ground, Bernice was sure she heard the bald woman officer whisper, 'An angel,' before turning guiltily back to her god.

'Byee!' called the drone as they gained speed.

Renée and Braxiatel looked out in astonishment over the arid valley before them.

'So this is where you were heading,' she said.

'Apparently so,' he agreed.

It looked as if every spaceship in the quadrant was parked

on these few square kilometres of Dellahan soil. Milling around the ships were what Braxiatel could only assume were their crews. Of course, John had spent almost his entire time making departure plans. Braxiatel wondered grimly if there was anyone he'd met recently that he hadn't either misjudged or misunderstood.

The nearest group of people was already heading towards them. 'Hello there,' the woman at their head called out to Braxiatel, scrubbing her hands back through her close-cropped grey hair. It was Captain Lorna Stewart. 'You're later than John said you'd be.'

Braxiatel glanced at Renée. 'We were delayed.'

Captain Stewart scowled. 'It's not good. The Sultan's soldiers are right behind you.' She nodded towards Renée. 'It didn't take them long to work out that this lot had deserted. I estimate we've got an hour to get clear. Ready to begin the evacuation?'

Braxiatel looked out over the approaching horde of mingled refugees and former New Moral Army troops. No one was missing; even those shot by Renée had merely been stunned, he had discovered. He was rather proud to think that he had actually managed, admittedly with a little help, to bring everyone to safety unscathed. 'More than ready,' he said.

The air reeked of the ozone tang of take-off. The once arid valley was now scorched a deep black from the exhausts of all the ships which had left it.

Braxiatel was on the last remaining ship. Standing beside him was a very impatient Captain Stewart. 'We've got to go,' she said, for the tenth time. 'The Sultan's troops are just the other side of that hill. They'll be here in minutes.'

Braxiatel shook his head stubbornly. 'We've got to wait for Bernice,' he said. He owed her that, at least.

Then he saw the ant figures of the New Moral Army crawling over the ridge of the valley. The captain was watching them, too, through her binocs. 'Shit!' she said. 'They've got rocket launchers!' She turned to Braxiatel. 'That's it, Professor, we're out of here. I was paid for an evac, not a suicide mission.'

After a second, Braxiatel nodded reluctantly. 'Do what you have to, Captain Stewart.'

The captain grimaced sympathetically at him as she began to strap herself into her pressure couch. 'I think you've done pretty well, Professor,' she said. 'There's nearly four thousand souls we've got off-planet. Losing just one isn't such bad going.'

Braxiatel didn't reply. He had recently come to doubt the validity of such calculations.

Clarence cradled Bernice's body carefully in his arms. She was bruised and battered, and he wished that she'd let him take her to a doctor. But she had insisted that she wanted one last look at the planet that had become her home.

'Why?' she said finally, wearily.

There were too many possible answers to that. Most of them, Clarence suspected, were things Bernice didn't want to hear right now. He settled for the safest option. 'I think they were our gods, once,' he said. 'But we cast them out. Imprisoned them.'

'Why Dellah?' she persisted.

Clarence shrugged, then wished he hadn't when he heard Bernice's gasp of pain at the movement. 'I think they thought it was safe,' he said. 'The population once believed in powerless gods, you see; they must have hoped that would contain the entities' power. But over time the entities were able to warp the religions of those around them. Until all it took was one small trigger . . .'

'And God wasn't able to check up as much as he intended because of the Treaty. How terribly inconvenient that must have been for him,' Bernice said bitterly. 'Still – lucky old me – he had his woman on the ground to keep an eye out for any trouble.'

Far beneath them the surface of the planet looked calm, unchanged. A brown-green-blue plain troubled by only the occasional visible pin-prick of civilization. So many problems, Clarence thought, all too small for the naked eye to see. 'Then when you did spot some trouble,' he said, 'God left you to deal with it alone.' He wondered if he sounded anything like as bitter as Bernice.

She squirmed round in his arms to stare at him, her face so close to his that it made him feel cross-eyed to look at her. He did it anyway.

'Why did you come for me, Clarence?' she asked.

Ah. That question. He decided she could probably handle at least part of the truth. 'God told me you'd die. Eventually, I realized that he meant you'd die if I didn't come to you. He was manipulating me.'

Bernice's eyes said, Of course, but she didn't bother vocalizing it. Clarence was grateful.

'He couldn't send me here. But, if he let me get enough information that I chose to come here myself, well . . . And, if I disobeyed the Treaty that way, I'd cease to be a Person. Cease to be his responsibility.'

'So you've burnt your bridges,' Bernice said softly.

Clarence sighed. 'Once I realized that whatever you were facing was probably our fault, I had to come,' he said.

Bernice's eyes narrowed in thought. 'Very convenient that you were immune to the entities' powers though, wasn't it?' Clarence was hurt to detect a slight hint of suspicion in her voice. Although, after everything she'd been through, he couldn't blame her for being a little paranoid.

'Eugenics,' Clarence said. 'The wild psi gene that's found in your race but never in mine. I think it's the same gene which creates the crack in your psyche that lets the gods in. And I think it's a gene which God started to breed out of us, long ago, to make sure the beings he'd driven away could never return.'

He could see Bernice nodding. 'And then there are the Also People,' she said, 'the mechanical intelligences who never had that gene in the first place.'

'And then there's me,' Clarence said. 'A gene-less organic, a religious ikon, and a former Ship: the safest bet God could make, in the circumstances.'

'And now God's made sure that you can't go back,' Bernice said.

Clarence saw that a strand of dark brown hair had become stuck to the corner of her mouth, and lifted a finger to gently brush it away. 'No, I can't,' he said. Then he grinned. 'But I'm not completely alone. I've brought a friend I'd like you to –'

'Sorry to interrupt a tender moment,' a voice said from right beside his ear.

He just about managed to avoid jumping out of his skin. Bernice, who had no doubt already suffered one shock too many over the last few weeks, let out a low yelp of surprise. She regarded the two-foot silver robot hovering on an anti-grav platform in front of her with barely concealed alarm.

'– meet,' Clarence finished sheepishly. '*B-Aaron*, I'd like to introduce you to my friend Bernice.'

The *B-Aaron* held out a stubby silver hand and, after a second's hesitation, Bernice shook it. 'I'm afraid you're not seeing me at my best,' the *B-Aaron* told her. 'I'm usually a bit of a kick-ass warship, but we couldn't really slip away in that without God noticing. The rest of me is still back on the Worldsphere, keeping up appearances. You know,' he added to Clarence, 'I'm still not sure I chose the right drone body. I mean, don't you think the sea-monster suited me better?'

Clarence didn't smile. A comedy ending didn't seem appropriate, in the circumstances.

The Grel datarunner was quiet. Only the low hum of the information systems provided the merest of background sounds as Shemda moved silently on to the flight deck.

He approached the core systems and began the lock-out. The knowledge protection systems were easily accessed (Demka had forgotten to block his clearance codes) and the former servitor began the elaborate process. Former servitor. Shemda knew he had changed a great deal since his arrival on Dellah. Now he only saw the datarunner as a ship, a useful vessel in the current crisis. It was no longer a tool for a higher, purer purpose.

He thought of re-engaging the data-stream. No. Grellor didn't need to know what was going on. Their curiosity might lead them into error. The same sort of error that had cost Grenke so dear at the hands of his former master. Better that they didn't know anything more than they already did. Ignorance would do them good, no matter how much it might annoy them.

The core systems acknowledged the lock-out, and Shemda smiled. Now he could relax a little. Demka could no longer use the ship at the behest of his masters. The quarantine might hold. For a while at least.

He scanned the recent communications on the data-stream and saw the call to Grellor. The request for assistance. A great find on Dellah: top priority. They would be coming. Datarunners from across the sector would scream in, eager for the promised knowledge. And Demka would lead them down his own path.

It had to be stopped. Quickly.

He accessed the deployment subroutines and keyed in the necessary coded sequence. The datacore asked for his clearance. He inputted the symbols and then spoke his mother's name clearly into the microphone. A brief flash of red filled the room, replaced swiftly by the comforting green auxiliary lighting. The core systems had shut down. Only manual systems would work now as the information buffers kicked in.

A distant clang from the aft section reached him. The buoy was away. A beacon to hang over Dellah and keep his race away, joining those already launched to warn the humans of the quarantine. None of his people would risk an information virus; the very thought would freeze their tentacles. They wouldn't stay in the system longer than it took to re-calibrate their jumps. Demka would have to wait a long time to see more of his kind.

He padded quietly out of the flight deck and into the observation port. The large round window offered a dramatic view of the planet below. It looked so peaceful. So blessed by the heavens. A deceptive gem.

All around the datarunner, the other ships were still gathered. Filled with people who had seen what he had seen. Experienced the horror and made it out. A tiny proportion of those who had lived happily on the planet below.

He leant on the rim of the spherical viewing port and gave a start. He was still not used to the prosthetic. He looked at his new right hand, moved the white, synthetic fingers, and wondered whether he would have a chance to return to Grellor for a regen limb. He would have to get used to it.

He carefully placed it back at the window's edge and looked out once more.

Catching the bright sunlight briefly, he saw Clarence, the angel, cradling Bernice in his hands. Not for the first time he wondered how he could hang like that, fly, and protect her and himself from the vacuum of space.

He decided to take some things on faith and chuckled to himself, still staring at the vulnerable human woman wrapped in the powerful figure's arms.

'Bernice,' he whispered, and then headed off to his berth.

Extract from the diary of Bernice Summerfield

I suppose I might have been a little hard on God. In the heat of the moment and all that. I just hate not knowing and this was very much the big one. Something about leaving us all here, running off, and hoping that everyone would work it out for themselves still sickens me. Even if he had been planning for it for years.

Clarence the religious ikon. The joke that only God got. Well, now we know the power of the image, the punch line of the joke. God looking after us in his own mysterious way. They can't deny the transparently holy: his effect is too primal. People can see the good in him and, for a moment at least, it can break the spell.

But I have a distinct worry that what I assume to be New Moral Army troops were new to their job and their god. The grip wasn't tight enough then, but it will be. I saw the change in James, the total subversion. He lost himself in his faith and gave everything to Maa'lon. I don't think imagery would have shaken his resolve.

But perhaps God's plan goes deeper yet.

The People's legacy is after all hemmed in on Dellah. Earth's aware of the problem and no one should come near with all those warning beacons. We just don't know how many believers they need to free themselves totally.

Maybe they don't have enough.

Extract ends

Elspeth sat miserably in the hold of the ship to which, she knew, she owed her life. So, she'd finally got off Dellah. But not, she reminded herself, before she'd betrayed all of her principles. She'd been one of the brightest students in her class; now she was just another useless refugee.

A lonely refugee. None of her friends had made it off-world. She'd been lucky to be in the spaceport when Braxiatel had led the evacuation. It seemed to her that her life over the past few weeks had consisted entirely of following other people, although at least Braxiatel had proved a reasonably sensible person to follow. She hoped the friends she'd left behind could say the same things about their chosen gods. Because, trapped on Dellah, she suspected that they'd find themselves following them for a very long time.

That was the problem with putting your safety ahead of your principles: you had to go on doing it, day after day, for the rest of your life.

Her brooding might have continued at the same pitch of self-pity for some time, if she hadn't suddenly seen him.

'Oh, my god!' she shouted. 'Emile! Emile!'

His distinctive friendly round face turned slowly towards her.

She ran, nearly tripping over the supine bodies of her fellow refugees in her haste to reach him. 'Emile! They told me you were dead!'

She skidded to a halt in front of him, reached her arms towards him, then dropped them, fazed by his lack of response. 'Emile?' she said, less certainly. 'What's wrong?'

At last, he smiled. 'Nothing,' he said. 'Nothing at all.'

Now he did reach out his arms, gripping her in an embrace which was almost suffocatingly tight. 'Tell me, Elspeth, do you still believe?'

ALSO AVAILABLE
IN
THE NEW ADVENTURES

OH NO IT ISN'T!
by Paul Cornell
ISBN: 0 426 20507 3

Bernice Surprise Summerfield is just settling into her new job as Professor of Archaeology at St Oscar's University on the cosmopolitan planet of Dellah. She's using this prestigious centre of learning to put her past, especially her failed marriage, behind her. But, when a routine exploration of the planet Perfecton goes awry, she needs all her old ingenuity and cunning as she faces a menace that can only be described as – panto.

DRAGONS' WRATH
by Justin Richards
ISBN: 0 426 20508 1

The Knights of Jeneve, a legendary chivalric order famed for their jewel-encrusted dragon emblem, were destroyed at the battle of Bocaro. But when a gifted forger is murdered on his way to meet her old friend Irving Braxiatel, and she comes into possession of a rather ornate dragon statue, Benny can't help thinking they're involved. So, suddenly embroiled in art fraud, murder and derring-do, she must discover the secret behind the dragon, and thwart the machinations of those seeking to control the sector.

BEYOND THE SUN
by Matthew Jones
ISBN: 0 426 20511 1

Benny has drawn the short straw – she's forced to take two overlooked freshers on their very first dig. Just when she thinks things can't get any worse, her no-good ex-husband Jason turns up and promptly gets himself kidnapped. As no one else is going to rescue him, Benny resigns herself to the task. But her only clue is a dusty artefact Jason implausibly claimed was part of an ancient and powerful weapon – a weapon rumoured to have powers beyond the sun.

SHIP OF FOOLS
by Dave Stone
ISBN: 0 426 20510 3

No hard-up archaeologist could resist the perks of working for the fabulously wealthy Krytell. Benny is given an unlimited expense account, an entire new wardrobe and all the jewels and pearls she could ever need. Also, her job, unofficial and shady though it is, requires her presence on the famed space cruise-liner, the *Titanian Queen*. But, as usual, there is a catch: those on board are being systematically bumped off, and the great detective, Emil Dupont, hasn't got a clue what's going on.

DOWN
by Lawrence Miles
ISBN: 0 426 20512 X

If the authorities on Tyler's Folly didn't expect to drag an off-world professor out of the ocean in a forbidden 'quake zone, they certainly weren't ready for her story. According to Benny the planet is hollow, its interior inhabited by warring tribes, rubber-clad Nazis and unconvincing prehistoric monsters. Has something stolen Benny's reason? Or is the planet the sole exception to the more mundane laws of physics? And what is the involvement of the utterly amoral alien known only as !X.

DEADFALL
by Gary Russell
ISBN: 0 426 20513 8

Jason Kane has stolen the location of the legendary planet of Ardethe from his ex-wife Bernice, and, as usual, it's all gone terribly wrong. In no time at all, he finds himself trapped on an isolated rock, pursued by brain-consuming aliens, and at the mercy of a shipload of female convicts. Unsurprisingly, he calls for help. However, when his old friend Christopher Cwej turns up, he can't even remember his own name.

GHOST DEVICES
by Simon Bucher-Jones
ISBN: 0 426 20514 6

Benny travels to Canopus IV, a world where the primitive locals worship the Spire – a massive structure that bends time – and talk of gods who saw the future. Unfortunately, she soon discovers the planet is on the brink of collapse, and that the whole sector is threatened by holy war. So, to prevent a jihad, Benny must journey to the dead world of Vol'ach Prime, and face a culture dedicated to the destruction of all life.

MEAN STREETS
by Terrance Dicks
ISBN: 0 426 20519 7

The Project: a criminal scheme so grand in its scale that it casts a shadow across a hundred worlds. Roz Forrester heard of this elaborate undertaking, and asked her squire to return with her to sprawling and violent Megacity – the scene of her discovery. Roz may be dead, but Chris Cwej is not a man to forget a promise, and Bernice is soon the other half of a noble crime-fighting duo.

TEMPEST
by Christopher Bulis
ISBN: 0 426 20523 5

On the wild and inhospitable planet of Tempest, a train is in trouble. And Bernice, returning home on the luxurious Polar Express, is right in the thick of it. Murder and an inexplicable theft mean that there's a criminal on board; the police are unable to reach them; and so the frightened staff and passengers turn to a hung-over, and rather bad-tempered, archaeologist for much-needed assistance.

WALKING TO BABYLON
by Kate Orman
ISBN: 0 426 20521 9

The People – the super-advanced inhabitants of a Dyson sphere – have a problem: to stop an illegal time-travel experiment they must destroy ancient Babylon and all its inhabitants. If they do not, war will break out with the dominant power of the Milky Way, and whole galaxies will be destroyed. Their only hope is that Bernice can travel back to the dawn of civilization, and find the culprits – or Earth history will never be the same again.

OBLIVION
by Dave Stone
ISBN: 0 426 20522 7

A man called Deed is threatening the fabric of the universe and tearing realities apart. At the heart of the disruption, three adventurers, Nathan li Shao, Leetha and Kiru, are trapped. Their friend Sgloomi Po must save them before they are obliterated, and in his desperation he looks up some old friends. So Bernice joins her feckless ex-husband Jason and her old friend Chris on the rescue mission; but then Sgloomi picks up someone who should really be dead.

THE MEDUSA EFFECT
by Justin Richards
ISBN: 0 426 20524 3

Medusa, an experimental ship missing for twenty years, is coming home. When one of the investigation team dies mysteriously, Bernice is assigned to help discover what went wrong. But to do so she must solve a riddle. Somehow the original crew are linked to the team put on board – their ghosts still haunt the ship. And the past is catching up with them all in more ways than one.

DRY PILGRIMAGE
by Paul Leonard and Nick Walters
ISBN: 0 426 20525 1

Thinking she has been offered a blissful pleasure cruise on Dellah's southern ocean, Benny gladly accepts. After all, she has some time on her hands. But, trapped on a yacht with an alien religious sect who forbid alcohol, she soon discovers that all is not well. And, as the ship heads towards a fateful rendezvous, she must unmask a traitor or risk the system being torn apart by war.

THE SWORD OF FOREVER
by Jim Mortimore
ISBN: 0 426 20526 X

Forced to leave her home on Dellah for Earth, Bernice finds work on an Antarctic dig. Once there she uncovers a link between an ancient reptile race, a secret society and a desperate megalomaniac – as well as the fabled Ark of the Covenant. A desperate race has begun, and she soon realizes her deadly knowledge affects not only her own life, but the destiny of the entire human race.

ANOTHER GIRL, ANOTHER PLANET
by Martin Day and Len Beech
ISBN: 0 426 20528 6

Lizbeth Fugard, an archaeologist working on the backwater planet of Dimetos, is in trouble. Someone is following her – watching her. Terrified, she calls on an old friend to help. On arrival, however, Bernice becomes involved in politics, gun-running and a centuries-old love affair, and soon realizes that unless she can find the truth a cycle of violence and hate will jeopardize more than one planet's future.

BEIGE PLANET MARS
by Lance Parkin and Mark Clapham
ISBN: 0 426 20529 4

It's the 500th anniversary of Mars' colonization, and Bernice
Summerfield, expert on the planet's archaeology, has been invited
to speak at an academic conference. On arrival, however, she is
immediately distracted by a murder and its link to an old betrayal
has never been forgotten. Her own life threatened, Bernice soon
discovers that the events of the famous Siege of Mars are far from
ancient history.

Should you wish to order any of these titles, or other
Virgin books, please write to the address below for
mail-order information:

> **Fiction Department**
> **Virgin Publishing Ltd**
> **Thames Wharf Studios**
> **Rainville Road**
> **London**
> **W6 9HT**

ANNOUNCING
PROFESSOR BERNICE SUMMERFIELD:
STARRING IN
BRAND-NEW AUDIO DRAMAS

Big Finish Productions are proud to announce that they have secured the audio drama rights to the New Adventures and their first two releases are available to buy now! These are fully dramatized plays, with original music and sound effects, based upon the novels *Oh No It Isn't!*, by Benny's creator and award-winning novelist Paul Cornell, and *Beyond the Sun* by television scriptwriter Matt Jones.

Featuring a full, professional cast, the double-cassette plays, with an approximate running time of two hours per story, will be on sale from September.

Available in Forbidden Planet and other specialist stores or via mail order.